JANET
EVANOVICH
and

PHOEF
SUTTON

WĬCKED
CHARMS

headline
review

Published by arrangement with Bantam Books, an imprint of
Random House, a division of Penguin Random House LLC,
New York.

First published in Great Britain in 2015
by HEADLINE REVIEW
An imprint of HEADLINE PUBLISHING GROUP

1

Cataloguing in Publication Data is available from the British Library

ISBN 978 1 4722 2545 0 (Hardback)
ISBN 978 1 4722 2546 7 (Trade Paperback)

Typeset in Minion Pro by Avon DataSet Ltd

Printed and bound in Great Britain by
Clays Ltd, St Ives plc

Headline's policy is to use papers that are natural, renewable and recyclable
products and made from wood grown in well-managed forests and other
controlled sources. The logging and manufacturing processes are expected to
conform to the environmental regulations of the country of origin.

HEADLINE PUBLISHING GROUP
An Hachette UK Company
Carmelite House
50 Victoria Embankment
London EC4Y 0DZ

www.headline.co.uk
www.hachette.co.uk

WĬCKED
CHARMS

CHAPTER ONE

My name is Lizzy Tucker, and I live in a small, slightly tilted historic house that sits on a hill overlooking Marblehead Harbor in Massachusetts. I inherited the house from my Great-Aunt Ophelia when I was twenty-eight, and I'm not much older now. I share the house with a tiger-striped shorthaired cat. When he was rescued from the shelter his tag said Cat 7143, and it's stuck as his name. Cat has one eye, half a tail, and I'm pretty sure he was a ninja in a past life. I'm a Johnson & Wales culinary school graduate, and when I'm not being asked to save the world I work as a pastry chef at Dazzle's Bakery in Salem.

It was ten o'clock at night, Cat and I were watching

television in bed, and a big, scruffy, incredibly hot guy walked into my bedroom.

"What the heck?" I asked. "Where did you come from?"

"Originally? Switzerland, but I was mostly raised in Southern California."

"That's not what I mean. What are you doing in my bedroom?"

He kicked his shoes off. "I'm undressing. And then I'm going to bed."

"No! Not allowed."

"Extenuating circumstance," he said, peeling off his shirt. "I'm between places of residence."

"I don't care if you're between a rock and a hard spot. You can't stay here."

His jeans hit the floor. "Of course I can. We're partners."

"We're not that kind of partners. We work together. We're not supposed to be . . . you know."

"Don't get your panties in a bunch. I have total self-control."

I leaned forward for a closer look. "Are those parrots on your boxers?"

"I got them in Key West. Cool, right?"

Okay, I have to admit it. The whole package was cool. The guy's name is Diesel. That's it. Only one name. And the name suits him because he plows over you like a freight train. He's over six feet of hard-muscled male perfection. His dark blond hair is thick and sun-streaked and perpetually mussed. His eyes are brown and unreadable. His smile is like Christmas morning. His attitude is deceptive—casual on the outside but intense on the inside. His moral code is all his own.

"All right. You win," I said, knowing there was no way I could physically remove him. "You can sleep on the couch."

He stuck his thumb into the waistband on his boxers. "I don't fit on the couch."

"Hey," I said. "Wait a minute!"

Too late. The boxers were on the floor with his shirt and jeans.

I clapped my hands over my eyes. "I can't believe you just did that."

"I sleep nude. Women don't usually mind."

"I mind!"

"I get that," Diesel said. "Move over."

I have a queen-size bed. Plenty big enough for me and Cat. Not big enough for me and Cat and Diesel. Truth is, I wouldn't mind getting romantic with Diesel, but we have an odd relationship. Diesel isn't normal. And it would seem that I'm not normal, either. I thought I was normal until Diesel popped into my life shortly after I moved to Marblehead. Now weird is the new normal.

The way Diesel tells it, there are some people on Earth who have *enhanced abilities* that can't be explained in ordinary ways. They might be useful abilities, such as Diesel's talent for opening locks. Or they might be hellacious powers, such as calling down lightning or levitating a garbage truck. Crazy, right? It gets even better. Supposedly there are seven ancient stones that hold the powers of the seven deadly sins. They're known as the seven SALIGIA Stones. If these stones fall into the wrong hands, all hell will, quite literally, break loose. I'm one of two people in the world who have the ability to locate the stones. Sort of like a human divining rod. Lucky me. So far, Diesel and I have acquired two of the stones, nearly getting blown up and kidnapped and chopped into tiny pieces with a broadsword in the process. When we find a stone, Diesel sends it off to some higher power for safekeeping. At least that's his story.

"We're not supposed to sleep together," I said.

"Sleeping is okay. Getting busy, not so much."

Turns out if two people with enhanced abilities get busy, one of them will discover that their special powers have gone up in smoke. If I could be sure it was my special powers that would disappear, I'd be happy to take one for the team. But what if it was Diesel who got cleaned out? I'd be on my own to save the world. This wouldn't be a good thing.

I grabbed a pillow and put it between us. "Just to be safe," I said.

"Sweetheart, if I decide to risk my abilities, that pillow isn't going to save you."

· · ·

6

My alarm went off at four-fifteen in the morning, and I rolled over into Diesel. He was deliciously warm, he smelled like gingerbread cookies, and the pillow was missing.

"Hey," I said. "Are you awake?"

"I am now."

"Something's poking at me under the covers," I said. "That better not be what I think it is."

"Maybe you should take a look just to be sure you've identified it correctly."

"That would be awkward."

"I could deal," Diesel said.

"It might lead to . . . things."

I sensed him smile in the dark room. "No doubt."

He moved over me and kissed me. There was some tongue involved, and heat flooded into every part of me. So maybe I could save the world on my own if it came down to that, I thought. Maybe I didn't care if one of us lost our abilities. Maybe I just cared about running my hands over every fantastic part of him, and then following it with my mouth, and then the inevitable would happen. Oh boy, I really wanted the inevitable.

"Damn," Diesel said.

"What? What damn?"

He slipped out of bed and got dressed in the clothes that were lying on the floor. "There's a problem," he said.

"Can you solve it?"

"Absolutely." He laced up his shoes. "I'll be back."

CHAPTER TWO

Three weeks later, Diesel still hadn't returned. Who cares and good riddance, I told myself. My life was humming along just fine. Maybe it was a little dull compared to chasing down enchanted objects with Diesel, but at least no one was trying to kill me or kidnap me.

Salem is half small-town USA, with its steepled churches, family neighborhoods, and traditional New England values, and half spook-town USA, with whole chunks of town devoted to the tourism industry built around the Salem witch hunts of the late 1600s.

Personally I don't buy into the witch thing, but Glo, the counter girl at Dazzle's, is smitten with the possibility that she might secretly be Samantha Stephens of *Bewitched*.

Truth is, if Glo channels anyone from that television series, it's Aunt Clara. Glo is four years younger than me and an inch shorter. So that puts her at five foot four. She has curly red hair chopped into a short bob. She lives with a broom she hopes will someday take her for a flight over Salem. Her wardrobe can best be described as goth meets Sugar Plum Fairy.

I'm not nearly as colorful as Glo. I have blond hair that is almost always pulled back into a ponytail. My eyes are brown, my metabolism is good, and my wardrobe lacks imagination. White chef coat, jeans, T-shirt, sneakers, and a sweatshirt if it's a chilly night.

Glo and I had closed up shop for the day, and her latest boyfriend, Josh Something, was giving us an after-hours tour of Salem's Pirate Museum. Josh works as a guide in the museum and was in period dress—a white puffy-sleeved shirt, black-and-red-striped breeches, and a grungy leather knee-length frock coat. His brown hair was long and tied with a slim black ribbon at the nape of his neck, and he usually wore a patch over his left eye. Since we were the only ones in the museum, his patch was up on his forehead.

"And look here, my lassies," Josh said to Glo and me, pointing to a grim replica of an unfortunate pirate prisoner. "This be a fine example of pirate justice. 'Tis a nasty way to end a life. The lad would have been better off thrown to the sharks."

The prisoner's leatherlike skin was stretched tight over

his skull and bony frame, and his mouth was open in a perpetual silent scream. The creepy mannequin was dressed in the sort of rags you'd expect to find on a desiccated corpse. And this phony-looking, partially rotted *thing* was stuffed into a flimsy cage that hung from a rusted chain attached to the ceiling. The rest of the room was filled with artifacts, both real and not so real. Cannons, cannonballs, maps under glass, cutlery, jugs of rum, a stuffed rat, coins in a small open chest, timbers, ropes, and weapons were all displayed in dim light.

"It's hard to get emotional over something that's so obviously fake," I said.

"Aye," Josh said. "He be a bit worn. The scurvy dog has been in that cage a good long time."

"I could try to put a spell on him to perk him up a little," Glo said.

A while back Glo found *Ripple's Book of Spells* in a curio shop, and she's been test-driving Ripple's recipes ever since, with varying results.

"It might help if you gave the cage a coat of Rust-Oleum," I said.

I reached up and touched the cage, there was some creaking, dust sifted down on us, and the chain separated from the bars. The cage crashed to the floor and broke into several pieces. The imprisoned dummy flopped out, its peg leg fell off, the skull detached from the neck, and its arm snapped in half.

We all gaped at the mess in front of us. The prisoner's leathery skin was split where the arm had cracked, and a bone was protruding.

"Aargh," Josh said.

"I think that be a human bone," I whispered.

It took the first cop five minutes to get to the museum. He was followed by three more uniformed cops, two plain-clothes cops, a forensic photographer, and two EMTs.

Everyone stared down at the broken cage and the ghoulish guy with the bone sticking out of his arm, and everyone said pretty much the same thing . . . *I was here a couple days ago with my brother-in-law, and I thought this was a fake.*

By the time the coroner arrived, a museum official was on the scene, the area had been roped off with crime scene tape, and the body, which looked more like a giant Slim Jim than a human being, had been photographed and outlined in chalk.

The coroner was a pleasant-looking guy in a wrinkled gray suit and wrinkled white dress shirt. He was my height, probably in his late thirties, wore Harry Potter glasses, had sandy blond hair, and was soft enough around the middle to look cuddly. His name was Theodore Nergal.

Nergal slipped under the crime scene tape and knelt beside the corpse. "Yep," he said. "This guy's dead."

One of the plainclothes cops looked over the tape. "It's a real flesh-and-blood body, right?"

Nergal nodded. "It was flesh and blood before someone decided to try his hand at mummification. Now it's tanned hide and partly calcified bone." He pulled on disposable gloves, picked the skull up, and examined it. "There's an entrance wound in the back of the head where he's been shot." He shook the head, and there was a rattling sound, like dice in a cup. He tipped the head forward, and a small lump of misshapen metal fell out of the man's mouth and plopped into the coroner's hand. "This is a Lubaloy round manufactured only in the 1920s," Nergal said. "This man was shot some ninety years ago."

"Wow," Glo said. "I guess you'll put out an APB for a perp with a walker and a hearing aid."

"Aargh, again," Josh said.

Nergal set the skull in the vicinity of the corpse's neck and stood. "Who found this?"

"We did," I said. "Josh works in the museum, and he was giving us an after-hours tour. I touched the cage, and it came crashing down."

"And you are who?"

"Lizzy Tucker," I said. "I'm a pastry chef at Dazzle's Bakery."

His eyes widened. "Do you make the red velvet cupcakes?"

"I do."

"I *love* those cupcakes!"

Nergal went back to examining the Slim Jim, and Glo elbowed me. "He loves your cupcakes," she said.

"I heard."

She leaned close. "He's cute!" she whispered.

"And?"

"He's not wearing a wedding ring."

"And?"

"Neither are you."

"I don't think he's my type," I told Glo.

"Okay, so he examines dead people all day," Glo said. "Nobody's perfect. He probably has all kinds of interesting hobbies."

"Excuse me," I said to Nergal. "Can we go now?"

"Of course," he said, "but don't leave town."

"Really?"

"Really," he said. "I'm addicted to your cupcakes."

Glo elbowed me again. "I think he might be flirting with you," she whispered.

"It's the cupcakes," I said. "It has nothing to do with me. I'm leaving."

"I can't leave," Josh said. "I have to stay to lock up the museum."

"I'll stay with you," Glo said to Josh. "This is just like one of those *CSI* shows."

I gave everyone a wave goodbye and walked out of the museum into the warm July night. The streetlights cast little pools of light onto the shadowy sidewalk. One of the lights flickered just as I reached it, blinking out twice before flaring back to life, brighter than ever.

I felt a chill ripple down my spine and goosebumps erupt on my arms. A man was standing under the streetlight. He was deadly handsome in a scary sexy-vampire sort of way. He had pale skin, piercing dark eyes, and shoulder-length raven-black hair that was swept back from his face. He was dressed in a perfectly tailored black suit with a black dress shirt. I knew him, and there had been times when I thought his soul might be black as well. His name is Gerwulf Grimoire. Mostly known as Wulf. He entered my life shortly after I moved to the North Shore. He'd introduced himself, touched his fingertip to the back of my hand, and left a burn mark. The scar is still there.

"Miss Tucker," he said. "We meet again."

"Nice to see you, Wulf."

"I'm sure that's not true," Wulf said, "but I appreciate the lie. I'm here to relieve you of the coin you just found."

"What coin? What are you talking about?"

Wulf studied me for a beat. "You really don't know, do you?"

"I assume you're not looking for a nickel or a dime."

"Hardly. You'll know soon enough about the coin. I'm sure my cousin Diesel is looking for it as well and will enlist your aid. If you're smart, you won't get involved. Consider this a warning."

"I'm not afraid of you." Another lie.

"I'm the least of your worries," Wulf said.

There was a *pop* and a puff of smoke, and Wulf was gone. Vanished.

A text message from Glo buzzed on my phone. *Locking up in ten minutes. Going to Ship's Side on Wharf Street for Jose Cuervo for me, and bringing cute coroner for you. Meet you there.*

The Ship's Side was a glorified clam shack with the requisite gray shake siding on the outside and decorated with nets, buoys, and lobster traps on the inside. We were seated at a round table on the back porch overlooking Salem Harbor. Josh was still in costume and still in character.

"I'll have a grog," he said to the waitress.

"Sorry, hon," she said. "We don't carry grog. You'll have to settle for beer."

"You see this?" Josh said. "This is another example of how mainstream society refuses to serve the needs of my people."

"Your people?" I asked. "Do you mean pirates?"

"We prefer the term 'Buccaneer Americans,'" Josh said.

"So does the Buccaneer American want beer?" the waitress asked.

"Aye," Josh said.

"I can't help noticing that you talk like a Buccaneer American even when you're not at work," Nergal said to Josh.

"'Tis a terrible curse," Josh said. "I speak Buccaneer all day, and then I can't stop. My brain doth think in Buccaneer."

"I like it," Glo said. "Sometimes he says I'm winsome."

"True enough, ye be a winsome lass," Josh said to Glo.

"Fortunately, I can stop speaking in coroner," Nergal said.

Josh nodded. "Speaking in coroner after hours wouldst be a bummer."

"It seems like an odd occupation," I said to Nergal. "Why did you become a coroner?"

"I was in debt after med school and this opportunity happened along. I know it seems gruesome to the average outsider, but it's really very interesting work. Why did you become a baker?"

"I flunked gravy when I was in culinary school, but I was good at making cupcakes."

I felt someone lean into me, and a long arm reached out for the breadbasket. I recognized the arm. It belonged to Diesel. He scraped a chair up to the table and positioned himself between Nergal and me.

"So what's new?" Diesel said, giving my ponytail a playful tug.

I was momentarily dumbstruck.

"Where the heck were you?" I said to him. "One minute you were in my house and then next thing you were gone. For all I knew you were dead. I haven't heard a word from you in weeks. You didn't even say goodbye."

"I was on a job. And I'm pretty sure I said goodbye."

"The last thing you said to me was 'I'll be back.'"

"And?"

"'I'll be back' is *not* 'goodbye.'"

Diesel took a roll from the breadbasket. "This is why I don't work with women."

"You *do* work with women. *I'm* a woman."

"Yeah, but I have no choice. I only had two options and Wulf snagged option number one. He got to Steven Hatchet first."

I thunked my forehead with the heel of my hand. *"Unh!"*

Steven Hatchet is the only other person with the ability to recognize a disguised stone. It's sort of insulting that Diesel would consider Hatchet to be the number one choice since Hatchet is flat-out nuts. He looks like an underbaked dinner roll with legs. He has scraggly red hair, is around my age, and thinks he's a medieval minion, serving his liege lord Wulf.

"You're crowding the table," I said to Diesel. "This table only has room for four."

"You're bummed, right?" Diesel said.

"Yes! Go away."

The waitress returned with our drinks and asked if we wanted to order food.

Glo ordered a burger, Josh ordered fried clams, Nergal ordered a lobster roll, and I ordered rice pudding.

"I'll have a lobster roll, too," Diesel said.

"No, he won't," I said to the waitress. "He's not with us."

"He's sitting with you," the waitress said.

"He's a squatter," I said. "Don't encourage him."

The waitress gave him a full body scan. "If it was *me* I'd totally encourage him."

"I'll have a beer with my lobster roll," Diesel said.

"No, he won't," I said.

"What kind of beer do you want?" the waitress asked Diesel.

"Surprise me," he said. "And I'll have a second lobster roll to go. My monkey's in the car and he's hungry."

"That is so adorable," the waitress said. "What's your monkey's name?"

"Carl," Diesel said. "And it would be great if you could hurry things along because Carl is probably gnawing on the steering wheel. We just got back from Sri Lanka, and he's still freaked over the elephants. There were lots of elephants."

"This is Theodore Nergal," I said to Diesel. "And the guy with the patch on his forehead is Josh the Pirate."

"Aargh," Josh said to Diesel. "Who be you?"

"I be Diesel," Diesel said.

"What were you doing in Sri Lanka?" Nergal asked Diesel.

"This and that," Diesel said.

"Ah, one thing and another," Nergal said.

Diesel ate half his dinner roll. "You got it."

"Was it difficult getting your monkey into the country without a quarantine period?" Nergal asked.

There was a long pause where no one spoke and everyone looked at Diesel.

"He's a service monkey," Diesel finally said.

Not to mention, Diesel doesn't fly by ordinary means.

"You'll never guess what happened tonight," Glo said to Diesel. "Josh was giving us a tour of the Pirate Museum and one of the exhibits came crashing down at our feet, and it turned out to be a real dead guy. That's how we got to meet Dr. Nergal. He's a coroner, and he was awesome. He figured out that the guy had been shot, and he knew all about the gun and everything. And he figured out the guy had been shot over ninety years ago."

"Impressive," Diesel said.

Nergal shook his head. "Not at all. It was obvious."

"The head fell off when the dead guy hit the floor," Glo said. "And it was as if the instant Dr. Nergal touched the head he knew all this stuff!"

"He had a bullet hole in the back of his skull, and the round was still contained in the cavity," Nergal said to Diesel.

The waitress brought the food, and we all dug in. Nergal was halfway through his lobster roll when his phone buzzed. He read the text message and tapped in a response.

"This has been fun," he said, pushing back from the table, leaving his share of the bill, "but I have to be going. Duty calls."

"He seems nice," Diesel said to me when Nergal left. "You should consider going out with him."

"You think?" I asked.

A half hour later we left the restaurant. Josh walked Glo to her car, and Diesel and I walked up Wharf Street to my tan Chevy clunker.

"I sense a disturbance in the Force," Diesel said.

"Gee, I can't imagine why. Maybe it's because one minute we're in bed together, and then all of a sudden you get dressed and leave, and I don't hear from you for three weeks. And then I find out you've been in Sri Lanka."

"Well, where did you think I was?"

"I don't know . . . a drugstore. I thought you were going out for condoms."

"Yeah, looking back I could see where that might have been a possibility." He slung an arm around me and nuzzled my neck. "Maybe we should take up where we left off."

"You're actually willing to risk one of us losing our abilities?"

"I think I could work around it."

"No way. I'm not taking the chance. Besides, I'm not even sure I like you."

"Of course you like me. I'm fun."

"I had an earlier run-in with Wulf, and now you're here," I said to Diesel. "What's going on?"

"Do you know about Martin Ammon?"

"I know he's a billionaire."

"Martin Ammon is a publishing and media giant," Diesel said. "He owns a bunch of newspaper and media outlets in England and the U.S. He also has a reputation as a devourer of companies, big and small. He's an eccentric, power-hungry megalomaniac. His great-grandfather was Billy McCoy, a notorious rumrunner during Prohibition. McCoy's partner was Peg Leg Dazzle."

"Was Peg Leg related to the bakery Dazzles?"

"I imagine all the Salem Dazzles are related, but I don't know where Peg Leg fits in. Anyway, McCoy and Peg Leg at some point in their illegal endeavors came across a diary and an accompanying coin. The diary belonged to a pirate name Palgrave Bellows, and it detailed a treasure he'd hidden on an island off the coast of Maine. The coin was supposed to help read Palgrave's treasure map. Unfortunately for McCoy and Peg Leg, the map wasn't with the diary and the coin, and they were never able to find the treasure.

"A bunch of years ago the diary fell into Ammon's hands,

and he became obsessed with finding the treasure. He bought a house on Marblehead Neck, and he buddied up with a history professor. The two of them put a lot of time and money into the project, but nothing came of it."

"How do you know all this?"

"It wasn't a secret. There were newspaper articles about the diary and the lost treasure of the *Gunsway*."

"The *Gunsway*?"

"That was the name of the ship that Palgrave plundered. It originated in the Far East, and according to the diary it contained unimaginable riches both ordinary and magical."

"Wow. Magical."

"Yeah, that's where Wulf and I come into the picture. The magical part of the treasure, if the diary is to be believed, is the Avaritia Stone. The Stone of Avarice. Ammon never made a big deal about the stone in all his interviews, but I suspect his real goal was to get his hands on it. He's made joking references in the past about his drive to acquire more and more money, and says that it's appropriate his parents named him Martin. If you combine his first initial with his last name it spells 'Mammon,' one of the seven princes of hell and the personification of wealth and greed."

"That wouldn't be my first choice for a prophetic name."

"Yeah, me either. I'd rather my name was B. Eergut."

It took me a beat to figure it out. "That's gross," I said.

Diesel grinned and tucked a loose strand of hair behind my ear, his touch giving me a rush that went from my ear to my doodah.

"Want me to try again?" Diesel asked.

"No. I want you to finish telling me about the treasure."

"Ammon managed to get hold of the map that Palgrave Bellows fashioned. It was discovered during a ship restoration project. Ammon tucked the map under his arm, and he still has it."

"So now Ammon has the diary and the map."

"Yep. Problem is, the directions to the treasure are in code, and the code can't be read without the special coin. Ammon hired a team of cryptographers, but they weren't able to crack the code without it. So all attention turned to finding the coin."

"How long have they been looking for the coin?"

"Years. Ammon's had a private investigator on the case."

"Looking for the coin?"

"Yes, but eventually looking for Peg Leg. After interviewing a lot of people, the PI discovered that the coin and the diary were originally found together, but because McCoy and Peg Leg didn't completely trust each other, McCoy took the diary and Peg Leg took the coin. Shortly after that, Peg Leg disappeared and was never seen again. It was thought he was shot over a keg of rum, but it never went beyond rumor. Last week the Pirate Museum hung the prisoner cage, and it caught the attention of the detective. The cadaver had been dressed in pirate rags, but the peg leg had clearly been made in more modern times."

"I didn't notice," I said. "It just looked like a wooden peg leg to me. And you know all this how?"

"The organization that employs me has had a man watching Ammon's detective."

Diesel is a sort of cop. At least that's what he tells me. He works for a loosely organized hierarchy of People with Special Abilities. His primary job was to keep his peers on the straight and narrow. When he was assigned the task of finding the seven SALIGIA Stones, the cop part of his job became secondary.

"I was being brought back to Salem to get you into the museum when you took matters into your own hands," Diesel said.

"It wasn't intentional. I was just on a tour with Glo's new boyfriend. How does Wulf know about this?"

"Wulf has his own underground and his own agenda. Hard to say how Wulf knows things sometimes . . . he just does."

"So the idea now is that the coin is somehow attached to the pirate skeleton?"

"Maybe. Or maybe the history of the skeleton will lead to the coin."

"When I touched the cage I felt a vibration just before it broke loose and fell to the floor. It wasn't especially strong, and I thought it was probably just my imagination."

"Honey, your imagination isn't that good."

"I happen to have an excellent imagination. Sometimes I imagine my life is normal."

"Yeah, that's a stretch," Diesel said. "So maybe the coin was in the cage."

"If it was, it had to be hidden somewhere. I didn't see a coin."

"Who had access to him?"

"The only one who actually touched the skeleton while I was there was Nergal. I'm sure the EMTs had their hands on him, but I left before they zipped him up and carted him off."

Diesel unlocked my car and opened the driver's side door for me. "I have stuff to do," he said. "I'll catch up with you later."

My house looks like it was sprinkled out with a lot of other houses from the big house saltshaker sometime in the 1700s. The neighborhood is a mix of small houses built by cod fishermen, shoemakers, carpenters, and mariners, and a few larger houses that were owned by merchants and ship captains. Most of the houses still have a wooden sculpture of a golden cod above their doorways, a symbol of good luck. My golden cod was getting a little worn around the fins, and I'd had "paint your fish" in my mental to-do list for a while.

I was later getting home than usual, and Cat was waiting

at the door. I snatched my mail from the mailbox, said hello to Cat, and went straight to the kitchen. I poured some kitty crunchies into Cat's bowl, adding a slice of cantaloupe as apology for his delayed dinner. I browsed through my mail while Cat ate.

Bills, junk mail, more junk mail . . . Uh-oh. Letter from a publisher. A while back I'd had an idea for a cookbook, *Hot Guys Cooking for Hungry Women*. I packaged up my ideas and recipes, and my manuscript was making the rounds of New York agents and publishers. Unfortunately, no one wanted it, and I'd come to dread opening the letters that were inevitably rejections.

"What do you think, Cat?" I asked. "Should I open it? Do you have a good feeling about this one?"

Cat was sinking his fangs into the cantaloupe and didn't appear to care a lot about the letter.

"Okay," I said to Cat. "Wish me luck."

I tore the envelope open and read the letter. Rejection. *Crap!*

"It's a great idea," I said to Cat. "And the recipes are perfect. I've kitchen-tested them. I don't know why no one wants to buy my book."

I went into my small living room and turned the television on. I flipped through channels until I came to the Food Network. I watched a half hour of cooking and moved on to *Property Brothers* on HGTV. They cooked in an entirely different way.

Cat had followed me into the living room and was curled up on the couch next to me.

"This is what I need," I said to Cat. "I need the Property Brothers. They work cheap, they always deliver on time, and they're cute."

I heard the front door open, and Cat gave a low growl. His ears rotated in the direction of the door, and he listened for a moment. He settled back with his nose tucked under a paw when Diesel and Carl walked into the room.

Carl jumped off Diesel's shoulder, scuttled over to Cat, and sniffed him. Cat opened his one working eye, and Carl shrank back and wrapped his arms around Diesel's leg. No one messes with Cat.

"Well?" I said to Diesel.

Diesel slouched onto the couch next to me, so that I was bookended between Cat and Diesel.

"I checked out the cage, and I went over the entire floor of the exhibit room," Diesel said. "The coin wasn't there."

"And the dead guy?"

"I took a look at him, too. He was taken to the morgue and stored for an autopsy. No coin on the dead guy."

"What about Wulf?"

"I talked to Wulf. He hasn't got it."

"There were two EMTs who handled the corpse. And probably someone checked him into the morgue."

"And there was Dr. Death," Diesel said.

"Nergal?"

"Yeah, my money's on Nergal."

"I thought you liked him. You told me I should date him."

"He would have gone over the body and collected evidence before they closed the bag. He's the logical person to have found the coin."

"Did you go through his office?"

"Yeah, and the coin wasn't there," Diesel said. "It also wasn't listed in the evidence log."

The Property Brothers signed off, and I stood and stretched. "Bedtime," I said. "I need to be at the bakery early tomorrow."

"No problem," Diesel said, taking charge of the remote. "I'll be up later."

" 'Up'? No. There's no 'up.' You need to go home."

"I was thinking *this* was home."

"This is *my* home. Don't you have a home?"

"I have a beach house in the South Pacific, but it's kind of a far commute."

"Where did you live in Sri Lanka?"

"Monastery. Longest three weeks of my life."

"You used to have your own apartment here. What happened to it?"

"The guy who owned it came back to town."

CHAPTER THREE

I shut the alarm off at four-fifteen. There was no big guy next to me. The sheets were cool. Nothing smelled like gingerbread. Hard to tell if I was happy or disappointed.

I showered, dressed for work, and trucked down to the kitchen. No big guy there, either. I gave Cat a fresh bowl of water and some kitty crunchies. I got coffee brewing, popped a frozen waffle into the toaster, and shrieked when Wulf appeared without warning.

"Jeez Louise," I said. "I hate when people just materialize. How did you get in here?"

"I have ways." He glanced at the waffle in the toaster. "Not a healthy breakfast, but then maybe you're not expecting to live that long."

"What's that supposed to mean?"

"You're playing on the losing team, and the stakes are high."

"Another warning?"

"An offer to come over to my side. There are dark forces who know about you, know about your special abilities. When they come for you, they won't be easy to evade."

"I'm just a baker. I don't even have a Facebook page. How would anyone know about me?"

"You aren't just a baker. You are an asset and a very rare and useful one. That kind of secret doesn't stay secret very long from people who crave power. How do you think I found you? How do you think my cousin found you? And are you so sure he isn't interested in the stone for himself?"

"I'll take my chances with Diesel."

"I could make your life very pleasant," Wulf said. "Or very uncomfortable. Which will it be?"

"Neither. Just leave me alone, and let me do my job."

"Finding the Avarice Stone for Diesel?"

"Making cupcakes."

Wulf's lips curved ever so slightly into a hint of a smile. His eyes were dilated totally black. There was a flash of light, and he was gone.

I looked over at Cat. His tail was bushed out like a bottlebrush. "It's a whole-wheat waffle," I said to Cat. "It's *sort* of healthy."

. . .

Dazzle's Bakery has been owned and operated by a Dazzle since Puritan times, and is now managed by Clarinda Dazzle. The shop is ancient, consisting of two rooms downstairs and a small apartment upstairs. The store part of the bakery fronts onto a narrow street that's close to the harbor. The floor is the original wide-plank pine. The walls are whitewashed. The glass display cases are filled with cupcakes and cookies. Wicker baskets holding a variety of breads and breakfast pastries line the back counter. Clara and I work in the kitchen behind the shop, and between the two of us we make everything that's sold up front.

I rolled into the bakery at five o'clock. I flipped the light switch, and dialed into '60s rock on my iPad. I love this part of my day when everything is a new beginning. I love that I'm the one to unlock the door and bring the bakery to life.

I slipped on a white chef coat and got the yeast dough started. I had just moved on to cupcake batter when Clara showed up at five-thirty. Clara is divorced, is in her early forties, and lives in the apartment above the shop. She has a wiry mass of black hair shot with gray that she tries to contain in a knot at the nape of her neck. Her nose is Wampanoag Indian. The rest of her is sturdy New England pilgrim stock. I've been told that special abilities run in her family, and that she used to be one of us. Several years ago she made an unfortunate choice in the bedroom, and Clara was the one to get stripped of her power.

"We have a lunch takeout for twelve with meat pies and cupcakes today," Clara said. "Plus Mr. Duggan will be here at ten for his standing order of pretzel rolls."

"I'm on it."

Two hours later Glo swept in with her tote bag on her shoulder and her broom in hand.

"Your tote bag has a big bulge in it," I said to Glo.

"I know. I made the most amazing purchase. I passed by a yard sale on my way to work just now, and a voice called out to me."

"Like when you bought *Ripple's Book of Spells*."

"Exactly! Only this voice belonged to Emily Shipton. It was her yard sale."

"What did she sell you?"

"A Magic 8 Ball. And she swore it could predict the future." Glo took the 8 Ball out and held it in her hand. "Emily said it was empowered by her distant relative Mother Shipton."

"Mother Shipton was an English prophet who lived in a cave and died in the 1500s," Clara said. "The Magic 8 Ball is a toy invented by Mattel in the 1950s."

"It could have been Mother Shipton's spirit," Glo said.

I looked over at Broom, and I swear I saw him twitch.

Glo dropped the Magic 8 Ball back into her tote. "I asked the 8 Ball if Lizzy would have another exciting night with Theodore Nergal, and it said, 'As I see it, yes.'"

"Who's Theodore Nergal?" Clara asked.

"I fixed Lizzy up with a date last night," Glo said. "It was a spur-of-the-moment thing, but he was very cool. A doctor."

"He's a coroner," I said. "And he smelled like formaldehyde."

I was working with the large pastry bag, piping pink cream cheese frosting onto a dozen cupcakes destined for a birthday party, when Diesel sauntered in.

"Are you ready to go?" Diesel asked me.

"Ready to go where?" I asked. "It's ten o'clock. I don't even get done till one."

"So, five minutes?" Diesel asked.

Clara looked over from her workstation. "Is it important?"

"You know how it is," Diesel said, picking up one of the cupcakes and taking a bite. "The end of the world, maybe."

Clara shoved a strand of hair back from her forehead with her forearm. "Only maybe?"

"Probably," Diesel said.

"If it's 'probably' then Lizzy can have another 'save the world' day, but you're using them up fast," Clara said.

I wasn't in a rush to get on with saving the world. I'd been there and done that, and I wasn't anxious to do it again.

"Why can't you save the world by yourself?" I asked Diesel. "Why do I have to go along?"

"You have to do your touchy-feely thing. I'm big and strong and smokin' hot, but I'm not touchy-feely."

This was all true.

"I'll be with you as soon as I finish this batch of cupcakes," I said to Diesel.

"I'll help," Diesel said, grabbing a second pastry bag off the counter.

"No! I don't need help."

"How hard can it be? You just squeeze the bag, and the stuff comes out."

Diesel squeezed the bag and pink frosting shot out and hit me in the head.

I rolled my eyes up, as if I could see the gunk that was now stuck in my hair.

"You did that on purpose," I said to Diesel.

Diesel smiled wide and swiped some frosting off my forehead with his finger. "No, but I like it. It's a good look for you."

Glo was standing in the doorway.

"It's true," Glo said to me. "Pink is your color."

"Okay, enough fun," Diesel said. "We need to get moving. Lots to do, and you have a meeting with Martin Ammon at four."

Everyone froze.

"Martin Ammon?" Clara asked. "*The* Martin Ammon?"

"He has a map and a diary that I'd like to see," Diesel said.

I went back to icing the cupcakes. "So why don't you just introduce yourself and ask if you can see them?"

"Because I might want to see them for an extended amount of time. And it's more than that. It could be helpful if you got friendly with Ammon. You could keep your eye on him."

"Why me?"

"You're cute. And you have a hook. You make magical cupcakes."

"Yes, but . . ."

"I was sitting in your kitchen, and I realized it would be easy for you to get friendly with Ammon. He's a publisher and you have a cookbook."

"You didn't!"

"Yeah, I did. You had a copy of your cookbook on the counter, so I messengered it over to him with a dozen cupcakes."

"Where did you get the cupcakes?"

"You had them in your freezer."

"Omigod. Crap on a cracker."

"It's all good," Diesel said. "I sent a note with the package saying how you had this amazing cookbook idea, and all he had to do was try one of your cupcakes to know they were like magic."

"And?"

"And his assistant called right away and said that Ammon would like to see you at four o'clock at his Marblehead house."

"That is so cool," Glo said. "He's like mega rich. He's a gazillionaire. I bet his house is made out of gold. What are you going to wear? Are you going to dress up like a chef?"

Everyone stared at me, taking in my outfit. Jeans, sneakers, T-shirt under a chocolate-smudged chef coat. Hair punked up with pink frosting.

"Maybe not a chef," Clara said.

"You should get something new," Glo said. "This is an important meeting."

I shrugged out of my chef coat. "While I'm at it, I should also get my hair done, buy some makeup, and lose five pounds."

"Don't forget a manicure," Glo said.

I checked my watch and gave up a sigh. "I have six hours, more or less, to whip myself into shape." I looked at Diesel. "How much time do you think it will take to save the world?"

Diesel grinned down at me. "Less time than it will take for you to lose five pounds."

I followed Diesel out of the bakery to his SUV, and saw that Carl wasn't in the backseat. "No monkey?" I asked.

"I left him at the apartment."

"You have an apartment already?"

"I have friends in high places. They have ways of getting things done fast."

I had no idea what that meant, and I wasn't going to ask. I'd reached the conclusion that it was best not to know too much about Diesel.

"Wulf popped into my kitchen this morning," I said.

Diesel looked over at me. "He have anything interesting to say?"

"Mostly it was dire warnings of my bleak future."

Ten minutes later, Diesel pulled into the lot attached to Salem Hospital and parked. We entered the hospital and found our way to the State Pathology Department. Nergal's office door was open, and Nergal was working at his computer when we walked in.

"Knock, knock," I said.

Nergal looked up and smiled. "Hey. Find any more mummies?"

"Nope," I said. "Just the one. We'd like some information on him."

"I haven't done the autopsy yet so there's not much to tell," Nergal said.

"Have you had a chance to look through his clothes?"

"Not since last night."

"Did you find anything last night?" Diesel asked him.

Nergal sat up a little straighter. "What do you mean?"

While Diesel was talking to Nergal, I walked around the room, skimming my hand across surfaces, looking for a vibration or a tingle or heat.

"Was anything interesting stuck in his clothes?" Diesel asked. "Like a coin?"

Nergal went silent for a beat. "Um . . ." he finally said.

I put my hand on Nergal's shoulder. Nothing.

"Try his pockets," Diesel said.

Nergal shrank away from me. "What's going on?"

"We think there might have been a coin on the dead guy," Diesel said. "And it's not on him now."

"How do you know?" Nergal asked.

"I looked," Diesel said.

Nergal jumped to his feet. "You're not allowed to look. How did you get in to look?"

"I'm special," Diesel said.

I ran my hand over Nergal's pants pocket and felt a definite vibration.

"He's got it," I said.

Nergal moved away from me. "You're freaking me out. Who *are* you? *What* are you?"

I looked over at Diesel. "You want to field this one?"

"You have the coin in your pocket," Diesel said to Nergal.

"So what?" Nergal said. "It's not a crime. It's evidence."

"I've seen the evidence list, and the coin isn't on it," Diesel said. "So it looks to me like you stole some evidence."

"It's just an old coin," Nergal said. "It's not even a whole coin. It's just a piece of a coin." He pulled it out of his pocket and held it in the palm of his hand. "Why are you so interested in this?"

"It's a small but important piece of a puzzle," Diesel said. "Why did *you* want it?"

"You wouldn't believe me if I told you," Nergal said. "It's too weird."

"Try me," Diesel said.

Nergal adjusted his Harry Potter glasses. "If I touch a dead body, I can sense the last thing he or she was thinking before death." He shifted foot to foot. "I know that's crazy. I used to think it was my imagination, but sometimes I learn things that turn out to be true."

"Wow," I said, "that's amazing."

He shrugged. "Most people's last thoughts are pretty mundane. I get a lot of people wishing they'd worn clean underwear. Or wishing they'd deleted their browser history. Folks are surprisingly pragmatic."

"So they don't get all profound at the end?"

"Not so much," Nergal said. "Still, every now and then someone tells me something interesting. Like the guy in the cage. I guess I shouldn't have taken the coin, but I didn't see any harm in it. I didn't think it had real value."

"Do you have any other talents besides the dead thing?" Diesel asked him. "Can you fly? Can you talk to grasshoppers?"

"No. I can't do either of those things."

"He's not listed in our database," Diesel said to me.

"What database?" Nergal asked.

"The one that records people with enhanced abilities," I said.

Nergal's mouth dropped open, and his eyes got wide. "You mean there are others?"

"Yep," I said. "We're called Unmentionables."

"Not officially," Diesel said.

I looked over at him. "You told me we were called Unmentionables."

"That's more of a nickname. Like calling people from Massachusetts 'Mass-holes.'"

"Well, what's the official name for people with enhanced abilities?" I asked.

Diesel shrugged. "People with enhanced abilities?"

"I thought I was the only one," Nergal said. "I never told anyone. And now I find out there are others like me."

"Not exactly like you," I said. "We all have different talents. I can locate certain empowered objects. Some people can bend spoons. Others can make it rain."

"That's so cool," Nergal said. "And you guys have, like, a club?"

"No club," Diesel said.

"Do you have parties?" Nergal asked. "Mixers?"

Diesel grinned. "Sorry, dude," he said. "No mixers."

"So if you don't have parties, how did Lizzy get frosting in her hair?" Nergal asked.

"It's work-related," I said, gesturing toward my head.

"Tell me about the pirate prisoner," Diesel said to Nergal. "What did you learn from him?"

"The first thought I got was 'peg leg.' That's how I found the piece of the coin. I heard the thought, and I looked down at the man's wooden leg and saw that a piece of a coin was lying next to it. It must have fallen out."

"Did he have any other thoughts?"

"The last thought he had before he was shot was 'At least McCoy will never be able to find the treasure without all eight pieces of the coin.' And his attitude was odd. The guy was almost happy. No, not happy. *Gloating.* That's the closest I can come to it." Nergal exhaled a long breath. "I can't tell you how good it feels to talk about all this. Can I have the names of other people in the club? Do we have a Facebook page?"

"No and no," Diesel said, taking the piece of coin from him.

"This is going to be a real pain in the ass," Diesel said when we got back to the car. "Some idiot cut the coin up into eight pieces."

CHAPTER FOUR

Clara was rolling out cookie dough in the kitchen when we returned. "Have you finished saving the world?" she asked Diesel.

"Just starting," Diesel said. "I assume by now Glo's told you about the skeleton in the cage at the Pirate Museum."

"I know every detail," Clara said.

"We've been doing some detective work, and it looks like the skeleton in the cage might be Peg Leg Dazzle," I said to Clara.

Clara stopped in mid-roll. "Are you serious?"

"Pretty much," I said. "Do you know anything about him?"

"Peg Leg was my great-uncle," Clara said. "His real name was Collier. He was my grandfather's older brother. Gramps didn't know him very well because Collier disappeared when Gramps was just a kid, but we've all heard lots of stories about Collier. He was a cod fisherman who lost his leg when it got tangled in rigging during a storm. He chose a wooden peg leg over a prosthetic, gave up on cod fishing, and went into business with Billy McCoy.

"Gramps said Collier used to drive him to a soda fountain on Essex Street, buy him milkshakes, and tell him stories of pirates and buried treasure. He even gave Gramps a couple pieces of a coin that was supposed to be a clue to finding the most fabulous treasure of all time. Collier said he got the coin from a pirate named Bellows. And Gramps said the pieces matched up to a couple more pieces Collier kept in his peg leg."

I looked over at Diesel. "Oh boy."

"No kidding," Diesel said.

"Did you ever get to see the pieces of coin Collier gave to your grandfather?" Diesel asked.

"I did," Clara said. "Gramps used to show them to me all the time when I was a kid."

Diesel pulled the pirate prisoner's chunk of coin out of his pocket and placed it on the workbench. "Did they look like this?"

"Yes!"

"Do you know what happened to them?" Diesel asked.

"I assume Gramps still has them."

"He's still alive?"

"The Dazzles have surprisingly long lifespans," Clara said. "Unless you partner up with Billy McCoy. Collier isn't the first McCoy partner to mysteriously disappear. I suspect McCoy wasn't good at sharing the wealth."

"How old is Gramps?" I asked Clara.

"Gramps is ninety-eight, and he doesn't look a day over a hundred and ten."

"I'd like to talk to him," Diesel said.

"You'll have to wait until tomorrow," Clara said. "He's on a seniors' bus trip to Mohegan Sun Casino. He likes to play the slots. He won't get back until late tonight."

The front door to the shop opened and a beat later Josh poked his head into the kitchen. "Ahoy there," he said. "Permission to come aboard and procure cupcakes." His attention immediately moved to the fragment of silver on the counter. "Is that part of a doubloon?"

We all shrugged. We didn't know.

"My knowledge is limited to museum fakery and Google," Josh said, "but it looks to me like a Spanish doubloon."

"What does Google have to say about it?" Diesel asked.

"I don't know," Josh said. "I don't read the text. I just look at the pictures. You should show it to Quentin Devereaux. He's a professor at Salem State, and he's the resident consultant for the Pirate Museum."

"Sounds like a plan," Diesel said. "Devereaux was the expert Martin Ammon turned to when he inherited the Palgrave diary. Who's going with me?"

"I will!" Glo said.

"No, you won't," Clara said. "You have to wait on customers."

"You and you," Diesel said, pointing to Josh and me.

"Aargh," Josh said. "I'm due at the museum at noon."

"And I need to do something with my hair and get something to wear," I said.

"No problem," Diesel said. "This won't take long."

Salem State University has been around, under one name or another, since 1854, when it was called Salem Normal School. I thought the juxtaposition of "Salem" and "Normal" had to be considered ironic, even then. Salem hasn't been normal for a long, long time.

With all the construction and parking lots and gleaming glass buildings on campus, Salem State looks like any number of colleges that are springing up, like shiny mushrooms, all around the country. The Sullivan Building is the only old structure still standing, its red bricks and turrets lost in the middle of the north campus, as if someone forgot to tear it down and replace it with gleaming chrome.

Professor Devereaux's office was on the second floor. He was at his desk, bent over a book, when we walked in. His hair was streaked with gray, his frame was lean, and his face was lined and dotted with gray stubble. He was wearing an ancient tweed sports coat over a pale blue button-down shirt.

"Yes?" he said, looking up at us.

"We be lookin' for some answers," Josh said.

"Do I know you?"

"I work at the Pirate Museum," Josh said.

Devereaux nodded. "That explains a lot."

There were two old buckles, some ancient coins, and a battered copper telescope on Devereaux's desk. On the wall behind him was a pirate flag. Not the usual skull and cross-bones of the movies, but rather a white skeleton plunging an arrow into a red heart dripping fountains of blood.

"So what do you want to know?" Devereaux asked. "You want to know about pirates? I could tell you things that would shock you. Pirates had the first representative government in all of Europe. The captain and the quartermaster were elected periodically by the crew. All the hands got an equal share of the booty. They even had workers' compensation. Pirates placed a portion of their plunder into a central fund that was used as insurance for any injuries sustained by the crew. On occasion, women were even welcomed as members of the crew. Pirates were quite socially advanced for their time."

"Except for the raping and pillaging," Diesel said.

Devereaux nodded. "They did engage in some classic activities."

Diesel showed Devereaux the piece of coin. "What can you tell me about this?"

Devereaux studied it through a jeweler's loupe. "It's Spanish."

"It's a doubloon, right?" Josh said.

Devereaux shook his head. "No. It's a fragment of an eight-reales silver coin, commonly called a 'bust dollar.' It's got a bust of Charles III on it, and was considered legal tender in the U.S. until 1857."

"Why is it cut like a pizza?" I asked.

"It's how you made change," Devereaux said. "Coins were often cut into pie-shaped sections, or 'bits.' If you had two of these pieces you'd have two bits. Do you know any of the history associated with this piece of the coin?"

"We think it was passed on by a pirate named Bellows," Diesel said.

"Palgrave Bellows," Devereaux said. "The Gentleman Corsair. He was a middle-aged silversmith from Rhode Island who suddenly decided to take up piracy. His captives reported that Bellows continued to wear the powdered wig of a gentleman even after years in the tropical sun. The curly white wig contrasted vividly with his swarthy skin and made Bellows a striking figure indeed. They called him the Last of the Roundsmen."

"Roundsmen?" I asked.

"Bellows was one of the last buccaneers to sail the Pirate Round. It was a route that started in New England and went all the way across the Atlantic to the coast of Africa. Then down past the Cape of Good Hope, through the Mozambique Channel to Madagascar. The pirates were nothing if not intrepid," Devereaux said. "They often went round to the Red Sea, which put them in an ideal spot to intercept the shipping of the Mughal Empire. You've heard of the *Gunsway*, of course. The *Gunsway* was a trading ship belonging to the Mughal emperor, and it contained untold riches."

"How much be untold riches?" Josh asked.

"A lot. Some say the treasure even included the legendary Blue Diamond of Babur."

Josh sucked in some air. "The Blue Diamond of Babur. I like the way she sounds. I wouldn't mind having such a treasure."

"It might come with a price," Devereaux said. "It's told that the diamond carries a dreadful curse to all who don't worship the demon Mammon. Legend has it that a magical stone imbued with the power of greed, and the Blue Diamond, were kept in a Mughal temple dedicated to

Mammon, the Prince of Avarice. In the center of the temple was a large idol representing Mammon, and the Blue Diamond was the heart of the idol. The diamond and the stone are said to be forever wed, and the diamond glows blue when it's near the stone."

"Ah," Josh said. "'Tis a fine fairy tale."

Devereaux smiled. "It is indeed. And the tale gets even more interesting. During a time of war, the decision was made to move the stone and the diamond to a safer location. While they were being moved with the rest of the treasure of Mammon, pirates plundered the ship and stole the stone and diamond."

"Would that be Palgrave Bellows and the *Gunsway*?" Josh asked.

"It would," Devereaux said. "Bellows boarded the *Gunsway* and took her back to New England, where it was said he hid the treasure on an island off the coast of Maine. That he even made a map in special code, so no one person knew where it was."

"Was the treasure ever found?" Josh asked.

"Never found," Devereaux said. "Estimated to be around one hundred and ninety million dollars in today's money."

"That would be worth a hunt," Josh said.

"Perhaps, but it could just be a myth," Devereaux said. "A two-hundred-year-old rumor fueled by the ramblings of a crazy pirate and his diary."

"Aargh," Josh said. "Is our piece of coin valuable?"

"It's not worth a great deal of money, if that's what you mean," Devereaux said. "It's just a single bit, and it looks to me like a counterfeit. Might I keep this bit for further examination?" he asked Diesel. "I am intrigued."

"I'm afraid not," Diesel said. "I'm also intrigued."

CHAPTER FIVE

"So what do ye think?" Josh asked when we got to the car. "He's a smart one, right?"

"Right," Diesel said, sliding behind the wheel.

"A hundred and ninety million be a worthy treasure," Josh said. "I could stop talking like a pirate if I had such a treasure."

"You could stop talking like a pirate without it," I said.

"Ah, 'tis not that easy," Josh said. "A lad doesn't just lay aside the role of a pirate."

I checked my watch. It was almost noon. "It's also hard to lay aside the role of prospective cookbook author. I need to go shopping."

"Aargh," Josh said. "And I'll be walking the plank if I'm late for work."

"See if you can find out how the museum happened to be in possession of Peg Leg's body," Diesel said to Josh.

"Aye, Captain," Josh said, getting out of the car. "I'll give you a full report."

"Will you be working all day?" Diesel asked.

"No. 'Tis a part-time day at the museum. I spend an hour or two helping to get things set up, and then I walk the streets to make some spare change posing for pictures."

Diesel watched Josh walk away before turning to me. "Clara said there were a couple pieces of the coin in the peg leg, but we only have one. Call Nergal and ask him if he's come across another piece."

I placed the call, and after a short discussion about cupcakes I asked him about the pieces of coin.

"Sorry," Nergal said. "No second piece. I did a thorough external exam and a full-body X-ray and nothing else turned up."

"I'm confused about the coin," I said to Diesel. "My ability is very specific. I only feel vibrations from a SALIGIA Stone, but I felt a very faint vibration from the sliver of coin."

"I've seen depictions of the Blue Diamond," Diesel said. "When it was set into the idol it was encased in an elaborate silver setting. Palgrave Bellows was a silversmith, and I'm guessing he fashioned the counterfeit coin out of the diamond's silver setting. Then he made a map that could only be read with the help of the coin."

"Very clever."

"So do you really need to go shopping for something to wear when you meet Ammon?" Diesel asked.

"I suppose. I haven't exactly got a closet filled with clothes that are appropriate for gazillionaire meetings."

"Where do you want to go?"

I would have preferred to go to the mall or at least T.J. Maxx, but time was short, so I settled for downtown Salem.

"There's a small boutique on Derby Street where I might be able to find something," I told Diesel.

Twenty minutes later I was standing in a dressing room in my underwear, staring at a pile of discarded blazers, skirts, and tops.

Diesel knocked on the changing room door. "How's it going?"

"Not good. Everything I try on makes me look like Miss Hathaway from *The Beverly Hillbillies*."

"Incoming," he said, tossing a shocking pink fitted jacket with a matching tank top and simple black skirt over the top of the door.

I tried them on and they were perfect.

"How did you find this?" I asked him.

"I undressed the mannequin in the window."

I should have guessed. Undressing women was probably

one of his many exceptional abilities. I took my new clothes to the register and maxed out my credit card. We dumped the bags in the car and walked over to the Pirate Museum to see if Josh had learned anything helpful about Peg Leg Dazzle. I was moving on autopilot alongside Diesel, thinking about my meeting with Ammon, when a guy burst out of the Pirate Museum and slammed into me. We both fell to the pavement, and I realized that the idiot who knocked me over was Steven Hatchet, Wulf's minion.

Hatchet jumped to his feet, straightened his hammered metal helmet, called me a "stupid wench," and took off at a run down the street.

Diesel gave me a hand up. "Are you okay?"

"The whole 'wench' thing is getting old. And I think I skinned my knee."

"I could kiss it and make it better."

"That would be hard to do since I'm wearing jeans."

"Yeah, we'd have to wrangle you out of them."

"Jeez Louise."

"Just a suggestion," Diesel said.

The museum door was still open, and I could hear sea shanties playing inside. We stepped into the foyer and Josh came forward to greet us.

"Ahoy, mateys," Josh said. "Welcome aboard."

"Ahoy," I said. "I was just knocked over by a moron who was running out of the museum."

"Aye. He was rude in here as well, waving his sword, threatening the museum manager, demanding information on the poor soul in the cage."

"What did the manager tell him?"

"That the museum got the pirate in the cage from a haunted house in Salem Willows. If you're looking for more pieces of the coin, it would be a good place to start. I asked the manager if there were any fragments in the packing when the exhibit arrived, and he said there weren't."

"I'm not familiar with Salem Willows," Diesel said.

"I'm going off my shift," Josh said. "I can show you how to get there. It's one of my favorite places. And just in case that rude red-haired scurvy swab is there, I'll put him in his place."

Josh whipped out his cutlass and slashed the air.

"Great," Diesel said. "Just dial back on the slashing in the car, okay? It's a loaner."

"You can drop me off at the bakery on your way to the Willows," I said to Diesel.

"Not gonna happen," Diesel said. "I need you."

"You have Josh."

"Lucky me," Diesel said.

"I need to do something about my hair."

"Your hair looks great."

"It has cake frosting in it!"

"Yeah, it's making me hungry."

"They'll have food at Salem Willows," Josh said.

"Done deal," Diesel said, wrapping an arm around me, dragging me along.

Salem Willows is a derelict Coney Island–type of seaside amusement park that sits on a small spit of land stretching into Beverly Harbor northeast of the city. I thought it looked sleazy and disreputable and retro charming.

"Aargh," Josh said, spreading his arms wide. "Housed on these grounds ye have the largest collection of vintage pinball machines in all of Massachusetts. 'Tis a vast treasure that includes a 1960 Official Baseball, which, in my pirate opinion, is the finest arcade game ever made. Plus there be Skee-Ball, classic videogames, redemption games, claw crane games, electro-mechanical games, air hockey, rail shooters, as well as *Dance Dance Revolution* and *Drummania*."

We were standing at the edge of the parking lot, taking it all in.

"What are we looking for here?" Diesel asked.

"Dr. Caligari's Cabinet of Terrors," Josh said. "'Tis the wreck of a house standing in the lee of the arcade." He tipped his nose up and sniffed the air. "I doth smell something tasty, and I be craving a bite of food."

Diesel gave him a twenty-dollar bill. "Lizzy and I are going into the terror house, and you're in charge of lunch.

And if you don't stop talking like a pirate I'm going to punch you in the face."

"Okay then. Good to know," Josh said.

A big headless guy was at the Cabinet of Terrors entrance, selling tickets. His head was sitting on the floor by his feet, and I could see his eyes through the mesh in his shirtfront.

"If you want to go in it's three bucks a head," the guy said to Diesel.

"Really? A head?" Diesel said.

"The irony is not lost on me," the headless guy said.

Diesel bought three tickets and asked to see the manager.

"Who wants to know?" the headless guy asked.

"I do," Diesel said.

The headless guy lifted a walkie-talkie to his chest. "Spencer. Somebody to see you. Business."

A crackling voice came over the walkie-talkie. "Send them in."

The headless guy gestured with his thumb. "He's in there somewhere."

Josh ran up and handed us corn dogs.

"Meat on a stick. My favorite," Diesel said.

I took a bite. It was a little like eating fried sand until you broke through to the hot dog. Once you did that, though, it was pretty good.

"Careful where you drop the food," the headless guy

said. "We don't want no more rat problems than we already got."

He buzzed us in, and the front door automatically opened and closed behind us. The interior was pitch-black, and screechy old-fashioned horror-movie music blasted out at us. Lightning flashed, illuminating the room. Blood was splattered on the walls and a hooded figure stood by the sofa, where a dismembered body lay in picturesque disarray.

Diesel looked over at the man in the bloody hood. "Are you the manager?"

"No, man," he said. "He's in the back. He's playing the killer clown today, 'cause the regular killer clown got food poisoning. Oh, and 'Beware the Birthday Party.'"

We rounded the corner and went into the dining room where a bunch of corpses sat at a table. A skeleton of a turkey was the centerpiece. A banner over the table read HAPPY THANKS-KILLING.

"What's next?" I asked. "'Happy Horror-ween'? 'Merry Christ-massacre'? 'Happy Kill-ombus Day'?"

"'Happy New Year's Evil,'" Josh suggested.

"'Slash Wednesday,'" I said.

"Are you done?" Diesel asked.

"I think so," I said. "No, wait. 'Happy Ground-up Hog Day'?"

We walked through the Hall of Mirrors and finally reached the children's birthday party. Not so much scary as having a high *ick* factor. The balloons were bloodstained, the streamers were dotted with ants and spiders, and the birthday cake was moldy and had an animatronic rat poking his head out of it. A broken doll sat at the table. The doll's one eye gleamed in the candlelight. A fat clown stood behind the doll. His face was white with black diamonds painted around his eyes. He had a red nose and a dirty orange fright wig, and his belly was busting out of his clown suit. He looked like a clown who should cut back on the pork chops.

"Are you the manager?" Diesel asked him.

"Yeah, I'm Spencer Rossitto. Are you the guy that wanted to talk to me?"

"I'm looking into the origin of the pirate skeleton that was sold to the Salem Pirate Museum."

"I don't know much about it. It was always there, hanging in the torture chamber. Been there forever. Or at least as long as I've been here. Which is since the 1980s, which might as well be forever."

"Why did you sell it?"

"The Pirate Museum made me a good offer. I'm always open to a good offer. You see anything you want to buy? Make me an offer."

"I might be in the market for a coin," Diesel said. "Even a piece of a coin. Do you have anything like that?"

"Maybe. I got lots of coins. Exactly what kind of coin do you want?"

"A sliver of a silver real. It has a picture of Charles III on one side."

"I'm a businessman," the clown said. "What's the going rate for one of them slivers?"

We were all distracted by shouting in the hallway and the sound of someone running in our direction. We turned to the doorway, and Hatchet burst into the room, sword drawn.

"Halt, rude and lowly beasts!" Hatchet yelled. "Hand over the coin before I cleave every one of you in twain and dance on your entrails."

Josh pulled out his cutlass and pointed it at Hatchet. "Stand down or feel the bite of my blade."

Hatchet was dressed in green tights, yellow Nike running shoes, and a white peasant shirt with a brown jerkin. Josh was wearing black Jack Sparrow–style boot covers over Converse sneakers, red-and-black-striped pants, a puffy white shirt, and a black tunic. It was like a fashion parade of crazies.

Hatchet squinted at Josh. "What art thou?"

Josh looked over at Diesel.

"Go for it," Diesel said.

"I be a Buccaneer American," Josh said. "What art *thou*?"

"Hatchet is his liege lord and master's faithful minion." Hatchet waggled his sword at Josh. "Do you dare to match swords with me, peasant?"

"Aye, sirrah, and I'll rip you from belly to chin," Josh said, waggling his sword back at Hatchet.

Hatchet swung the bigger, heavier broadsword. Josh's cutlass was short but curved to an angry point. What the cutlass lacked in length I thought it must make up for in maneuverability.

"Methinks thou knows not about swordplay," Hatchet said to Josh.

"Thou thinks as a fool," Josh said. "Me took a course in fencing at North Shore Community College."

Hatchet lowered his sword a bit. "How didst thou do?"

"Sadly, this good and worthy buccaneer suffered the flu during final exam and dost got an incomplete."

"Seems unjust," Hatchet said.

"Aye. Much of the world is unjust."

"This is going nowhere," Diesel said. "Maybe you two should take it outside so we can get on with business."

"I will smite thee down first," Hatchet said, turning toward Diesel.

"Back off," Diesel said, "or I'll turn you into a toad."

"Can you do that?" I asked Diesel.

Diesel smiled. "I'd need permission."

Hatchet lunged at Diesel, and Josh whacked Hatchet on the back of his head with the flat of the cutlass. Hatchet stumbled, went down to one knee, and farted.

"I believe I doth break wind," Hatchet said. "Sincere apologies."

We all took a step back from Hatchet and fanned the air. Spencer bumped into me, and I felt a vibration.

"The clown is vibrating," I said to Diesel.

Diesel grabbed Spencer and shoved his hand into one of the big pockets in the baggy checkered clown pants.

"Hey, if I'm gonna get groped at least let the girl do it," the clown said.

Diesel came up with some loose change, a throat lozenge, and a set of car keys. "You're lucky you're not getting searched by my monkey."

"No kidding?" Spencer said. "You've got a monkey? Do you got an organ to grind?"

"Doesn't everyone?" Diesel said, moving on to another pocket. He pulled his hand out of the pocket and held a pie-shaped piece of a coin between his fingers. "Tell me about this," he said to Spencer.

"It fell out of the cage," Spencer said. "The one that held the body. When I was loading it into the truck, it fell out. I didn't think it was worth anything. I only kept it as a good luck charm."

Diesel flipped the coin to me, and I caught it with one hand and felt the vibration.

"This is it," I said. "This is the second piece of the pie."

The lights went out, and we were plunged into total blackness. I felt an arm wrap around my waist, I was lifted off my feet, and I was effortlessly swept across the room. Wulf's voice whispered against my ear, his voice so soft it was barely above a thought.

"You're still playing on the wrong team," he said to me. "It won't end well for you."

He smelled faintly of cloves and woodsmoke. I felt his lips brush along my neck, and a chill ran down my spine followed by a rush of heat. His hand closed over mine, and I was no longer in possession of the coin.

"Hey!" I said.

There was a flash of fire, and after a beat the lights came on in the room.

Wulf was gone but Hatchet was still with us. He tipped his head up and sniffed the air.

"Sire?" Hatchet asked.

"He t-t-took the c-c-coin," I said.

Diesel was hands on hips. "He should take his act to Vegas."

CHAPTER SIX

Martin Ammon's house on Marblehead Neck was ten minutes from my house, and I was going to arrive precisely on time. I'd combed most of the frosting from my hair, and I was dressed in my new clothes. I'd taken a moment to swipe on some mascara and lip gloss. I had butterflies in my stomach, and a nervous twitch in my left eye. My car's gas gauge read empty, but the red light wasn't on, so I felt pretty confident I could make it to the Neck and back.

The Neck was an island at one time, but now a road built on a causeway connects it to the mainland. There are a couple yacht clubs on the harbor side. The rest of the

Neck is high-end residential. The oceanfront properties are especially pricey, and that's where Ammon lived. His large stone house, with its multiple chimneys and turrets, was partially hidden behind a high stone wall. I pulled up to an intricately scrolled wrought iron gate. The plaque in the middle of it bore the name CUPIDITAS. A red light was blinking in a call box at the edge of the driveway.

"Lizzy Tucker to see Martin Ammon," I said to the call box.

The gate slowly swung open, and I drove through to the house and parked in the circular driveway. The massive front door was opened by a man in a navy blazer, a crisp white dress shirt, and a red tie with the Ammon logo on it. I was afraid to ask if he was the butler, because if he said yes I might burst out laughing out of sheer nervousness.

He was somewhere in his thirties and slightly overweight, around five foot ten. He had mousy brown hair cut in a traditional square-back style, side part. Hazel eyes with skimpy mousy brown eyelashes and eyebrows. Thick lips and a nose that was almost too small for his face. If you saw him on the street you might think he reminded you of Practical Pig in a blazer.

"My name is Rutherford," he said, smiling wide, showing lots of teeth. "I'm Mr. Ammon's devoted assistant."

Devoted assistant? Okay, that's weird. Does that imply love? Sexual relationship? Minion status?

"Mr. Ammon is expecting you," Rutherford said. "This way."

I was led up a red carpeted staircase and down a cherry-paneled hallway to a set of double doors that looked like they belonged in Downton Abbey.

"This is Mr. Ammon's home office," Rutherford said. "It's his private space, and not many people are privileged to see it. You must be quite special. I understand you've submitted a cookbook for Mr. Ammon's consideration."

The possibility of getting my cookbook published had me breathless. I was desperate for the money it might bring in. My house needed a new roof, and my car was ready for the junkyard. Diesel had used the cookbook and the cupcakes as a ploy to get me into Ammon's house, but what if Ammon really liked my book! Okay, take a step back, I told myself. It would be very cool to get the cookbook published, but let's not lose sight of the true purpose for the visit. I needed to help Diesel find the stone, so I could get on with my life. That meant locating the map and the diary. Focus, Lizzy!

The home office was huge, and every wall was lined with bookshelves. The floor was glossy dark wood covered with Oriental carpets. The furniture looked comfortable. Overstuffed club chairs covered in burgundy chenille. Mahogany leather couches. A desk the size of a king-size bed. All right, maybe that's an exaggeration, but not by much.

A massive stone fireplace dominated one wall. A black rose was engraved in the center of the mantel, with some Latin phrase carved underneath it. A framed piece of parchment hung over the mantel. The parchment was obviously important to Ammon since it held the place of honor in the room.

"What is this?" I asked Rutherford.

"It's a treasure map," Rutherford said. "Mr. Ammon is a history buff."

That had my full attention. This could be *the* map.

"It doesn't look like a treasure map," I said. "It's round."

"Yes, yes, that's the amazing part of it. It's unique. And so far it hasn't given up its treasure, but Mr. Ammon has hopes of cracking the code someday. High hopes."

Hot damn, am I good or what? I only just got here and I might have located the map.

On the other side, the room opened onto a porch with a spectacular view of the Atlantic. Martin Ammon was on the porch. He had a dazzling white smile, which was the result of either superior breeding or superior dentistry. His eyes were an unsettling pale blue in a narrow spray-tanned face. His frizzed bleached-blond hair was carefully combed over his balding head. His online biography placed him at fifty-two. He was slim and about five foot six in his expensive Italian leather boots. He was dressed in a gray suit, the jacket thrown casually over a wicker chair. In his tailored vest and blue shirt with the sleeves rolled up, he looked like a movie star between takes. More Christopher Walken than George Clooney.

Ammon was standing beside a glass-topped bistro table. A stack of dog-eared pages that I feared was my manuscript was on the table. Even from a distance I could see there was so much red ink on the top page that it looked like fresh roadkill.

"Thank you for making the trip out here," he said. "I have an office in Salem, but I rarely use it. I find it more efficient and enjoyable to work from Cupiditas."

"No problem. This is an incredible house. I can understand why you wouldn't want to leave it."

"Truth is, I'm only here sporadically. It was fortunate that your manuscript was brought to my attention while I was in residence."

My heart did a flip. He said it was fortunate! That was good!

"So you like my book!" I said.

He looked down at the pages on the table. "No, I hate it. Actually I despise it. I thought it was ridiculous. The whole concept of it. Who wants to see hot guys cooking? I don't. Guys don't. Women don't. They want to see someone like themselves cooking."

I'd had my share of rejections with this project, but they all paled in comparison to this. This was like getting hit in the face with a frying pan. The heck with the map and the diary and saving the world . . . this was freaking insulting. I sucked in some air and made an attempt to steady my voice.

"Let me see if I have this straight," I said. "You brought me here to tell me you hated my book?"

"Yes, the book is trash."

He picked the manuscript up and heaved the pages over the railing, off into space. They fluttered in the breeze for a moment and then swirled gracefully to the ground in a paper blizzard. Rutherford and two housekeepers in gray dresses and white aprons ran out onto the lawn, gathered the pages up, and shoved them into garbage bags. I watched in frozen horror, and within minutes it was as if there had never been a manuscript at all.

"Uh, gosh," I said.

"Much better," Ammon said. "Now we can start fresh. I don't want the book, but I *do* want *you*. I hated the concept, but I love your writing. You have a way of bringing cooking to life. It's delightful. It's conversational. It's funny. It's sexy. It's like we're right there in the kitchen with you, watching you create wickedly delicious dishes. I want you to start over with a new idea. We're not going to publish just a book . . . we're going to publish *you*. We're going to push Lizzy Tucker as a brand. Lizzy Tucker is going to be the new millennium's Martha Stewart and Rachael Ray and Julia Child all rolled into one."

"That's a lot to roll into one."

"That's just the beginning. We're going to put you

on television worldwide. You'll be more famous than Santa Claus."

"I don't think I want to be more famous than Santa Claus. And to tell you the truth, I don't know if I have the time to write a new cookbook."

"It's not just about cooking. If you don't have time to start over I'll hire someone to do it for you. This is going to be about Lizzy Tucker laundry baskets, and Lizzy Tucker crockpots, and Lizzy Tucker wine. I own a vineyard in New Zealand that's begging for a brand."

"I'll have to think about it."

"I'll give you a five-hundred-thousand-dollar advance."

I went thumbs-up. "Let's get started."

Martin Ammon looked at his watch. "I have an hour before I have to get dressed for a dinner engagement," he said. "We can use the time to review your life story. My publicity and marketing department has already laid the groundwork of a bright young woman who goes to the big city and enrolls in a prestigious cooking school only to drop out due to sexual harassment."

"Actually I graduated and there was no sexual harassment."

"We might want to massage the truth a little. Everyone loves sexual harassment."

"I don't think I can go there."

"No problem. We'll skip over the sexual harassment and go straight to the fact that you saved Dazzle's Bakery, singlehandedly making it a success with your magical cupcakes."

"It was doing just fine without me."

"We'll smooth it out with editorial."

"Why me?" I asked him.

"I told you. I like your writing style. And you're cute. You're going to look great on television, and you'll package up perfect. You're a twenty-first-century Doris Day."

"Lucky me."

"Exactly," Martin Ammon said.

He leaned close, and his strange pale blue eyes narrowed a little. "We're going to spend some time together, Lizzy Tucker. I'm going to learn all about you. There will be no secrets."

Eek.

"And now I have a surprise for you," he said.

Crap. I didn't need another surprise.

Ammon crossed to an elaborate silver and glass serving cart positioned against the wall. The serving cart held a single canister, which I now realized had my picture on it. Below the picture, in gold and black lettering, were the words LIZZY TUCKER GOODIES. Ammon lifted the lid of the canister and helped himself to a cookie.

"*Mint* chocolate chip cookies," Martin said, holding the cookie aloft. "From page 101 of your manuscript. As soon as I read that page, I had to try the cookies to see if they were really as good as the recipe looked."

"You made them yourself?"

"Don't be silly. I had my chef make them. But I told him to follow the recipe exactly, no embroidering, no improvising." He took a bite. "Fantastic," he said. "These cookies will be the first in our product line." He smiled so wide I was almost blinded by the brilliance. "Lizzy Tucker, you're going to be rich beyond your dreams. We're going to be an unstoppable team."

I supposed this was good. This was sort of what Diesel wanted, right?

I gave him a forced smile. "Yep, we'll be a team."

"One last thing," he said. "The cupcakes. I probably wouldn't have looked at your cookbook if I hadn't eaten the cupcakes. They were wonderful. They made me feel happy. They were the best cupcakes I've ever had, and I fashion myself to be something of a cupcake expert. I had my chef make your cupcake recipe, but they weren't the same. Did you leave out an ingredient?"

"I left out the magic."

Diesel and Carl were in my kitchen eating cookies when I rolled in. Diesel was eating Double Stuf Oreos, and Carl was eating Fig Newtons.

"How'd it go?" Diesel asked.

"Okay, I guess. It was weird. Not what I expected."

"How so?"

"He hated my idea for a cookbook, but he liked my writing style. And he thought I was cute."

"And?"

"And he offered me a big bag of money."

"What did he want you to do for the money?"

"Rewrite the cookbook."

"That doesn't sound so bad."

I took a couple Oreos from Diesel. "It feels off. And I don't like him. He's creepy."

"From what I read, *no one* likes him."

"His butler likes him."

"He has a butler?"

"Actually I don't know what the guy is. His name is Rutherford, and he said he was Ammon's devoted assistant. *Devoted.* Like he lived to suck Ammon's toes."

Carl ate the last Fig Newton and stared into the empty bag. He turned the bag upside down and shook it. No Fig Newtons fell out. He looked over at Diesel and shook the bag some more.

"You ate the whole bag," Diesel said to Carl. "There aren't any more."

"Eeep," Carl said, and he gave Diesel the finger.

I took another Oreo from Diesel's bag. "I think I saw the

treasure map. It was hanging over the fireplace in Ammon's home office. The office is on the second floor, and it opens onto a wonderful balcony that looks out over the ocean."

"Did you see the diary?"

"No. And there wasn't an opportunity to insert it into the conversation."

"Clara's going to take us to talk to Gramps tomorrow. Hopefully he'll still have his piece of the coin."

CHAPTER SEVEN

Diesel sauntered into the bakery a little before one o'clock. Clara had just finished scrubbing down her workstation, and I was bagging leftover muffins.

"Give me a minute to change my clothes, and I'll be ready to go," Clara said to Diesel.

Clara lives in the little apartment over the shop, so a wardrobe change was easy. Mine was even easier. I took off my apron and chef coat and stomped the flour off my sneakers.

"Are you going to be okay here alone?" I asked Glo.

"No problem," she said. "I brought Broom to keep me company, and Clara will be back to help me close."

I followed Diesel out of the shop and stood staring at the bright orange Dodge Charger parked in the lot.

"Yours?" I asked him.

"Yep."

"What happened to the SUV?"

"I don't know. The cars come and go."

"That's very strange."

"No stranger than anything else in my life."

Clara exited the building by her private entrance. She locked the door and walked over to us.

"Gramps is at the Salem Aquarium today," she said. "He has a day care lady who takes him there once a week."

The Salem Aquarium is a pleasant little public aquarium nestled in bustling Salem Harbor. It was built inside an old brewery, where the area with the boil kettles and fermenting tanks was nicely converted into coral reefs and shark tanks.

We found Clara's grandfather perched on a Rascal scooter, watching the sharks and stingrays. With a few long strands of thin white hair plastered to the top of his head, pink wrinkled skin hanging from a stooped bone structure, and a nose like an eagle's beak, he looked like Mr. Burns on *The Simpsons*. He was wearing a dark blue velour tracksuit with the pants hiked up to his armpits. He wasn't currently sucking oxygen, but he had a tank and face mask in his scooter basket just in case the need should arise. A small Hispanic woman was sitting on a bench a short distance away.

Clara approached the woman.

"Hi, Benita. How is he today?"

"He asked me to marry him. He said he was feeling frisky."

"Are you going to marry him?"

"No way. The man would bury me."

"Hey, Gramps," Clara said. "How's it going?"

"A little slow. Benita won't marry me."

"Did he take his meds?" Clara asked Benita.

"Yes, ma'am. If he didn't take his meds he'd be hitting you with his cane."

"That's a lie," Gramps said. "I don't hit pretty girls." He pointed at Diesel. "I'd hit *him* a good one. He looks like trouble."

"These are my friends Lizzy and Diesel," Clara said. "They want to ask you about Collier."

"Collier's dead," Gramps said. "Dead as a doornail. I suppose I miss him, but at least I don't have to listen to that damn poem anymore. He insisted I memorize it. He brought me down to the harbor near every day before he disappeared and made me recite it. The man never read a book in his life but he was obsessed with that poem. 'I must go down to the seas again, to the lonely sea and the sky / And all I ask is a tall ship and a light to guide her by / I must go down to the seas again, to the dazzling gypsy life / to the tern's way and the whale's way where the wind's like a whetted knife.' I'm sure the poem means something but damned if I know what it is."

"Did he ever tell you about the treasure he was hunting?" Diesel asked him.

"Sometimes, but not much. Once he brought me back two pieces of a Spanish coin. He said to guard 'em with my life, and they'd bring me luck. And I guess they did because I made some money in my time. I invested in the stock market and made a fortune. Of course, I lost it all when I bought some swampland in Florida. But then I invested in GM. Started another fortune. Lost that. Lost another one to the dot.com bubble."

"Anything else?" Diesel asked, smiling, enjoying himself.

"I produced a Broadway play in the sixties. Lost a bundle. It was made into a movie in the eighties and I made a bundle. Donated it all to this aquarium, so I could watch the sharks." He pointed at the tank where a tiger shark swam around a prop treasure chest that was sitting on the sandy bottom of the fake sea. "I call that one Smiley," Gramps said.

"Where are the Spanish coin pieces now?" Diesel asked.

"You're looking at them," Gramps said. "Collier was always going on about treasure chests, so I had one made, put the pieces of eight in it, and had it sunk there in the tank. You give people enough money and they most likely will do you a favor. Those pieces of eight are sitting at the bottom of the shark tank, protected by all that water and shark poop."

Diesel looked at the Rascal. "I like your wheels."

"Had it painted special," Gramps said. "The ladies love it."

The Rascal was fire engine red with yellow and orange flame detailing.

"I had it souped up," Gramps said. "I can do fifteen miles per hour in this baby. Truth is, I don't need it, but it gets me a lot of attention, and Benita has to run to keep up with me. I like to see her run. It makes her boobs bounce up and down."

Gramps rolled off to look at the penguins, and Benita followed him. Diesel, Clara, and I remained behind at the shark tank.

"The way I see it, the problem is all that water," Diesel said, staring at the treasure chest resting on the bottom of the shark tank.

"I'd think the problem would be the sharks," Clara said.

Diesel shook his head. "The sharks are tame. They're well fed. They won't bother me if I'm quick about it. The sign says the sharks get fed at three-thirty. That's ten minutes from now. If I go in then it'll look like business as usual. Especially if you two create a disturbance that takes everyone away from the tank."

Diesel left, and Clara and I started counting down ten minutes.

"What about the guy standing in the corner?" Clara

asked. "He's been staring at us off and on for fifteen minutes. Do you know him?"

The man was slim. Receding hairline. Looked to be in his early thirties. Dressed in a black long-sleeved T-shirt and black jeans.

"Nope," I said. "I don't know him."

We moved into the next room and checked out the coral reef. The man moved with us. We walked back to the shark room, and he followed.

"He's definitely tailing us," I said to Clara. "And he's really bad at it."

There was a brief announcement over the public address system of feeding time at the shark tank, and a handful of people moved up to the glass. Two scuba divers carrying mesh bags full of dead fish splashed into the tank from above. One of the divers looked directly at me and nodded.

"Showtime," Clara said.

I took a deep breath and told myself this was all part of the grand scheme of things and probably necessary in terms of saving the world. I turned, walked up to the guy dressed in black, set my hands onto my hips, and glared at him. "Why are you stalking me?" I yelled in his face.

"Who, me?" he said, panic in his eyes.

"You've been stalking me all afternoon."

"No. I swear. I don't know what you're talking about, lady."

I leaned forward and raised the volume. "What did you call me?"

"Nothing. I swear."

Clara was beside me. "What did you call my friend?"

"I might have called her 'lady.'"

Everyone was staring at us. Some people were hurrying from the room. Some were behind Clara, straining to get a better look at the crazy woman yelling at the crazy man. No one over the age of five was looking at the shark tank.

"Security!" I shouted. "This man is following me and calling me disgusting names."

An elderly security guard came over to us. "What's the problem here?"

I cut my eyes to the shark tank to see one of the scuba divers swimming down to the treasure chest and lifting the lid.

"These women are crazy," the man in black said. "They came up to me and started yelling at me for no reason."

"Did you or did you not call my friend a 'lady'?" Clara demanded.

"Yes, but—"

"He admits it!" Clara said.

"Is that so bad?" the security guard asked.

"It's the way he said it," I said. "Sneaking up behind me and whispering 'lady.'"

"There was no whispering," the guy said. "Honestly, I didn't whisper."

I made a show of getting a shiver. "It was *frightening*."

Dear lord, I thought. Isn't Diesel *ever* going to get out of the stupid shark tank! How long did I have to keep this thing going?

"And I think he was taking pictures of us," I said to the guard. "Up our skirts."

"You're wearing jeans," the guard said.

"So we outsmarted him!" I said.

"Check his cellphone," Clara said. "See if there are pictures of us."

"No way," the man said. "I have my rights."

I reached around him to his back pocket and searched for his phone.

"She's grabbing my ass!" he said.

"Pervert!" Clara shouted, getting into the mix, shoving her hand into his other back pocket. *"Pervert alert!"*

There was a lot of yelling and wrestling around, then the guy broke free and took off at a run with the security guard in pursuit.

"Thank goodness he got away," I said.

"Yeah," Clara said, bending down, picking a phone up from the floor. "But he dropped his phone in the scuffle."

I looked over her shoulder and saw Diesel and the other diver swim up and out of sight.

"What a nightmare," I said to Clara.

The guard came back. He was red-faced, sweating, and out of breath. "Couldn't catch him," he said. "Sorry, but I

see at least you got his phone. Have you checked for pictures?"

"Not yet," I said. "I'm sure he's deleted them."

The guard took the phone and tapped the camera icon.

"Nope, they aren't deleted," he said. "And he was for sure
following you *ladies* . . . if you'll pardon the expression."

He handed the phone to me, and I scanned through the
photos. Pictures of me. Pictures of Clara. Pictures of Diesel.
Pictures of Clara's grandfather. Pictures of the treasure
chest in the shark tank.

CHAPTER EIGHT

Clara and I met up with Diesel at the car.

"Did you get anything out of the treasure chest?" I asked.

"Yeah," Diesel said. "Two more pieces of the coin."

"You don't seem very excited about it."

"I'll be excited when I have all eight and figure out what to do with them."

"Do the two new pieces look like they fit with the piece we already have?" I asked Diesel.

"At first glance, yes." Diesel pulled the pieces out of his pocket and handed one to me. "Does this do anything for you?"

"Yep. It's vibrating."

"Hold it up to the sun."

I held it up, and Clara and I squinted at it. A small hole had been punched into the silver.

"Cool," I said. "Very Indiana Jones."

"I now have three pieces of the coin, and they each have a hole punched in them," Diesel said.

I gave the piece of coin back to him. "I keep thinking about the poem Gramps recited. It seems odd that Peg Leg would have been so obsessed with it."

"Gramps has complained about it so much that I know it by heart," Clara said. "It's a poem by John Masefield called 'Sea Fever.' It wasn't until I was in college that I realized he had it wrong. The real line is 'And all I ask is a tall ship and a star to steer her by.' Gramps always said 'a light to guide her by.'"

We dropped Clara off at the bakery, and Diesel and I drove the short distance to Kosciuszko Street for pizza. We got an extra-large pizza with extra cheese and extra pepperoni, and we took it to a table outside. We had a good view of the Derby Wharf and of the wooden frigate that served as a floating museum of Salem's maritime history. The Derby lighthouse stood off in the distance at the end of the jetty.

"How did you manage to get into the shark tank?" I asked Diesel.

"I hypnotized the divers by showing them magical pieces of paper."

"Fifty-dollar bills?"

Diesel sprinkled crushed red pepper on his pizza slice. "They held out for a hundred each."

"Saving the world is expensive."

"Yeah, I just hope this leads to something. We probably need all eight pieces to read the map that will take us to the stone. And we're already down one of the pieces."

"Maybe Wulf will give his piece back to us."

"Maybe hell will freeze over. Wulf is psycho. He's like an animal who gets on a scent and follows it with a bloodlust."

"Jeez. He's your cousin."

"Insanity runs in my family," Diesel said. "My Great-Uncle Gustav thinks he's a fruit bat."

"Is he?"

Diesel shrugged. "Not always. He looked pretty normal at my cousin Maria's wedding."

"Well, at least he'd be vegetarian."

"True." Diesel eyed the pizza. "Do you want the last piece?"

"No. I'm stuffed."

Diesel reached for the pizza and a phone rang. Not my ringtone. Not Diesel's ringtone. It was the stalker's phone. I pulled it out of my purse and stared at it. The caller ID read BLOCKED. I put the phone on the table and pressed the SPEAKER function.

"You seem to have my phone," a man said.

"Who is this?" I asked.

"Names aren't important. However, I do have something you might value."

We heard angry chattering in the background. Carl!

"I'm willing to trade this unpleasant monkey for the pieces of eight you've acquired and a small service from Ms. Tucker."

"Get serious," Diesel said. "Keep the monkey."

"Here's the deal. You are going to meet me at the Derby lighthouse in an hour. If you don't follow instructions we'll begin chopping off pieces of your monkey's tail and mailing them to you."

"Eeep!" Carl said.

The caller disconnected.

"How awful!" I said.

"Yeah. Hope they send it overnight. Monkey tail could get funky after a couple days."

"Do you think this guy is working for Wulf?"

"No. This isn't Wulf's style. There's another player in the game." He looked down at the phone on the table. "Where did you get this?"

"There was a guy following Clara and me around the aquarium, and I used him to create the diversion. There was a scuffle, the cellphone got dropped onto the floor, and Clara retrieved it."

"And the guy?"

"He ran away. A guard ran after him but couldn't catch him. It turned out the guy was taking pictures of all of us. Plus he took some pictures of the shark tank."

"I'm surprised the guard let you keep the phone."

"He was all done in from the chase. I think he was just happy to be rid of us. Unfortunately it's a prepaid phone. No ID. No phone numbers on it. There's nothing to trace."

"He wanted something else besides the coin pieces. He wanted a service from you. And I don't think he wants cupcakes."

The Derby lighthouse isn't the traditional, narrow cylindrical lighthouse you see in all the calendars. It's squat and square and made of whitewashed brick. It's twenty-three feet tall and looks like it was built out of Legos by a six-year-old kid with no imagination.

We reached the end of the narrow spit of land, and the red beacon on the top of the lighthouse began to flash every six seconds. The door at the base of the lighthouse was unlocked, so we pushed it open and stepped into a small, dark room. Diesel flipped the light switch, and we saw that the room was empty with the exception of a metal spiral staircase that led to the rooftop lantern room.

The guy from the aquarium was standing at the top of the staircase. A burlap sack was at his feet, a nasty-looking semiautomatic was in his hand, and he had a booted foot on the sack, holding it in place while something squirmed inside.

Diesel stood hands on hips, looking up at the guy. "I'm guessing my monkey's in that sack."

"You guess right," the guy said. "And if I get alarmed I might kick him over the side, so don't try anything stupid. There's more of the coin hidden here somewhere. As soon as I heard the poem the old man was blathering on about I had a hunch. A light to guide her by. That's this lighthouse, right? I was thinking about the lighthouse even before I heard the poem because Peg Leg spent a lot of time here. When he was working as a cod fisherman he would some-times tend the light during winter months. I was going to try a metal detector, but you're even better. You're the special person who's got the power."

"How do you know about that? Someone's a big blabbermouth."

"Yeah, word gets around."

"Does your hunch tell you where I should start looking?"

"There's nothing in here but walls and floor. Start with the walls, and do it fast. I haven't got all day."

I ran my hands over the brick walls. I was on the third wall when I felt a vibration.

"It's here," I said. "The third brick from the bottom."

"Dig it out," the guy said.

I looked up at him. "Do you have a power drill on you? Jackhammer? Nail file?"

He tossed a medium-size screwdriver over the railing. "The jackhammer wouldn't fit in my pocket. Get to work."

Diesel retrieved the screwdriver and chipped away at the mortar around the brick. After five minutes he was able to pop the brick out. The back was partially missing and the inside was hollowed out and stuffed with wadded-up cloth. Diesel pulled the cloth out, tipped the brick over, and two bits of the coin fell out into his hand.

"Bring the pieces to me," the guy said. "Send them up with Miss Magic."

Diesel handed the two pieces over, and I climbed the circular stairs, stopping when I was within arm's reach of Carl and his captor.

I dropped the two pieces into the monkey-napper's hand and reached for the burlap sack.

"Not so fast," the guy said. "I know you have more pieces."

"I have one more," Diesel said. "Catch."

Diesel tossed the piece up to the guy, and when he lunged for the piece of coin I reached for Carl. The guy snagged the coin, and I slipped the knot on the sack. Carl wriggled free and launched himself at the man's face. Carl was screeching and the man was screaming and batting at Carl, ineffectively flailing his arms with the gun still in his hand. The gun discharged and time stood still for a beat when we all realized he'd shot himself.

Diesel whistled and Carl disengaged, leaping from the top of the stairs onto Diesel's shoulder.

"Oh crap," the guy said, looking down at his stomach, where a bloodstain was beginning to show.

His eyes rolled back and he crumpled, falling headfirst over the metal railing. There was a loud *crack* and a *thud* and then total silence. We rushed over to see if we could help, but he was beyond anything we could do. He was beyond anything *anyone* could do. He still had the gun in his hand, his head was mashed into his neck, and blood was pooling under him.

Nergal answered his phone on the fifth ring.

"So how's it going?" I said to him.

"Pretty good. How's it going with you?"

Diesel had laid the burlap monkey sack over the guy's face and what was left of his neck, and I was trying not to look in that direction. "It's going okay," I said. "So what are you doing tonight?"

"Not much. Watching television."

"Do you think you would be able to come out?"

"Are you having one of those *special-people* mixers?"

"Sort of."

"Great. Where is it?"

"The Derby lighthouse."

"That's a terrific place for a party," he said. "I'm not far away. I'll be right there."

"This is totally horrible," I said to Diesel. "How are we going to explain this?"

"It's either accidental suicide or death by monkey. I'm going to push for suicide."

Ten minutes later there was a knock on the door, and Diesel went to answer it.

Nergal stepped in and handed Diesel a bottle of wine. "Am I late?" he asked. "Where is everyone?"

"It's just getting started," I said.

"Yeah," Diesel said, "by midnight this place will be rocking."

Nergal looked over at Carl, and Carl flipped him the bird.

"Does the monkey have enhanced abilities, too?" Nergal asked. "Is he a powerful wizard under an enchantment?"

"This isn't Hogwarts," Diesel said, unscrewing the cap on the wine and chugging some from the bottle.

Nergal caught sight of the body on the floor and the blood leaking out from under the burlap. "Uh-oh," Nergal said.

"We have sort of a situation here," Diesel said, lifting the burlap sack so Nergal could appreciate the fact that the head was basically sitting on the man's shoulders.

"Whoa," Nergal said. "This isn't really a party, is it?"

"No, but we're a pretty fun group."

"I can see that," Nergal said, approaching the body.

"We didn't kill him," I said. "We just found him like this. More or less."

"Did you call the police?"

"Not yet."

"Most people think of that first thing when they find a body."

"Do you think you could touch him?" I asked, gesturing vaguely with my hands. "Do your thing?"

He hesitated. "This is very irregular. I usually do it with the police around. As a CSI."

"Think of it as a secret mission," I said. "For EAF."

"What's that?"

"The Enhanced Abilities Force."

"Is that a real thing?"

"It could be," I said.

Nergal went down to one knee and put his hand on the body.

"This guy died pretty pissed off."

"He had a bad day," I said.

Nergal tilted his head, as if he were listening. "I'm getting a lot of complaints about a monkey."

"Way to go, Carl," Diesel said.

"And he's thinking he made a bad decision to go off on his own," Nergal said.

"On his own where?" I asked. "What does that mean?"

"That's what I'm getting," Nergal said. "And he wished he hadn't shot himself."

After we were done communing with the dead, we made an anonymous call to the police and left. Nergal wanted to go out for a drink, but I asked for a rain check. I gave him a sterile kiss on the cheek and thanked him for the wine. Diesel drove me back to the bakery so I could get my car, then he and Carl followed me home.

"There's something I should tell you," Diesel said when we were at my front door. "It could be a mess in there."

I looked at him with raised eyebrows.

"I left Carl in your house today, so that's where he was snatched. Probably there was a tussle."

"A tussle?"

"Unless the monkey-napper had a bag of doughnuts, Carl wouldn't voluntarily go into that sack."

I opened the door and gasped. The house was a wreck, and Cat was standing his ground with his fur bushed out like a porcupine's quills. He saw Diesel and me, and he relaxed.

The couch cushions were on the floor, and furniture was overturned. In the kitchen, canisters were emptied onto the counter with flour and sugar sifted out everywhere. Boxes had been torn open and emptied. Trash was spread across the floor.

"This was more than a struggle to get Carl," Diesel said. "This was a search for the coin pieces."

Diesel was still carrying the bottle of wine. I took it from him and chugged some.

"Let's clean this up," I said. "By morning this will be an ant factory."

Two hours later, we had the kitchen scrubbed clean, and the wine bottle was empty.

"Hey, handsome," I said to Diesel. "Let's go to bed."

Diesel grinned over at me. "You drank almost that whole bottle of wine."

"I did. And it was yummy."

"You might be a little snockered."

"Not me," I said. "I can hold my liquor."

I sidled up to him, nuzzled his neck, and kissed him just below his ear.

"You smell delicious," I said. "I could eat you up . . . all over, if you know what I mean."

The grin widened. "My lucky day."

I slipped my hand under his T-shirt and ran my fingers over his perfectly defined abs. "Mmmmm," I said, dipping my hand inside his jeans. I heard him give a sharp intake of air, and I continued to explore uncharted territory.

"Am I doing okay?" I asked. "What I lack in experience I make up for in enthusiasm."

"Had me fooled. It feels to me like you know what you're doing."

"I like these soft round things."

"Yeah, I can tell. Listen, maybe we should go a little slower."

I wrapped my hand around his joystick. "Going to warp speed, Captain. Brace yourself. We're in launch mode."

"Eeep!" Carl said.

"Oh crap," I said. "The monkey is watching."

"Ignore the monkey."

"I can't ignore the monkey. I feel like a porn star."

"Is that good or bad?"

"It's bad."

Carl was sitting back on his haunches, three feet away, his eyes wide, taking it all in.

"Maybe we should do this some other time," I said to Diesel.

"Honey, you've got me in launch mode."

"Yeah, but you can abort the mission, right?"

Diesel grabbed Carl and locked him in the broom closet. He returned to me, pulled me close, and kissed me. His hand was under my shirt, his thumb traced a path across my nipple, and his tongue touched mine.

Bang, bang, bang! Carl didn't want to be locked in the broom closet.

"I can't concentrate with all that banging," I said to Diesel.

"Do you need to concentrate?"

"Yes!"

Diesel let Carl out of the broom closet, took my hand, and tugged me up the stairs to my bedroom. He closed and locked my bedroom door, leaving Carl on the outside.

"Are you sure this is going to be okay?" I asked him. "I don't want to have to save the world all by myself."

"We'll only do certain things."

"Does that include launching?"

"Yeah, we're *both* going to launch."

"Okay, but I hope you know what you're doing."

"I've never had any complaints."

CHAPTER NINE

My alarm went off as usual at four-fifteen. Diesel reached over me, grabbed the clock, and threw it across the dark room.

"If it's broken you're going to have to buy me a new one," I said.

"If it *isn't* broken I'm going to smash it with a hammer until it's dead."

I felt around under the covers. We were both naked.

"Uh-oh," I said.

"If you keep feeling around like that you're going to be late for work," Diesel said.

"Are we . . . damaged?"

"I don't feel damaged."

I rolled out of bed and touched one of the pieces of coin that were on the nightstand. It vibrated under my touch.

"I'm okay," I said.

"Honey, you're way better than just okay."

That was good to know. And it had me smiling. Still, I thought I should try to stay sober and not take a chance a second time. Not to mention it would be a disaster of major proportions if I should fall in love with him. And this morning I was thinking it would be easy to fall in love.

Twenty minutes later I was showered and dressed and only slightly hungover. The bed was empty when I came out of the bathroom. No Diesel. No Cat. No Carl. Everyone was in the kitchen waiting for breakfast.

I got the coffee brewing, filled the toaster with frozen waffles, scrambled up a bunch of eggs, and opened a can of cat food.

"I'm off to work," I said to Diesel. "What's your plan for the day?"

"I have the name of the monkey-napper. It made the local news this morning. They said he died from a self-inflicted gunshot wound and a broken neck. I'd like to get some background information on him."

It had been a slow day at the bakery. This was bad for Clara, but good for me. I brought home a big bag of left-over meat pies, muffins, and cheese scones. My house felt benign when I rolled in. No overturned furniture. No bad guys lurking in closets. No monkey. I love Carl, but he creates chaos. I said hello to Cat and gave him part of a sausage turnover. The rest of the food went into the fridge.

I closed the refrigerator door, turned around, and bumped into Martin Ammon.

"Holy bejeezus!" I said, jumping away from him. "How did you get into my house?"

"You didn't lock your door. Not smart in this day and age. Anyone can walk in."

"No kidding."

"I had a free moment this afternoon, so I thought I'd drop off your contract."

"In person?"

He looked around. "I was curious to see how you lived. This is small, isn't it? And your kitchen is quite antiquated. Do you actually cook here?"

"Occasionally."

He pulled a multipage contract out of a slim briefcase and placed it on the counter with a pen. "You need to initial each page and sign on the back page."

"I should read this first."

"If you must," he said. "It's standard. Nothing unusual. I give you money, and you give me a cookbook. And also cupcakes. Cupcakes on demand. I trust you won't mind that. I'm not here year-round."

I started to read the first page and my eyes glazed over. "Is this written in English?"

"It's lawyer talk. Perhaps you'll want to engage a lawyer to translate it for you. Or you could sign with an agent. Most agents take fifteen percent."

I looked at my decrepit stove and chipped Formica countertop. I didn't want to give up 15 percent. I needed all the money Ammon was paying me.

"I'm having a fundraiser at my house on Saturday," Ammon said. "Something to do with the environment, I believe. You're invited. In fact, I would like you to make the desserts. We'll have media there, and it will make a good launch opportunity for the Lizzy Tucker brand." He checked his watch. "I have to run. Rutherford is circling the block. There's no place to park in this neighborhood. The city should bulldoze some of these dilapidated houses and put in some parking."

"This is the historic section of town. These houses are hundreds of years old."

"Obviously." He tapped his finger on the contract. "Have you finished reading yet?"

I scanned the document and saw that the ultimate payment was circled in red. Five hundred thousand dollars. I signed.

. . .

Ammon left and Clara called ten minutes later.

"I've been thinking about the poem," Clara said. "I wrote out the version Gramps always repeated, and I looked up the original version. There are several differences. Not sure if the differences are significant, but Glo's going to bring both versions to you when we close the shop."

I thanked Clara and disconnected.

"What do you think?" I asked Cat. "Are the clues to the treasure hunt found in Gramps's poem?"

Cat looked uncertain.

"Here's a bigger question," I said to Cat. "Is any of this going to lead us to a SALIGIA Stone?"

Cat stared at me.

"Exactly," I said. "There's no guarantee, right? We could be on a big wild goose chase."

I shared some apple slices with Cat and began a list of repairs I would be able to make on the house. A new roof was the top priority.

"I love my house," I said to Cat, "but I can't really afford it. Even without a mortgage payment, the taxes and main-tenance bills are killing me."

Cat's ear pricked forward, and he gave a low growl. The back door opened, and Carl bounded in, followed by Diesel. Cat looked them over, decided they were no threat, and hunkered down with his half tail tucked in.

"How'd it go with the monkey-napper sleuthing?" I asked.

"The guy's name was Bernie Weiner, and he happens to be the detective that Ammon hired to find the coin. After some digging I located his ex-wife. I thought we could go talk to her."

"Now?"

"Yeah. It won't take long. She lives in Lynn."

Lynn is a little southwest of Marblehead and has a lot of hardworking people in it, plus some people who don't work at all. Weiner's ex lived in a small house in a modest neighborhood. There was a Big Wheels trike in the minuscule front yard. The woman who answered the door looked exhausted. She had a baby balanced on her hip and a toddler wrapped around her leg.

"What?" she said.

Diesel introduced himself as an insurance investigator and told her he was doing some background work on Bernie.

"I haven't got a lot of time," she said. "The baby is teething, and the toddler has the poops. Bernie was an idiot. I don't know what else to tell you. I wasn't that surprised to hear he was . . . you know. He could get talked into anything. He should never have taken that job for Martin Ammon. It became an obsession. He thought he was Indiana Jones off looking for some holy relic. If he spent as much time with me as he did looking for that stupid coin, we'd still be married."

"Thanks," Diesel said. "This has been helpful."

"I don't suppose there's any money in this for me?" she asked. "Did he have a policy? Was I listed?"

"I don't have that information," Diesel said. "I hope it works out for you."

We returned to the car, and Diesel drove back to Marblehead.

"That was depressing," I said. "I feel bad for her."

"It looks like she's struggling with the money, but she has two healthy kids, aside from the poops, and I bet she's a good mom," Diesel said. "She'll be okay."

"According to Nergal, Bernie's last thought was that he regretted going off on his own. So it sounds to me like he might not have been working for Ammon at the end."

"I had the same thought."

Diesel parked in front of my house, and we migrated to the kitchen. I gave Cat and Carl a snack, and I watched Diesel place his five coin pieces on the counter and fit them together. Even though pieces were still missing it was clear that an image of a crown was engraved on one side of the coin. Diesel turned the pieces over, and I could see a face engraved on the other side. Charles III of Spain. Each of the pieces had a tiny hole punched into it.

Someone rapped on my back door, and Diesel opened it to Glo and Josh.

"Howdy," Josh said. "How's it going?"

"Slow," Diesel said.

Glo gave me the two versions of "Sea Fever." "Clara said she picked out three discrepancies. She has them circled. She asked her gramps about the changes, and he said that's just the way the poem was always said to him."

Star had been changed to *light*. *Steer* had been changed to *guide*. To the *vagrant* gypsy life had been changed to the *dazzling* gypsy life.

"Do you think these changes are relevant?" I asked Diesel.

"The first two changes got my monkey back."

We all looked over at Carl, and Carl gave us a hideous, teeth-baring monkey smile.

"These coin pieces have holes in them." Glo said. "Is that normal?"

I shrugged. I didn't know. Diesel didn't know. Josh didn't know.

"We could check in with the professor," Josh said. "He might still be at work."

CHAPTER TEN

Diesel parked in front of the Sullivan Building, we climbed the stairs to Devereaux's floor, and I knocked on his closed door. No answer. Josh opened the door and we peeked inside. No one there.

"Do you have Devereaux's number?" Diesel asked Josh.

"Sure. We're practically friends now. He's called a couple of times asking about the coin."

Josh punched in the number. Devereaux picked up, and Josh put him on speakerphone.

"We're in your office," Josh said. "Where are you?"

"I had to leave. Why did you come to see me?"

"We had a question about the pieces of the coin."

"Are you still in my office?"

"Yes."

"You need to leave. It's dangerous for you to stay. Run. Get out! I can't talk now. I'll call back."

We exchanged a look, and we didn't exactly run, but we didn't waste any time leaving. We hurried out of the building and stood in the middle of the grassy quad, looking up at Devereaux's office window.

"Maybe we've been punked," Josh said.

Barooom! Flames shot out of the open window, and the fire alarm went off.

"I was wrong," Josh said. "That's not the work of a punker."

The alarm was blaring, people were pouring out of the buildings, sirens screamed in the distance, and Josh's phone buzzed.

"I can't hear you," Josh yelled into the phone. "Can you repeat that?"

We all stared at Josh.

"It was Devereaux," Josh said, sliding his phone back into his pocket. "I couldn't get everything, but he wanted us to meet him at the museum ship. The *Friendship of Salem.*"

We made our way around the clumps of gawkers and first responders, loaded ourselves into Diesel's orange Charger, and Diesel drove us off campus.

"I don't want to take everyone onboard the *Friendship,*"

Diesel said to Glo and Josh. "I'm going to drop both of you off first."

The *Friendship of Salem* was the name of the replica frigate docked at Derby Wharf and used as a museum. We drove to the wharf, left the car in the lot, and walked toward the frigate. It was early evening, and the sun was low on the horizon. The tall masts and rigging were dark against the sky. The squat Derby lighthouse flashed red at the end of the wharf.

The gate at the end of the gangway was unlocked. Diesel opened it, and we stepped onto the empty deck of the *Friendship*. Ropes creaked with the movement of the ship, but all else was silent. We prowled from one end to the other, found an open hatchway, and went below. Diesel flipped a light switch, and we were transported from the eighteenth century to the twenty-first century. We were in a shining white room filled with state-of-the-art navigation equipment and a complicated-looking control panel. Professor Devereaux was at the consul.

"What's up?" Diesel said.

"Are you alone?" Devereaux asked. "Did anyone follow you?"

"Yes, we're alone. And no, we weren't followed," Diesel said. "And, by the way, someone blew up your office."

"Bastard," Devereaux said. "Was anyone hurt? Did the building burn down?"

"Not sure if anyone was hurt," Diesel said. "It looked pretty well contained to your office."

"It's Martin Ammon," Devereaux said. "He hates me. He sent one of his goons to tell me to stop looking for the treasure. I told him I wasn't looking for it, that I was merely a historian. And he said historians are the worst treasure hunters of all. And then he said he was going to make sure I understood the consequences of my actions. I assumed he was going to break my arm or slash my face, and I was about to call for security when one of my colleagues came in, and Ammon's thug left. When you called I was worried you would get caught in the crossfire. It didn't occur to me that he would blow up my office."

"Why did you come here?"

"I was in the middle of some research, and I didn't feel safe in my office or my apartment. I knew I could use the equipment here and be undisturbed. As you know, I have a history with the ship. I'm no longer officially involved, but I still return on the sly from time to time."

"Why does Ammon hate you?" Diesel asked.

"Ammon inherited a diary that belonged to Palgrave Bellows. The diary spoke of a fabulous treasure that had been plundered from the Mughal ship *Gunsway*. Problem was, Ammon didn't know how to find the treasure. It wasn't enough to just have the diary. The treasure was hidden and could only be found with the help of a map and a coin.

"I'd received some publicity while I was working on the *Friendship* restoration, and Ammon approached me, offering to share the treasure if I could locate the map and the coin. It was the opportunity of a lifetime. I would have funding to research the lost *Gunsway*.

"After almost a year of searching I ran across the map in a curio shop in Boston. I gave the map to Ammon and continued to search for the coin but had no luck. It was a total dead end. I was disillusioned by then anyway. In the beginning of our professional relationship I thought Ammon was a wealthy eccentric. As I got to know him better I came to realize he's criminally insane. He has delusions of grandeur, and he'll stop at nothing to get what he wants.

"The diary listed, among other riches, the Avaritia Stone as part of the Mughal treasure. This was Ammon's true reason for funding my research. Ammon had become obsessed with the idea that he might possess the Avaritia Stone. He'd begun to believe that he could awaken the sleeping Mammon within himself if he had the stone. He hates me because I know this about him, and because I don't worship Mammon."

"Did you ever see the diary?"

"Yes. I had an opportunity to read it, and I think

Palgrave Bellows had his own streak of insanity running through him. I'm now told Ammon keeps the diary under lock and key, like it's a sacred book."

"I believe I've seen the map hanging in Ammon's office."

"It's a lovely piece of history," Devereaux said, "but worthless as a treasure map without the coin. Directions to the treasure are written in code, and the coin is the key to the code."

"And when we came to your office with a piece of a counterfeit coin you thought it might have been fashioned by Bellows."

"Exactly," Devereaux said. "I didn't know for certain, but I hoped I was finally seeing part of the coin. And because you are the one who found the fragment, I had hopes that you could find the rest. You have special abilities."

"How do you know about my special abilities?" I asked him.

"It's not exactly a secret," Devereaux said. "People talk."

"Yeah," I said. "I keep hearing this."

In most places in this country people would roll their eyes and smile, and any rumor of my abilities would be filed away next to extraterrestrials landing in Arizona. This was Salem, however, and people were willing to believe just about anything.

"Unfortunately, Martin Ammon, with all his fortune and influence, has eyes and ears everywhere," Devereaux said. "When it was whispered that pieces of the coin had surfaced, it fueled his obsession to find the treasure."

"And he wants you out of the game," I said.

Devereaux nodded. "Yes."

Devereaux left to check on his office, and Diesel and I were alone on the ship. I could hear voices in the distance. Quiet conversations carrying across the water to us from harborside restaurants. I looked out to sea and thought it would be nice to sail away and leave my strange, confusing life behind.

Diesel slipped his arms around me and drew me in close against him. "You wouldn't like it," he said, reading my mind. "You'd get seasick. And you'd miss your purpose."

"Don't you ever want to abandon all responsibility?"

"Yeah, all day, every day."

"What keeps you in the game?"

"You don't wear responsibility like clothes. You can't take it off and put it on when you feel like. You wear responsibility on the inside, and it isn't that easy to remove. You have to learn how to live with it."

"Wow."

"Profound, right? How valuable is that nugget of wisdom? Will it get you undressed?"

"No!"

"In that case, it's all bullshit. I stay in the game because at some level I enjoy it. I just don't enjoy it at *all* levels."

I suspected both explanations were true for Diesel, and neither of them was true for me.

CHAPTER ELEVEN

G lo bustled into the bakery exactly at nine o'clock. She had a newspaper in her tote bag and Broom stuck under her arm.

"Did you see the paper?" she asked Clara and me. "The explosion made the front page. And it was on the news this morning on television."

Clara stopped working and looked at Glo. "You read the paper and listen to the news?"

"No. I ran into Mr. Bork on the street, and he told me about the explosion story, so I bought a paper." She pulled the paper out of her bag and laid it on a workbench. "There are pictures and everything. They said it was some kind of homemade bomb that had been set on a timer. Nobody was hurt, but there was a lot of damage."

Clara and I went to the workbench and looked at the pictures. I was relieved to find I wasn't in any of them.

"You should have been there," Glo said to Clara. "We were in Devereaux's office, and Josh called him, and Devereaux told us to get out of the building, so we ran out, and *BOOM!* Devereaux's office exploded. And then Josh got a phone call from Devereaux except he couldn't hear what he was saying."

"Scary," Clara said. "It would have been terrible if you hadn't gotten out of the office in time."

"Who do you think would bomb an office?" Glo asked.

The same person who just bought my cookbook, I thought. My phone chirped, and I checked my text messages.

"What's wrong?" Clara asked. "You look like someone just died."

"It's a text from Martin Ammon reminding me that I'm supposed to cater a party at his house on Saturday. I'd completely forgotten about it."

"Do you need help with the party?"

"Yes!"

An hour later I took off for the Wednesday farmers' market on Pleasant Street. We use local produce whenever we can, and this morning I bought apples for turnovers, herbs and onions for the meat pies, and I got a bargain on raspberries. I arranged for delivery, and on my way back to the bakery a hand grasped my shoulder from behind, and I felt a sharp stabbing pain in my butt cheek. I whirled around and saw Hatchet with a needle in his hand.

"Surprise," he said.

When I regained consciousness I was stretched out on a deck chair on a large yacht. The Salem waterfront was visible in the distance. Hatchet was at the rail. Wulf was seated at a small table nearby laid out with fresh fruit, croissants, and coffee.

"I trust you're well," Wulf said. "Hatchet is an expert on paralytic poisons. You should have no ill effects from your nap. I'm having a late breakfast. Would you like to join me?"

"Just coffee. And I'd like to know the reason for the drugging and kidnapping."

Wulf snapped his fingers and Hatchet rushed over, poured a cup of coffee, and handed it to me.

"Cream or sugar?" Hatchet asked.

I shook my head no.

"I asked Steven to escort you to my boat," Wulf said. "The method was his choice."

"He gave me a needle in the butt."

"Thee were moving," Hatchet said. "Hatchet needed a large target."

I narrowed my eyes at him. "How'd you like me to punch you in the face?"

"Thou art an impertinent shrew," Hatchet said.

Wulf cut his eyes to Hatchet, and Hatchet shrank back into the shadows of the salon entrance.

"I'm sorry if this caused you discomfort," Wulf said to me. "I wanted to speak to you about Martin Ammon. You signed a dangerous contract with him."

"How do you know about the contract?"

"I know many things. For instance, I know that there are those who think Martin Ammon is Mammon. Martin is one of them."

"Do you mean Mammon-like or the actual Mammon?"

"The actual Mammon."

"I realize when you add his first initial to his name it spells 'Mammon,' but I can't see him as a prince of hell. I don't think a prince of hell would get a spray tan."

"I've seen the contract you signed. Martin Ammon effectively owns you."

"My soul?"

"No. Your livelihood. In perpetuity."

"Why are you telling me this?"

"I want you to understand your position and the degree of evil you're facing. Martin Ammon must not get his hands on the Stone of Avarice. He's not interested in your cookbook. He's using the book as a ploy to stay close and to control you with your own greed. He needs you to gather together the eight pieces of the coin. If he gets the whole coin he can use it to read Palgrave Bellows's map. Once he reads the map it's only a matter of time before he possesses the stone."

"If you're so concerned, why don't you snatch the map? You could sneak in like smoke, grab the map, and disappear in a flash of light."

"I appreciate the vote of confidence, but it's not that simple. There are other forces at play in that house, and my annoying cousin is more suited for larceny."

"Are you suggesting that Diesel should steal the map?"

"I'm suggesting that at all costs you should *not* help Martin Ammon."

Wulf snapped his fingers again, and Hatchet scurried over to us.

"Miss Tucker would like to depart."

Hatchet whipped out a syringe.

"If he takes a step in my direction I'm going to jump over the side and swim," I said.

"He loves his toys," Wulf said.

"He's a nut job."

"We won't be needing pharmacology," Wulf said to Hatchet. "Drop Miss Tucker off at the wharf."

I followed Hatchet into the launch, and looked back at the yacht when the launch pulled away. Wulf wasn't in sight. The name on the boat was *Sea Wulf.* I put as much distance as I could between Hatchet and me. When we pulled up to the wharf I carefully moved past him.

"Is that a dolphin next to the boat?" I asked.

Hatchet turned to look for the dolphin, and I hit him hard with my tote bag and knocked him overboard into the water. I scrambled out of the launch and walked off without a second glance at Hatchet.

Diesel and Carl were at the bakery when I returned.

"The produce arrived a half hour ago," Glo said. "We were starting to worry about you."

"I ran into Wulf."

"And?" Diesel asked.

"And we had an interesting conversation. He said the contract I signed with Martin Ammon was not in my best interest. And then he said there were some who thought M. Ammon was actually Mammon. And that Martin was one of them. We sort of already knew all of that."

"Mammon is a demon," Glo said. "I read all about him in *Ripple's Book of Spells*. It has a chapter on devils and demons. Mammon is the demon of greed."

Diesel was slouched against one of the workbenches. "Wulf said he thought Martin Ammon was Mammon?"

"Not exactly. He said, 'There are those who think he's Mammon.' And he said there were 'other forces at play' in Ammon's house."

"That's a pretty cryptic message," Diesel said. "Did Wulf say anything else?"

"He said Ammon wasn't interested in my cookbook. He said it was a ploy to get close to me and use my greed to find the eight pieces of the coin. Once Ammon gets the entire coin he can use it to read Palgrave Bellows's treasure map, and the map will lead him to the Stone of Avarice. We knew this, too."

"It's kind of cool that you know a demon," Glo said to me. "Has he ever exhibited any demon behavior? Do his eyes glow? Does he have horn nubs?"

"None of the above. He's a strange, unpleasant man with perfect teeth."

"And billions of dollars," Clara said.

We all went silent for a moment.

"Mammon, the demon of greed," Glo said. "Think about it."

"I personally know an elf and a tree fairy," Diesel said, "but I'm having a hard time with the demon of greed."

"Wulf sort of suggested that you might want to steal the map," I said to Diesel. "He said you're better at larceny than he is."

"You could steal it on Saturday," Glo said. "We'll all go to the party disguised as dessert caterers."

"We *are* dessert caterers," I said.

"That's why it's the perfect cover," Glo said. "Diesel can

walk off with the map while everyone is snarfing down desserts."

"Do you have a license to steal?" I asked Diesel.

"It's more in the vicinity of *vague permission.*"

"Aside from being fun, do you think there's a reason for Diesel to steal the map?" Glo said. "It isn't as if it's any use to us. We only have five pieces of the coin. Wulf has one more, and nobody has any idea where to find the other two."

"Okay, let's think about the last two pieces," I said. "The pieces were hidden by Peg Leg Dazzle. Where would he hide them? He would have kept the last two pieces close, just like he did the other six. Two were on him. Two were with Gramps. Two were in the lighthouse."

Clara thunked the heel of her hand against her forehead. "The Dazzle Speakeasy! It's been abandoned since Prohibition ended. Peg Leg practically lived there . . . at least until he disappeared. It was his pride and joy. You can get there through the Underground."

"What's the Underground?" I asked.

"It's a series of tunnels built by smugglers. They run underneath the whole city. The rumrunners used them, but they date from way before that. Salem has a long history of civil disobedience. Most of the tunnels go back to the first Jefferson administration, when he imposed customs duties on molasses. One of the tunnels runs right under Dazzle's.

You can get there through that door right there in the back."

We all moved to the back of the kitchen. Diesel opened the door and stared down into the dark stairwell.

"What's down there?" Diesel asked Clara.

"Not much," Clara said. "Mostly mechanical stuff. Technically it's a storeroom, but it's not very convenient. It connects to the Underground, so I keep the door locked."

Diesel made his way down the rickety stairs and yanked the chain that turned the single overhead bulb on. We all followed Diesel and watched while Clara pushed an empty shelf unit aside on the far wall.

"It's a hidden entrance," Clara said.

"It's a black, yawning corridor of doom," Glo said.

Clara grabbed a flashlight off the shelf and switched it on, splashing light around a cavernous hallway. It was lined in ocher-colored bricks with iron arches every few yards. Carl dashed in front of us. He smiled and gave us the finger when the light hit him.

Diesel took the flashlight from Clara and walked into the tunnel. "Do you know where this leads?"

"Yes. I haven't been down here in years, but I used to play in the tunnels when I was a little girl. I was able to go from my parents' house to the bakery without going aboveground. The tunnel also goes to Gramps's house. And to the speakeasy."

Diesel moved further into the corridor. "Is the speakeasy still in use?"

"Only by Gramps. There's a direct access from his broom closet. He calls it his rumpus room. Gramps's house was originally owned by Peg Leg, and for a short time Peg Leg ran the speakeasy."

Glo returned to the bakery, and Clara, Diesel, and I followed the tunnel until we came to an iron door.

"This is it," Clara said. "We can't get in because it's locked from the other side."

"No problem," Diesel said, placing his hand on the door handle.

The lock clicked and Diesel pushed the door open.

"How do you do that?" Clara asked.

"I'm told it has something to do with my magnetic field," Diesel said.

It wasn't a large room in terms of a public space. It was about the size of the store part of the bakery. Clara flipped the light switch, and we looked around Gramps's rumpus room. It was a classic man cave, and I suspect as a younger man Gramps had used it for poker games and heavy drinking. The bar was polished oak. The wood floor was scuffed. The green felt on the poker table was faded and stained. Two overstuffed chairs sat in the middle of the room where, I imagined, high-top tables once held illegal drinks.

Diesel looked around and smiled.

"What?" I asked him.

"I like it. I might rent it out next time I'm in town."

"You could invite Nergal," I said. "Have a mixer."

Diesel wrapped an arm around me. "I have a job for you."

"Oh boy."

"I'd blindfold you, but I don't have a blindfold on me, so we'll save that for later, if you know what I mean."

"Everyone knows what you mean."

The smile widened. "I want you to move around the room with your eyes closed. Just feel around and see if anything speaks to you. Usually you have to hold something in your hand to feel the vibration, but you felt the coin fragment behind the brick at the lighthouse, so let's see if you pick up any vibrations here."

Diesel guided me around the room. I felt the soft felt of the poker table. I felt the brick in the walls. And I felt a very faint hum as I ran my hand along the oak bar.

"Here," I said.

I opened my eyes and traced along with my fingertip until I isolated the spot.

"This wood has a lot of grain and it has a dark stain on it, but it looks to me like it's been plugged where you're feeling the vibration," Diesel said.

He drilled into the bar with a corkscrew, popped the plug out, and then used the corkscrew to pry two pieces of coin out of the hole. He dropped the pieces into my hand, and I felt them hum.

"They're empowered," I said.

Diesel took the five coin pieces out of his pocket and placed them on the bar top. I added the two new pieces, and they were a perfect fit. All the markings lined up.

"If I had Wulf's piece of the coin, Charles III would have a whole head," Diesel said.

He pocketed the seven pieces of empowered coin. We retraced our steps back to the bakery, pushed the shelf across the tunnel entrance, and climbed the stairs.

Diesel used his thumb to swipe a flour smudge off my cheek. "I have some errands to run, and then I'll meet you at the house."

"I might be home late," I said. "I need to put together a menu for Ammon's party. And I should get a head start on the baking."

CHAPTER TWELVE

G lo locked the shop door at four o'clock, hung the
CLOSED sign in the window, and joined Clara and me
in the back.

"I've been doing research on demons," Glo said, watching
me roll out piecrust for the tarts. "I have a couple excellent
anti-demon spells. We don't want to be caught short without protection."

"I pretty much don't believe in demons," I said.

"I believe in everything," Glo said. "I'm a free-range
believer. I even found some tests we can do on Ammon to
prove his demonicness."

"I can't see Ammon submitting to demon testing."

"Exactly, so I found a spell that will make him cooperative.

It's foolproof. I'm going to stop in at the Exotica Shoppe after work and get the ingredients." Glo looked at the piecrust. "How many tarts do you have to make?"

"Four hundred."

"Yowza. That's a lot of tarts."

"I'll make four different fillings. Plus I'll have four large cookie trays, four large trays of miniature cupcakes, and a bananas Foster station."

"I can't wait," Glo said. "I love parties. I promised Broom he could come. I hope that's okay."

"Sure. He can help sweep up afterward."

Glo left, and Clara packed up and left a half hour later. I stayed until five. I stored my tart shells, shoved my party menu into my tote bag, cut the lights, and locked up. I had my hand on the door handle of my car when I heard rustling behind me. I turned and saw Hatchet rushing at me. His eyes were crazy wide, his hair stuck out every which way, and his damp tights looked mostly dry but droopy. He had his sword in his hand.

"Bitch wench!" he yelled at me. "How dare thee dunk Hatchet? Thee art a cowardly sow to attack Hatchet from behind. Prepare to have Hatchet smite thee!"

Crap! I wrenched the door open, jumped into the car, slammed the door shut, and punched the lock button. Hatchet brought the blade of the sword down hard on the roof of the car and recoiled from the impact. I cranked the engine and roared away with Hatchet running after me. I lost him after a block and a half. My heartbeat returned to normal after three blocks. Lucky for Hatchet, he didn't actually get to smite me, because Wulf wouldn't have been happy. And ugly things can happen when Wulf isn't happy.

I walked into my house twenty minutes later. Diesel and Carl were already there. Cat was keeping his eye on them.

"What's new?" Diesel asked.

"Had an incident with Hatchet. He tried to smite me, but I was too fast for him. What's new with you?"

"I have to pull the plug on someone on the West Coast, but I want to do a show-and-tell for you first."

"Pull the plug? Is that like whacking someone?"

"No. 'Whacking' would imply death. This is more like cutting off someone's electricity because they didn't pay their bill."

I thought this was a conversation I didn't want to pursue. Sometimes you don't want to know too much.

We all went into the kitchen.

"Can you cook at all?" I asked Diesel.

"I can scramble an egg, make a sandwich, and open a beer bottle. I leave the fancy stuff to other people."

I was obviously one of those people who made the fancy stuff, so I pulled a couple chicken breasts and a bunch of root vegetables out of the fridge.

"How serious was the Hatchet incident?" Diesel asked.

"Hard to say. Serious enough to get my heart rate up. As it was, he put a big scratch in my car. Not that it matters."

"Do you know what caused him to attack you?"

"I sort of knocked him off the launch and into the bay earlier today, and I think it ruined his hairdo."

Diesel grinned. "Nice."

I washed the vegetables and set them on the counter to chop. "So we're one coin fragment and a map away from finding the stone. All that stands between us is a demon and Wulf. Our troubles are over."

"The map will be easy, but I might have to trade you off to Wulf in exchange for his piece of the coin."

"*What?*"

Diesel was close behind me. He leaned in and kissed me just below my ear.

"I was kidding," Diesel said. "I wouldn't give you to Wulf. You're worth more than one piece. He'd have to throw in Hatchet to sweeten the deal."

I elbowed him in the chest. "Jerk."

"Yeah, but I'm hot," Diesel said.

"When will you be back from your plug pulling?"

"Hard to say. It shouldn't take long. I'll be back in time to steal the map on Saturday."

I took my chef's knife out of the drawer and diced the heck out of a carrot.

"You've got some serious aggression going there," Diesel

said. "If you need to relax, I can offer something better than carrot mutilation."

I looked at him with one raised eyebrow.

Diesel was hands in his pockets, back on his heels. "Just sayin'."

Whack. I halved an onion.

"Maybe later," Diesel said.

CHAPTER THIRTEEN

At four o'clock sharp on Saturday, Glo hung the CLOSED sign on the bakery door and we all assembled in the kitchen. We needed to load the van and arrive at Cupiditas for setup by six o'clock at the latest. The party was from seven to nine. I'd been told it was a fundraiser for the preservation of the Eastern spadefoot toad. I suspected most of the people attending didn't give a flying fig about the toad. They'd forked over five thousand for a ticket to a Martin Ammon party and to get a look at his house.

Josh and Glo were going to help me serve. They were dressed in standard caterer attire. Black slacks, white shirt, and red tie for Josh. Black skirt, white shirt, and red tie for

Glo. I was wearing my one and only little black dress. So far Diesel was a no-show.

We had the van packed and ready to roll a little after five o'clock, and Diesel strolled in. He was wearing a black suit, black dress shirt, and black tie. Wulf dresses like that and looks like a Hollywood vampire. Diesel looked more like a bodyguard for Madonna.

"Who are you?" I asked him.

"I'm your van driver. Once the party gets under way I'll be a guest who will wander unnoticed around Ammon's house and borrow his map."

"Good luck with that one," I said.

I couldn't imagine Diesel ever going unnoticed. He was big and scruffy in a rugged movie star handsome kind of way, and he walked in a cloud of testosterone. You would have to be dead not to notice Diesel.

Twenty minutes later, Diesel drove the van through Ammon's gated entrance and parked in front of a garage bay. Rutherford and two household staff were waiting to help us unload. By seven o'clock we were set to serve. Guests were directed to the large formal living room and from there onto a terrace that looked out over the ocean. I had my desserts displayed on several tables on the terrace. My bananas Foster station was indoors, in front of a bay window. Josh and Glo were circulating with sterling silver trays filled with cookies and homemade chocolates. Diesel was lurking in a corner.

At seven-thirty Ammon called everyone into the living room and drew their attention to me.

"I would like to introduce Lizzy Tucker," Ammon said. "Ammon Industries will be bringing out an entirely new line of products inspired by Lizzy Tucker and her magical kitchen skills. Every recipe in her brand-new cookbook, *Kitchen Magic,* will eventually be available under the Ammon brand."

Everyone applauded, and I had to grip the serving trolley to steady myself. Wulf's warning that Ammon now owned me was echoing in my brain.

"Miss Tucker will now be performing culinary magic, serving bananas Foster," Ammon said. "Enjoy."

He gave me his dazzling white smile, turned on his heel, and marched off to mingle.

Glo was beside me. "Are you okay?" she asked. "You went white just now. Was it because you were standing next to a demon?"

"He's not a demon."

"We don't know that for sure. His skin is a strange color."

"It's spray tan!"

People were clustering around me, lining up for bananas Foster.

"You'd better get cooking," Glo said. "These people don't look like they have a lot of patience. And I hope you brought a lot of bananas because everyone in the room is in line."

"I could use an assistant. Stay here and help me serve."

I had a single burner on the serving trolley, and there were two hundred people waiting for their bananas. I lit the burner, grabbed a sauté pan, melted unsalted butter, and mixed in brown sugar and spices. I added sliced bananas and reached for the rum. No rum.

"Where's the rum?" I asked Glo. "It's not on the trolley."

"I've got it," Glo said. "I'm ready to assist."

"Okay, sprinkle a little rum on the bananas, and I'll light the butane torch."

I flicked the torch on, and Glo dumped half a bottle of rum on the bananas.

"Too much!" I said.

She jerked the bottle away and rum went everywhere. The bananas burst into flame, and the blue flames leaped from the pan, ran down the legs of the trolley and across the Oriental carpet, and ignited the heavy brocade drapes behind me.

It was instant mayhem. The fire alarm was blaring. People were screaming, shoving, running out of the room onto the terrace. A lot of black smoke was coming off the drapes. Little runners of fire were racing across the wall. I'd like to think I'd be good in an emergency, but truth is I stood frozen, rooted to the spot, watching Rutherford and half a dozen employees rush in with fire extinguishers.

"I think the party is over," Glo said. "I just got a text from Josh saying that Diesel has the motor running."

I looked around the room. The fire was mostly out, and it hadn't spread beyond the back wall. I didn't see Ammon.

"I guess we could leave," I said. "The bananas Foster station is closed."

We put our heads down and quickly walked into the hall, through the empty kitchen, and into the garage where Josh was waiting, making hurry-up motions. We crossed to the van, Josh and Glo climbed into the back, and I took the seat next to Diesel.

"Why the rush?" I asked Diesel. "Did you get the map?"

"Yeah. Unfortunately, when you set the house on fire, Ammon rushed up to his study to save the map and caught me leaving with it. There was a brief discussion over who was going to retain ownership, and Josh smacked him with a serving tray."

"I saw him leave the room, and I followed him," Josh said. "Good thing I did."

"Omigosh. Was he hurt?" I asked.

"He be a bit stunned," Josh said, reverting to pirate talk.

"More like he be a bit knocked out," Diesel said, putting the van in gear, "but he was coming around when we left."

Police cars and fire trucks were screaming in the distance.

"We need to get out of here before we're blocked in," Diesel said.

It wasn't a very long driveway, but there was valet parking

and cars were lined up on either side. Diesel carefully drove toward the gate, and halfway there a man burst out from between two cars and jumped in front of us. It was Martin Ammon. He was crazy mad, waving his arms and shouting.

"Help! Police! Rutherford!"

"This is a real pain in the ass," Diesel said.

Diesel inched the van up to Ammon, but Ammon wouldn't budge. He banged on the hood and kept shouting.

"What are you going to do?" I asked Diesel.

"Run him over," Diesel said.

"You can't do that! You'll kill him."

"And?"

"You don't have permission to kill."

"Extenuating circumstance," Diesel said.

Ammon gave the hood one last thump and moved to the driver's side door, trying to pull it open.

"You're not leaving with my map," he yelled.

"My Magic 8 Ball is telling me that in five minutes this place is going to be swarming with police," Glo said.

"I'll have you arrested, and you'll rot in jail," Ammon said. "The police are on their way. I can hear their sirens."

Diesel rolled the van forward. Ammon staggered back, pulled out his cellphone, and dialed.

"This isn't good," I said. "He's calling 911."

"We'll have to take him with us," Diesel said. *"Get him!"*

Glo, Josh, and I jumped out of the van and ran at

Ammon. He took off down the driveway, and Josh tackled him at the gate. Diesel pulled the van up, we wrestled Ammon into the back, and Josh and Glo sat on him while I climbed into the front. There was a lot of grunting and swearing and scuffing going on in the back of the van while Diesel motored off the property and headed for the causeway. There was a loud *"Unh!"* And *thunk.* And then there was quiet.

"What just happened?" I asked, trying to see beyond the racks for dishes and holding trays.

"The Magic 8 Ball jumped out of my hand and beaned Ammon," Glo said. "Ammon seems to be sleeping."

"Omigod, we knocked Martin Ammon out cold, *twice,* and now we've kidnapped him!" I said. "We're all going to prison. My mother will have to be sedated."

"I have *Ripple's* with me," Glo said. "I can put a forgetful spell on Ammon, so he won't remember anything."

There was a moment of silence. No one had a lot of confidence in Glo's spell-casting abilities.

"Here it is on page thirty-seven," Glo said. "And I have almost all the ingredients with me."

"Almost?" I asked.

"I'm missing the powdered newt snot, but I don't think it will matter. Powdered newt snot is mostly used as a binding agent."

Diesel smiled, and I bit into my lower lip to keep from whimpering.

"Candle burn, smoke expire, Martin's brain will now retire," Glo said.

"Do you have a candle back there?" I asked her.

"I have a Bic lighter," Glo said. "I didn't bring a candle."

I heard some pages rustle.

"Whoops," Glo said. "I lost my place."

More pages rustling.

"Here it is," she said. "Brain of dog, trusted friend, remember not the sad end but act as ever."

"That doesn't sound right," I said to her.

"It's dark back here," Glo said, "but I'm pretty sure I got it correct."

The first police car flew past us on the other side of the road. It was followed by two more police cars and a fire truck.

"Maybe we should drop Ammon off at the hospital," I said to Glo. "How bad is he?"

"He's okay," Glo said. "His nose has stopped bleeding, and he sort of has his eyes open."

"I've got his hands tied with some rope we had back here," Josh said. "I think he's secure."

"So if we don't take him to the hospital, where *do* we take him?" I asked Diesel.

"Your house. I'm hungry."

"No, no, no. I don't want him in my house."

"Lizzy is right," Glo said. "I'm pretty sure he's a demon, and he might infect Lizzy's house with demon cooties. For a second there when we were rolling around I thought I caught a glimpse of a double pupil in his eyes, and then they might have glowed red."

Diesel turned off Ocean Avenue onto Atlantic. "He isn't a demon. He's a narcissist with demonic ambition."

"What if we take him to my house and a SWAT team shows up and crashes through my windows and breaks down my doors?" I said. "That would be awful."

"I won't lock the front door," Diesel said. "Then they can just walk in."

Ten minutes later we carted Ammon from the van and set him in my kitchen. Cat glared at him from a vantage point on the counter and Carl gave him the finger. Diesel went off to find a parking space.

Glo had her Magic 8 Ball out.

"Magic 8 Ball tell me true, is Martin Ammon a demon?"

"Well?" I asked. "What does it say?"

"It says 'Signs point to yes.'"

CHAPTER FOURTEEN

Ammon was standing in the middle of my kitchen, swaying slightly, his eyes glazed, his hands tied in front of him.

"Demons don't like salt," Glo said, grabbing a box of salt from my cabinet.

She poured the salt onto the floor in a circle around Ammon.

"Okay," she said to Ammon. "Step out of the salt circle."

Ammon didn't look like he was totally with the program.

"Maybe he's confused because I put the forgetful spell on him, and he doesn't remember he's a demon," Glo said.

"Maybe he's confused because he was knocked out twice

and has a concussion," I said. "What happens to demons who cross the salt line?"

"I think they melt," Glo said, "but that's secondhand information."

Josh gave Ammon a shove, and Ammon stumbled across the salt line.

"Hunh," Glo said. "He's not melting."

Ammon tipped his head back and howled.

"Omigod," Glo said. "He's a demon werewolf. We need to shoot him with a silver bullet. Who's got a silver bullet?"

Josh and I shuffled around. We didn't have a silver bullet. We also didn't have a gun.

"He hasn't got fangs like a werewolf," I said. "Are you sure you did the right spell?"

Glo thumbed through *Ripple's*. "Here it is . . . uh-oh."

"What uh-oh?" I asked. "I *hate* uh-oh."

"I might have made a mistake when I lost my place in the van. I think I might have put the man's-best-friend spell on him."

Ammon was on his knees licking up the salt. He moved to the work island and lifted his leg.

"Bad dog!" I said. "No!"

He put his leg down and looked up at me.

"Do something!" I said to Glo. "Change him back."

"That could be a problem," Glo said, "since I seem to have made a combination of two spells. But here's the good news. I didn't have any powdered newt snot, so the spell is most likely temporary."

Diesel walked into the kitchen, set the map on the counter, and went to the refrigerator. "How's it going?"

"Not so good," I said. "Ammon thinks he's a dog."

"Not my bad," Diesel said, grabbing a meat pie. "And I'm not walking him."

"So this is the map," Josh said, staring down at it. "Hard to believe it will lead to such riches."

Diesel ate the meat pie cold like a sandwich and washed it down with a beer. He removed the map from the frame and placed the map back on the countertop. I thought Josh was right. The map didn't look like anything that would lead us to a treasure. It was a round piece of old parchment. On one side was the inscription *"Denarius clavis ad chartum est."* There was also a rudimentary sketch of a collection of islands below the inscription. One of the islands had an X drawn onto it. The other side of the map was filled from top to bottom with seemingly random letters. A series of concentric circles drawn on the round map were the only things that seemed to separate one group of letters from another. It looked like an archery target.

"This isn't a slam dunk," Glo said. "The treasure could be buried anywhere on those islands. We could dig holes for a thousand years and never find anything."

Diesel turned the map over to the side with the letters. He put the coin on the parchment. Nothing magical happened. Josh tried to rub the letters with the coin, as if it was a scratch-off lottery ticket. Nothing happened.

"How did you get the seven pieces of coin to stick together?" I asked Diesel.

"Superglue."

"Maybe it's like a Ouija board," Glo said. "Maybe we just need to put the coin on the map, and we all put our hands on it, and the coin will move around while we chant."

"It's some kind of a puzzle," I said. "I'm sure we have to figure out how to use these concentric circles."

I put the coin in the center circle . . . the bull's-eye. It was a perfect fit.

"Omigosh," Glo said. "There's a letter peeking out through one of the little holes in the coin."

I rotated the coin and there were more alphabet letters.

"The coin has to be perfectly rotated to have letters appear in the holes," I said. "Right now we have an 'E' and an 'O.'"

"We need the missing piece of the coin," Diesel said. "Without that piece it's impossible to know if the coin is oriented correctly, if we're missing letters, or even if we have the correct letters."

"What about the outer rings?" Josh asked. "They all have letters in them, too."

Diesel put the coin on top of the outermost ring. The width of the coin was exactly the width of the "doughnut ring," the space between the outside ring and the next one.

In fact, each of the concentric rings, though they formed smaller and smaller doughnuts, had the same exact width of approximately one and a half inches, the same width as the diameter of the coin.

"Try to rotate the coin in the outer ring and see if you can find letters in the holes," Diesel said to me.

I chose a random place within the doughnut ring and put the coin inside it. I rotated the coin slightly until letters were visible through the holes. I used that as my starting point and rolled the coin, like the wheel of a bicycle rolling down the road, so that it stayed inside the confines of the doughnut ring. It looked like a planet revolving around the sun. As the coin moved through its orbit, additional letters were revealed through the holes. I rolled the coin around all of the rings, and Diesel wrote down all of the letters.

"This makes no sense," Diesel said, looking at what he'd written. "We need the last piece of the coin from Wulf. We can't decipher the map without it."

Ammon was on his feet, looking around. He spied Cat, gave a *woof*, and chased Cat into the living room. Cat planted his feet, hissed, and swatted at Ammon, slashing a four-inch rip in Ammon's pants leg. Ammon yelped and jumped away from Cat.

I pointed at the couch. *"Sit!"* I said to Ammon.

Ammon got on the couch, scrunched around a little, and curled up.

"We have to do something with him," I said to Diesel. "He can't stay here. Either we turn him over to Rutherford, or else we take him to the animal shelter."

Crash! Ammon fell off the couch.

"What the heck?" I said. "Is he okay?"

"I think he tried to lick his dog balls and fell off the couch," Glo said.

Rutherford arrived fifteen minutes later. We were outside on the sidewalk with Ammon. Ammon was no longer bound, but Diesel had a grip on him so he wouldn't chase after cars or squirrels.

"I found him on my doorstep," I said to Rutherford. "He seems confused."

Ammon growled at Rutherford.

"He must be in shock from the traumatic fire," I said. "He's not himself."

"It's true," Josh said to Rutherford. "He thinks he's a doggy. You'll want to watch him on the carpets."

Rutherford gaped at Ammon. "He's bloody!"

"Yeah," Diesel said. "He might have fallen down."

Rutherford loaded Ammon into the Mercedes sedan, and they drove off with Ammon's head out the window, his nose pointed into the wind.

"Go figure," Glo said.

We drove the van back to Dazzle's. We all got into our own cars and drove home. I looked in my rearview mirror and saw that Diesel was following me. I parked in my space alongside my house, and Diesel parked on the street one house down.

"Not going home?" I asked him.

We were on the sidewalk in front of my house, and Diesel looked toward the front door. "I left my monkey here. And Wulf is here."

"How do you know Wulf is here?"

"I have a cramp in my ass."

Diesel went in first, flipped the light on, and I saw that Wulf was sitting in a chair in the living room. He looked deadly calm and perfectly at ease. He didn't blink in the sudden bright light. He didn't smile. He didn't scowl. He didn't look surprised to see Diesel.

"Hello, cousin," Wulf said.

Diesel gave a small nod of recognition. "Wulf."

"I've been admiring the map," Wulf said. "Pity it's useless without my piece of the coin."

"What's the deal?" Diesel asked him.

"You keep the treasure, and I get the stone if I give you my piece."

"Not gonna happen," Diesel said.

"Martin Ammon looks the fool right now, but he's no fool."

"He's also no demon," Diesel said.

"There's a demon inside all of us," Wulf said. "Ammon's demon is greed. He will always want more wealth and more power. He'll stop at nothing to get it. And there are those who follow him doglike, if you'll excuse the expression. Mammon has his disciples, whether they be misguided or not."

"And your point?" Diesel asked.

"My point is that for all purposes he now owns Miss Tucker. She's signed a contract that gives Ammon control of her professional future. She's been caught on security cameras kidnapping Ammon. She's in possession of stolen property from his house. He will use all this to blackmail her into helping him find the treasure. And if that doesn't work, he'll raise the stakes until she agrees. He'll burn down her house, kill her cat, and kidnap her mother and chop off her fingers one by one."

This was all said very matter-of-fact, without any emotional inflection or doubt that it would happen. It was the word of Wulf, and Diesel and I knew that everything he said was true.

"Better I get the stone than Ammon and his Mammon worshippers. I can control the power. Followers of Mammon will unleash it."

"We could just leave the stone hidden," I said. "Even someone as crazy as Ammon would understand that we're at an impasse."

"It won't stop them from chopping off your mother's fingers," Wulf said.

"Even a crazy person has to realize I have no control

over you, and can't get you to give me the last piece," I said to Wulf.

Diesel and Wulf exchanged glances.

"You *do* have control over him," Diesel said. "Wulf couldn't allow anything bad to happen to you or your family. He would have to act."

"Why?"

"For the same reason I couldn't allow it," Diesel said. "We're bound to you."

"Jeez," I said. "I don't even know what that means."

"It means there would have to be a price paid for destroying what I'm bound to protect," Wulf said. "And that would be a large, tiresome project if my targets were Mammon followers."

"I don't get it," I said to Wulf. "You threaten me all the time."

"There's me, and then there's them," Wulf said, laying his single piece of the coin on the coffee table.

Diesel took the piece and joined it to the other seven pieces. We put the coin on the map, and Diesel recorded the letters that resulted when we rolled the coin around the rings.

"What does it say?" I asked Diesel.

"'In the deep water west of Gull Rock lies Babur's cursed gemstone. It may find ye a treasure but the price be your bones.'"

"Oh boy," I said. "A cursed gemstone."

"*Whatever* it is, you need to find it," Wulf said.

Phuunf! There was a flash of light and some smoke and Wulf was gone.

"How does he do that?" I asked.

Diesel grinned. "To tell you the truth, I don't know."

"Did we just agree to give him the Stone of Avarice?"

"Yeah, and it doesn't make me happy, but his power is limited as long as we have two stones safely locked away. He needs all seven to do real damage."

"Wulf mentioned Mammon followers," I said to Diesel. "Do you think they exist?"

"It wouldn't surprise me. And I can understand why they would gravitate to Ammon as their supreme representative."

"You don't suppose he could actually *be* Mammon, do you?"

"No. I think his parents made an unfortunate choice of a first name."

"What would these Mammon followers look like?" I asked. "Would they be like a zombie army worshipping Ammon?"

"My money's on Rutherford," said Diesel. "He's always got Ammon in his sights. And if Rutherford is one of them, there are probably other acolytes on the household staff."

"Rutherford seems unusually devoted to Ammon, but I don't know if I could see him as a Mammon worshipper. He looks so normal."

"My Aunt Lydia looks normal, but she belongs to a coven that elected her Goddess of the Daisies."

"You have a strange family," I said.

"Not by California standards."

I poured myself a glass of wine and chugged half. "About tonight."

Diesel was relaxed against a counter, thumbs hooked into his pants pockets, tie loosened, top button to his shirt open. "You had to drink half a glass of wine before you brought it up?"

"Is there a problem with that?"

"Not on my end," Diesel said.

"Here's the thing," I said. "I'm sort of creeped out to stay here by myself. Wulf pops in whenever he wants, and I'm worried that Ammon will realize he's not a dog, and I have his map."

"So you want me to spend the night."

"Yes."

"Where am I sleeping?"

"Wherever you want," I told him.

"This is too easy."

"I thought you liked easy."

"I'm good at my job because I have superior instincts, and my instincts tell me this isn't going to end well."

"You're doing me a favor by staying here. The least I can do is offer you my bed . . . being that you don't fit on the couch."

"And?"

"And I'll sleep down here," I said.

"Because?"

"Because I don't want to take any chances on having to save the world all by myself."

"I thought we figured that one out," Diesel said.

"What if it was a fluke? Like, what if someone had just been asleep at the switch? There's a lot at stake right now."

Diesel helped himself to the wine and refilled my glass. "Let me know if you change your mind. I'm good on short notice."

I changed my mind at ten o'clock when we shut the television off.

"Maybe we could try the pillow thing again," I said. "You stay on your side, and I'll stay on my side."

He wrapped his hand around my wrist and tugged me toward the stairs. "It would be easier if I had Hatchet."

"He's a nut."

"True, but I have no desire to get him naked."

"I don't suppose you'd want to sleep with your clothes on."

He tossed his jacket over a chair. "Don't suppose I would, but feel free to wear whatever you want."

I grabbed some flannel pajamas and changed in the bathroom. Diesel was already in bed when I came out.

"It's July," Diesel said. "Don't you think you'll be hot in flannel pajamas?"

"They feel cozy."

"I bet."

CHAPTER FIFTEEN

My smartphone alarm buzzed me awake. The room was pitch-black. I could feel Cat curled at my feet. I was cuddled next to Diesel. No pillows. I checked my pajamas. Still buttoned. Still on me. I eased out of bed, found some clothes in the dark, and went into the bathroom. I was showered and dressed in fifteen minutes. Diesel was still sleeping.

"No, I'm not," Diesel said.

I turned the light on.

"That doesn't mean I want the light on," he said.

I turned the light off and went downstairs with Cat close on my heels.

I made coffee, fed Cat, and toasted a bagel. I hung my

tote bag on my shoulder, poured my coffee into a to-go cup, and took a bite of the bagel. Carl was asleep on the couch with a night-light on. I crossed the room, unlocked the front door, and was knocked back when the door was shoved open.

Josh and Devereaux rushed into the room. Devereaux held me at gunpoint while Josh went to the kitchen and returned with the coin, the map, and the paper Diesel had copied the letters onto.

"What the heck?" I said.

"One hundred and ninety million dollars be a lot of money," Josh said, heading for the door with the map tucked under his arm.

It was so unexpected it took a beat for me to put it together. They were stealing everything and going after the treasure.

"Diesel!" I yelled. *"DEEEEZELLL!"*

I dropped my coffee, bagel, and tote bag and ran after Devereaux, grabbing him by the back of his jacket. He whirled around and caught me on the side of my head with the gun butt.

Josh looked over at me. "Are you okay?"

"No," I said. Blood was dripping off the side of my face onto my sweatshirt, and my ears were ringing.

Devereaux raced toward a car parked half on the sidewalk in front of my house. "Get in the car," he yelled at Josh.

"Sorry," Josh said to me. "Ye be a comely lass, but I best do this."

"Ye be an a-hole," I yelled after him. "Best you get herpes."

"Aargh," he said. And they drove away.

Diesel came up beside me. "What's going on?"

"Devereaux and Josh just took off with the map and the coin."

I turned and looked at Diesel. He was naked.

"Holy cow," I said.

"You got me out of bed."

A car drove by and beeped. Diesel waved and closed the front door and locked it.

"You have a gash on the side of your head," Diesel said. "How'd that happen?"

I took my sweatshirt off, pressed it against the cut, and went to the kitchen. "Devereaux hit me with his gun. It stunned me long enough for them to get away."

"It's disappointing that Josh threw in with Devereaux. I didn't see that coming." He moistened a kitchen towel and cleaned the area around the cut. "It's not so bad," he said. "It's not deep, and the bleeding is stopping." He got a giant Band-Aid from my kitchen first-aid kit. "Relax while I get dressed."

Damn. He was going to get dressed. Bummer.

"That's the sort of thinking that will get you into trouble," Diesel said.

"You're reading my mind again!"

"I wasn't reading your mind," Diesel said. "You were licking your lips and staring."

Diesel was wearing washed-out jeans, a black T-shirt, and running shoes. His hair was still damp from a shower, and he had a two-day beard. He popped half a bagel into the toaster and helped himself to coffee.

I was rinsing my coffee mug in the sink when I sensed someone at the back door. I looked over and saw Rutherford staring in at us.

Diesel opened the door to him. "How's it going?" Diesel said.

"Well, the truth is it could be going better," Rutherford said. "Mr. Ammon is upset that his map is missing. And he would like to have it back."

"Sorry," Diesel said. "We don't have it."

"Perhaps you might check around just to be sure," Rutherford said. He was smiling and making patty-cake gestures with his hands.

"Not here," Diesel said.

Rutherford kept smiling. "Here's the thing . . . it isn't that I doubt your word, but we have video of you taking it."

"That was yesterday," Diesel said. "You're an hour late. Someone just stole it."

Rutherford gave a short burst of polite laughter. "Ah!

Ha-ha. Of course I believe you, but . . . ha-ha, Mr. Ammon might not believe it. That someone could, ah, just waltz in here and steal it?"

"Everyone waltzes in here," Diesel said. "It happens all the time."

"I was hit on the head with a gun," I said, pointing to my Band-Aid.

"I'm so sorry," Rutherford said, looking at the Band-Aid, his face a study in agonized concern. "I'll do my best to explain this to Mr. Ammon. Yes, yes."

Diesel closed the door after Rutherford left, and topped off his coffee. "You're getting a lot of traffic in here today."

I set my mug in the dish drain. "Do you think Devereaux and Josh will be able to find the island?"

"Devereaux probably always knew where the island was located. It was crudely drawn on the bottom of the map, and he had the map long enough to conduct research. Ammon has probably always known where the island is, too. And most likely both of them have searched every square inch of it and found nothing. They were dead-ended without the coin to read the message on the map."

"What about us? Do we know where the island is?"

"Yep. I took a picture of the map last night and sent it to a guy I know who's spent a lot of time sailing these waters. The cluster of small islands is in Penobscot Bay. My guy said it wasn't hard to find the target island because it has a unique shape. It's called Brimstone Island. And he also knew about Gull Rock."

"The name *Brimstone Island* doesn't exactly conjure up thoughts of a tropical paradise." I checked the time. "I have to run. I'm going to be late for work."

"Correction. You're going to be *missing*. You need to call in for another 'save the world' day. We need to get to Brimstone Island before Devereaux."

"Can we do that? He has a head start."

"I've mapped it out. It takes about four hours to get to Rockland, Maine. From there it's a two-hour ferry ride to the Fox Islands. Then it's necessary to hire a boat to get to Brimstone. It's about an eight-hour trip total. Fortunately we have resources that probably aren't available to Devereaux."

"And that would be?"

"A fast boat. Wulf is meeting us at the wharf in an hour."

I called Clara and told her I wouldn't be in. Sunday was a slow day, and she'd be able to manage the cider doughnuts on her own. Glo could help her with cleanup.

We took Diesel's car to Pickering Wharf Marina, parked, and walked to the dock.

"I don't see Wulf's boat," I said.

"It's the orange one on the end."

"That's not the boat I was on."

"The boat you were on is too slow for our purposes.

This is a fifty-one-foot Nor-Tech 5000 Vee. It tops out at 120 miles per hour. We won't be going that fast today, but we'll be going faster than Devereaux."

"How many boats does Wulf have?"

Diesel shrugged. "They come and go."

"Do you have a boat?"

"I have a hammock and a surfboard."

The boat was long and low with an open cockpit. Wulf was at the helm. Hatchet was in the copilot seat. There were three seats behind them. I counted eighteen dials on the console and more to the left of the wheel. The hatch leading to below decks was also to the left of the wheel. Decking was teak. Seats were red leather. I got on board and took a seat. Diesel stood behind Wulf. Wulf hit the ignition switch and the boat rumbled to life. Wulf maneuvered us away from the slip and into the harbor. He was in his usual black. His hair was pulled back into a ponytail at the nape of his neck. His eyes were hidden behind mirrored sunglasses. I wondered if he was wearing sunscreen. We reached open water, he pushed the throttle forward, and the boat took off. Diesel and Wulf looked like this was business as usual. Hatchet looked like he was going to throw up. And I was breathless.

We reached Penobscot Bay at midmorning. The sea was calm and the sun was shining. Wulf slowed and cruised along, following the coordinates from Diesel's boat guy.

"That's Brimstone straight ahead," Wulf said.

It looked like a cupcake with green icing. In reality it was a massive hunk of rock with just enough topsoil for trees to grow. We circled the island, keeping our eyes open for Gull Rock. Most of the coastline consisted of ledges and boulders, but we found a small sand beach on the north side of the island and a larger beach on the west side. The west-side beach was packed with people. A tiki hut had been erected on the beach and music carried across the water to us. Small boats were moored a few feet from shore.

"I thought this was supposed to be a lost deserted island," Diesel said.

Wulf scanned the beach with binoculars. "The sign on the tiki hut says BRIMSTONE BAR AND GRILL. It looks like a nudie beach for seniors."

Diesel took the binoculars from Wulf. "Whoa!"

He grinned and handed the binoculars to me, but I passed. I was happy to have old age creep up on me. I didn't want a full frontal preview.

We returned to the north side of the island where there were a lot of rock outcroppings.

"There," Diesel said, pointing out to sea. "Gull Rock, according to my source. It's the chunk of rock that looks like bird wings, and it's filled with gulls. There's probably good fishing around it."

Wulf motored around the rock, watching the fish finder and side-scan sonar. He enlarged his circle and found a wreck on the second pass. He cut the engine and dropped anchor.

"What's the depth on the wreck?" Diesel asked him.

"Not deep. Looks like about twenty-five meters."

"In feet?" I asked.

"About eighty," Diesel said. "I could free-dive that, but I can stay down longer with tanks."

"They're in the salon," Wulf said.

"Are you diving, too?" I asked him.

"No," Wulf said. "I drive, and he dives."

Wulf put out a dive flag, and Diesel changed into a wetsuit and scuba gear. He went over the side and disappeared into the dark water. He reappeared after twenty minutes and hoisted himself onto the boat.

"It's a relatively small wreck," Diesel said, shrugging out of the scuba gear. "Looked like a fishing vessel that was intentionally scuttled. Didn't look disturbed. Not much of value in it with the exception of this chest." Diesel handed Wulf a net pouch with a small barnacle-encrusted box in it.

Wulf took the box out of the net and opened it. "At first glance, I'd say I'm looking at the Blue Diamond."

Diesel took the diamond out of the box and put it in my hand. "Do you feel anything?"

"A small vibration and some heat."

"It's cold when it's in *my* hand," Diesel said.

"It's not glowing," I said. "Devereaux told us it glows blue when it approaches the stone."

"I'm sure it needs to be closer to the stone to do that," Diesel said. "There was nothing else down there, and clearly it's empowered by the stone if you feel a vibration."

"Boat approaching, sire," Hatchet said.

We all turned our attention to the boat. It was a center console, about half our size, and it was traveling at a good speed, pushed by two outboards.

Wulf had the binoculars up. "Professor Devereaux and a mate," he said. "Hatchet, raise the anchor and stow the dive flag."

The boat came up on us, swerved, and sped away. It whipped around and came to a stop at some distance with its prow aimed in our direction.

"What's going on?" Diesel asked.

"Devereaux is angry. The mate looks worried," Wulf said, binoculars still trained on them.

"I'm sure Devereaux isn't happy to find we got here first," Diesel said.

Wulf moved to the wheel and hit the ignition. "Devereaux just shouldered a handheld rocket launcher. We need to move *now*. Hang on."

CHAPTER SIXTEEN

The twin turbines roared and our boat jumped forward. I saw the flash from the rocket launcher, and then I was flying through the air. I went underwater, kicked my way to the surface, and struggled to stay afloat. Debris from Wulf's boat was all around me. A seat cushion floated by, and I grabbed hold. I was too stunned to hear the smaller boat approach, and still stunned when I was dragged out of the water. I lay on the floor of the boat, catching my breath, clutching the seat cushion.

"What?" I said, jostled by the motion of the boat as it raced through the water.

Josh was on his knees next to me. "Are you okay?" he asked. His face was white, and he looked shaken.

I pushed myself up to a sitting position, and Josh helped me get to my feet and pivot onto the bench seat in the back of the boat.

"What happened?" I asked.

"He blew you out of the water," Josh said. "He's nuts. He blew that boat to smithereens."

"Why?"

"The treasure. He's obsessed with it. I admit I joined up with him to get some money and go on a treasure hunt, but it's like all of a sudden he's nutso. It wasn't supposed to be like this. He said it would be a lark. A race to the finish with winner take all."

I looked back at the wreckage. "Diesel and Wulf . . ."

"They've surfaced," Josh said. "They're floating on something. There's a third mate, too."

"That would be Steven Hatchet."

I looked down at my hand. I was still holding on to the Blue Diamond.

"Whoa," Josh said. "What is that?"

Devereaux stepped away from the console and looked at the diamond. "It's the *finder*," he said. "It's the Blue Diamond of Babur. I never thought I would have this opportunity, but here I am. You were the critical missing element. And now I have everything I need to claim the treasure. And Ammon has nothing!"

"Wow, that's great," I said. "Good for you. Maybe since

you have it all we should go back and pick up the men who are floating in the ocean."

"I don't need them. I hope they drown."

Not an unexpected answer since the man blew up our boat, but it sent a chill through me all the same.

"You alone can find the treasure," Devereaux said. "It's in the diary. And it's in the writings of Mammon. The guide will find the way. You're the guide."

"I thought you weren't a follower of Mammon."

"I'm not a believer. I'm a historian. When I find the treasure my name will be listed with the greatest historians and treasure hunters of all time."

"Not to mention, you'll be shockingly rich."

Devereaux smiled. "That, too."

"If those three men drown back there you'll also be listed as a murderer," I said.

"Who will accuse me? Josh? He's an accomplice. And no one will believe you. You're just a hysterical, delusional female."

I was soaking wet and shivering, and I worried that he might be right about the delusional and hysterical part. There was definitely an element of unreality to all this, and I could feel the hysteria twitching in my chest, ready to burst out at any moment.

Devereaux returned to the controls and directed the boat toward shore. He had a semiautomatic pistol shoved into his pants pocket, and I thought he was wacko enough to use it.

"Here's how this will play out," Devereaux said. "I've studied the map, and I'm going to beach this boat in the most likely starting point that will lead us to the treasure."

"How does the finder work?" I asked.

"According to the diary, the finder will want to join with the stone, so it will emit energy as it gets closer."

"It will glow," I said.

"Yes, I thought the finder might be the Blue Diamond, but I wasn't sure. I personally feel like Palgrave Bellows made this whole treasure hunt more complicated than it had to be, but it is what it is."

"Suppose I don't want to do this?" I said.

Devereaux looked at Josh. "I'll kill him."

"Aargh," Josh said. "Best not be hasty."

"True," Devereaux said. "I'll just shoot off some fingers. Maybe an ear."

"It's not good to be missing an ear," Josh said. "I'm fond of them both."

Devereaux followed the rocky shoreline until he came to a small patch of sand in a protected cove. He nosed the boat in as far as he could, and when he started to churn sand he raised the engines.

"Take a line and pull us in," he said to Josh. "Secure the line to the tree at the edge of the shore. We're at dead-low tide. The boat will be floating when we return."

Josh grabbed the line and jumped into the knee-high water. He pulled the boat in as far as it would go, waded out of the water, and walked to the tree. When he got to the tree he looked back at us and put his hand to his ear. No doubt thinking he didn't want to lose it. He dropped the rope and ran off into the woods.

"Oops," I said.

Devereaux fired off two shots, but Josh continued to crash through the brush, so I assumed he wasn't hit . . . or at least not badly.

"This isn't going well," I said. "Why don't I give you the diamond, and you can find the treasure all by yourself?"

Devereaux hung a beat-up knapsack on his shoulder and pointed the gun at me. "Because that might not work. It's not clear if the diamond will glow for an ordinary person. Wade in to the beach and tie up the boat. I'll be right behind you, and I'll shoot you if you decide to follow him."

I tied the boat to the tree and set off on a path that led into the woods. I came to a fork in the path, Devereaux pulled a folded map of the island out of the knapsack, studied it for a moment, and told me to go left. I was still dripping wet and my shoes leaked water with every step. I looked at the chosen route and cringed. The rock-strewn trail wound uphill to a granite ledge.

"What's the finder telling you?" Devereaux asked.

"It's not telling me anything. It's a little warm but that's all."

"Keep moving," Devereaux said.

I was struggling to follow a narrow dirt path that was littered with rocks and sporadically overgrown with tangled vines. Thorny shrubs and stunted evergreens hugged the trail, obscuring the view. I could hear Devereaux laboring behind me. I reached the granite ledge, and the evergreens gave way enough for me to see the surf crashing onto the rocks far below me. The cove where we tied the boat was no longer in sight. I looked at the diamond and sucked in some air. The diamond was glowing. The light in the gemstone was very faint, but definitely there.

Devereaux saw it, too.

"I knew it!" he said. "It's going to lead us to the treasure."

His voice was hoarse and his face was red from the exertion of the climb. His eyes were glazed, his pupils narrow pinpoints of insanity.

"Do you have the coin on you?" I asked him.

"Of course."

"Is it in anything . . . like a lead box?"

"It's in my pocket."

"It's occurred to me that it might be affecting your behavior," I said. "I don't mean to be rude or anything, but you're a little nutso. You're not really yourself. Maybe you should sit and rest. Catch your breath."

"No time for that. Ammon could be following us."

I didn't think he had to worry about Ammon as much as he had to worry about Diesel and Wulf. I was confident that they were on the hunt, looking for me.

Now that I was on the granite ledge there was no path to follow. It was all rock with patches of scrub forest. I chose a direction at random and the diamond stopped glowing. I backtracked and went off in another direction, and the light returned. We were climbing over boulders and bushwhacking through brambles. I had scratches on my arms where I'd caught thorns, and my jeans were torn at the knee from skidding down a rockslide. From time to time I'd turn and check on Devereaux, hoping he'd fall behind enough for me to escape. So far he was keeping up, trudging along with the gun in his hand, his eyes bright with crazed excitement. I had to stop and backtrack again twice when the diamond went dim, but for twenty minutes now the glow had been getting steadily stronger.

I approached what at first looked like a dead end, but turned out to be a narrow canyon made by two slabs of granite. The distance between the slabs was three feet at best, and the walls were thirty to forty feet high. I stepped into the slot, looked up at the ribbon of blue sky far above me, and felt a rush of panic burn in my chest.

"I can't go in there," I said to Devereaux. "It's too narrow. We'll get trapped."

"There's plenty of room. What does the diamond say?"

I had the diamond in my pocket, so he couldn't see it, but the stupid thing was glowing through the denim.

"There has to be an easier way to get to the treasure," I said. "We should go back and try a different route."

"We're not going back. We're following the diamond. Give it to me. Hand it over."

I gave him the diamond, and it went cold. No glow. No heat. Nothing.

"I guess you're not the guide," I said.

"Lucky for you, but that doesn't mean you're not expendable. I've gotten this far, and I have a map. If you cease to be useful to me I'll eliminate you and go it alone."

"You won't find the treasure on your own."

"So be it, then."

I didn't like the word *eliminate*. The prospect of being *eliminated* was even less desirable than threading my way through the slot. I put my head down and walked forward, putting one foot in front of the other. I watched my feet. I didn't look up, and I didn't look ahead. The narrow passage-way seemed to go on forever, and then suddenly I was in bright sunlight and in an open space that was shaped like a bowl. The rocky sides of the bowl were maybe thirty feet high, and the bowl was thirty or forty feet across. Not huge, but I could breathe easier. Problem was I didn't see a way out of the bowl other than the way we came in.

"Now what?" I asked Devereaux.

"Walk around and see what happens to the diamond."

I set off around the perimeter of the pit, and a third of the way the diamond began to pulse with light. Two years ago I wouldn't have believed any of this, but since Diesel popped into my life I was willing to believe almost anything. And I have to admit it was hard not to get excited about the pulsing diamond. I looked up at the rim of the bowl high above me hoping to see Diesel or Wulf, but there was only blue sky.

"Keep walking," Devereaux said.

I continued picking my way along the bottom of the bowl, and after a couple minutes the diamond stopped pulsing.

"Go back!" Devereaux said. "The treasure must be back with the boulders."

There was an outcropping of loose rock and large boulders in the area where the diamond pulsed. A clump of scruffy bushes and scraggly evergreens grew in the thin soil around the boulders. Mostly there was granite ledge under our feet. No place to bury a treasure chest.

I kicked through the bushes and found a fissure in the rock wall behind a man-sized boulder. Devereaux took a couple flashlights out of his knapsack. He handed one to me, and he kept the other.

"Look around," he said. "What do you see?"

I stuck my head in and flicked the light on. The fissure appeared to form a natural tunnel. From what I could see, it was damp, dark, and no place I wanted to go. It was at best three feet wide, and it was difficult to determine the height. I might be able to stand, but there wouldn't be a lot of clearance.

"Well?" Devereaux asked.

"Looks like a dead end," I said.

"No, it doesn't. It looks like a tunnel. I can see from here. It's going to lead us to the treasure. Get in there."

"No way. Shoot me. I'd rather die here than in that tomb."

"It's not a tomb, you ninny. It's a treasure trove. It's the path to immortality."

He was very close to me, and the gun was shaking in his hand.

"This is too important for me to walk away," Devereaux said. "It's my destiny. My legacy. And you're going to help me."

"I don't think so. Take the diamond. Good riddance. Good luck."

I heard the *wup, wup, wup* sound of a helicopter overhead, and a shadow fell over Devereaux and me. My first thought was of Diesel and Wulf, but I looked up and saw AMMON ENTERPRISES written in black and gold on the white chopper. Hard to tell if I was relieved or even more terrified.

"Bastards!" Devereaux shouted.

He squeezed off two shots at the helicopter, and it disappeared over the edge of the bowl.

"They aren't getting my treasure," he said, pointing the gun at me. "We have to hurry. Lead the way to the cave, or I'll shoot you."

"How do you know the treasure is in a cave?"

"It's always either in a cave or buried. And nothing is

going to be buried on this godforsaken piece of rock. I'm counting to three, and then I'm going to shoot you in the foot if you don't start walking."

"How do you know the treasure is still there? It's been hundreds of years."

"Three," Devereaux said, and he fired off a shot at my foot.

The bullet caught the side of my sneaker and ripped a hole in it.

"Damn," Devereaux said. "Hold still so I can try again."

"Stop!" I said. "I'm going in."

CHAPTER SEVENTEEN

I edged my way into the tunnel and cautiously moved forward. Even with the flashlight it was difficult to see more than a few feet ahead. I kept telling myself that the tunnel had to lead somewhere, and that the somewhere would be better than this claustrophobic tube. I could hear Devereaux behind me, sliding on the slick, uneven rock surface. He was mumbling and swearing, and I was worried that he would lose his footing and accidentally shoot me.

After what seemed like an eternity I reached a fork. One side went left, and the other side was a hole in the ground. I moved left, and the diamond dimmed. I went back and looked at the black hole. It was like an elevator shaft dropping off into the darkness. I played the flashlight beam around the sides of the hole and saw that there were stairs carved out of the rock, spiraling down into the unknown.

"Go," Devereaux said. "We have to get to the treasure first. I have to claim it as my own."

"That's not going to do you any good if they come in and shoot you," I said.

"I'll shoot them first. I'll kill them all. I should have done that long ago anyway."

This was all Diesel's fault. My life was just fine until he barged into it. Now look at me. I'm being held at gunpoint by a homicidal maniac who's getting crazier by the minute.

"These stairs are narrow and slippery," I said, "and there's no handrail. My suggestion is to hide in the part of the tunnel that goes to the left and let Ammon and whoever is with him plunge to their death all on their own. Then we can get some equipment, like rock-climbing stuff, and safely explore the road to hell."

"You will go to hell *now*!" Devereaux said. *"NOW!"*

His face was contorted into a snarl, and his eyes glittered in the ambient glow from his flashlight.

"You're a little scary," I said to him. "You should try to calm yourself."

"I'll calm myself when I get my treasure. Now move. I hear voices. The demons must be in the tunnel."

"Demons?"

"Demon worshippers. Might as well be demons. Ammon

and his followers. He probably had the helicopter filled with the greedy bastards. They're all looking for that stupid stone that will turn Ammon back into his true form."

"And his true form would be . . ."

"Mammon, of course. The God of Greed."

I blew out a sigh. Diesel was missing in action and I was going to have to save the world all by myself. I couldn't stand by and let the God of Greed get the stone. I carefully tested the first couple steps, keeping my shoulder pressed to the rock wall. They weren't as slippery as I'd originally feared. If I took my time and didn't lose focus I thought I'd be okay. I counted as I crept down the steps. Twenty-six, and I still couldn't see the bottom. I paused to gather myself together, and Devereaux prodded me with the gun barrel.

"Move," he said. "They're getting closer. I hear footsteps."

His hearing was a lot better than mine. I couldn't hear anything over the pounding of my heart. I was in a cold sweat from the fear of falling and the exertion of controlling my panic. I went down four more steps and realized Devereaux was holding back. He was turned slightly, looking up at the shaft's entrance, his flashlight in one hand and his gun in the other. I suspected he was going to shoot whoever stuck their head over the edge. Not something I wanted to think about. My focus was on the next step and the step after that. I directed my light down for a moment and was able to see the bottom of the pit. That was a good sign, but I still needed to stay vigilant.

High above me a spotlight blinked on, lighting the entire staircase. Devereaux fired a shot at the spotlight, lost his footing, and stepped off into space. His arms windmilled out like a cartoon character's, he found nothing to grab, and he plunged straight down. I closed my eyes and didn't open them again until I heard him hit bottom. I fought back a wave of nausea and took another step. Get to the bottom, I thought. One thing at a time. If I could get to the bottom I might be able to find Devereaux's gun. I might be able to hide somewhere. If I could evade Ammon long enough, Diesel might find me.

I had maybe twenty steps left, and I heard a rope drop. Moments later the first man rappelled down. A second rope dropped, and two more men descended. By the time I reached the last step and was on bedrock, there were four men in total. Three were dressed in black fatigues, and they were all armed. The fourth man was Rutherford. He was also dressed in black fatigues, but he looked uncomfortable in them, smoothing them out when his feet touched ground. As far as I could see he wasn't armed.

Devereaux lay motionless on the ground. No one paid any attention to him. Just beyond him was a gaping black hole that I suspected was the entrance to another tunnel.

"Someone should check on Professor Devereaux," I said.

One of the men went over and took a closer look. "Dead," he said.

"Really?" Rutherford asked. "Are you certain? Well,

then, I suppose we should move on. After all, Mr. Ammon is waiting." Rutherford turned to me. "Mr. Ammon is very excited about this. This is a holy mission for him. Yes, yes. Actually for all of us who serve him."

"Serve him? You mean as his assistant."

"Yes, yes, of course. But also as a disciple. Mr. Ammon feels that he holds the sleeping beast within him. Once he has the Avaritia Stone and the ceremony is performed, Mammon will finally awaken and rule the earth." Rutherford wiped his sweaty palms on his fatigues. "It will be glorious. Glorious."

"So you believe in Mammon?"

"Very definitely. Mr. Ammon feels very strongly about Mammon. It came to Mr. Ammon in a vision shortly after he inherited the diary. He believes Mammon has been lying dormant in the males of his family for eons. Can you imagine? And when you examine everything it becomes obvious. The ruthless ambition. The relentless acquisition of power. Mr. Ammon's whole family history is a rogue's gallery of notorious villains. It's very impressive. If you have the opportunity you should ask Mr. Ammon about it. I'm sure he would enjoy telling you his history. It's fascinating. Fascinating. Mr. Ammon is quite taken with you, you know. He speaks of you often."

"Because I have the ability to identify the Avaritia Stone."

"No, no. Mr. Ammon is certain he'll recognize the stone once it's uncovered. Although you were helpful in finding the various pieces of the coin. I must admit we couldn't have done that without you. And goodness, it wasn't as if we hadn't tried." Rutherford rocked back on his heels, smiling wide. "Here's the fun part of the equation. Mr. Ammon is a big fan of your cupcakes."

It took a moment for this to compute in my head. I'd pretty much forgotten about the cupcakes.

"I can see you're surprised at this," Rutherford said, doing a lot more smiling. "Mr. Ammon is multifaceted. He's a shrewd businessman, and he knows a good product when he sees it. True, he inherited much of his wealth, but he also made many, many excellent deals on his own. And he has his eye on you. You're a lucky woman. I suspect you'll get rich and famous under the Ammon brand. Of course, it will be necessary for you to embrace our lord Mammon, but I'm sure you'll find that quite painless. We're a happy, fun-loving group. Though, now that I think about it, there's the possibility of a sacrifice . . . but, again, that shouldn't be too painful."

Someone whistled from far above us. "We're sending her down," they shouted.

I looked up and was blinded by the spotlight. I shaded my eyes and saw something descending, dangling from a rope. It was something in a short pink tutu-type skirt, black motorcycle boots, and an orange thong. It was Glo.

"We thought she might be useful," Rutherford said. "We understand that you have a special ability to find the stone, but this one seems to also have strange powers. There's a rumor that she can cast spells and see into the future."

Double oh boy. Glo had a book of spells that never worked as they should and a Magic 8 Ball she got at a yard sale. She was strapped into a harness that was attached to the rope. Her tote bag was slung over her shoulder. Broom was tucked into the tote bag.

"What the heck?" she said when her feet touched granite and she was able to stand.

I thought *What the heck?* about summed it all up. Beyond that I didn't know what to think.

"They kidnapped me when I wasn't looking," Glo said. She glanced at the body sprawled on the floor of the cave. "Whoa."

"It's Devereaux," I said. "He slipped and fell."

"He's not moving."

"It's a permanent condition."

"He's paralyzed?"

"He's dead," I told her.

"Bummer," Glo said. "Do you want me to say some words? I'm an ordained minister. I even have a certificate."

"What church?" I asked her.

"The Church of the Barley Goddess."

"I don't think that's a real church."

"They have a website," Glo said. "The World Wide Web wouldn't allow them on there if they weren't real."

"I suppose it wouldn't hurt," I said.

"I'm sure Mr. Ammon wouldn't mind if we took a moment," Rutherford said.

Glo bowed her head. "We commend the spirit of Quentin Devereaux to you, Great Old Ones and New Sprouts. Give him safe passage to the afterlife and if there's reincarnation we hope he doesn't come back as a snail or a spider because they're icky."

Everyone said "Amen," and looked to Rutherford for direction.

"Now that we have that solemn task behind us we can move forward," Rutherford said, going into jolly mode. "Mr. Carter can lead the way."

Mr. Carter tentatively stepped into the downward-sloping tunnel, and we all followed single file. Everyone but Glo had a flashlight. The tunnel was tight, and the man in front of me had to stoop. I had the diamond in my jeans pocket and could see its glow through the denim fabric.

We shuffled along in the dark for what seemed like forever, and then almost like a mirage there was light in front of us. Not enough light to make me believe we were going to be standing in an open field, but enough light to make me think we were coming to the end of the tunnel. Minutes later we stepped out into a massive cavern with a vast underground lake. Vents in the rock ceiling high above us beamed down shafts of sunlight.

Wooden pilings and a few rotting boards jutted out into the water, the remnants of an old dock. Beyond the boards

I could see an outcropping of rock and the tip of another dilapidated structure. The diamond was blinking and flashing in my pocket, and I could feel the heat it was generating.

"We're close," Rutherford said. "My goodness, this is a thrill."

I walked along the edge of the lake to the small mountain of rocks and stopped. The diamond had begun to hum, but I was at a dead end.

"It's on the other side of this jumble of rocks," Rutherford said to me. "Climb up on it." He gestured with his hands. "Up, up, up."

Glo had her Magic 8 Ball out. " 'Signs point to maybe,' " she said.

"Maybe what?" I asked her. "Maybe only a mountain goat could climb up on those rocks?"

"Mr. Carter will help you," Rutherford said, cheerfully. "He's quite the athlete. Mr. Carter was a marine."

I clenched my teeth and followed Carter as he picked his way over the rubble. Glo followed me, and everyone else followed Glo. The chunk of solid granite and loose rock was twenty to thirty feet high, and progress was slow. When we finally reached the top of the mound we looked down on the remains of a tall ship that had been beached in a small alcove. It was tipped on its side, the masts were broken off and resting on the shore, and much of the timber was rotted. It was like discovering the bones of a giant prehistoric beast.

We inched our way down to the shore, slipping and sliding on loose rock, and crawling over the larger boulders. I approached the ship, and the diamond continued to hum and blink. Still no sign of Diesel or Wulf, and I was feeling some anxiety. I felt certain that they were safe. I'd been told many times that they were hard to kill. My anxiety came from the fact that we were close to the stone, and I had no way to stop Rutherford from taking it. I could refuse to cooperate any further, but Glo was here now, and I suspected Rutherford might use her to make me stay on target. I suspected behind all the annoying, smiling good cheer, Rutherford was an insecure toad who would do anything to gain favor with his boss. If he had to slit my throat I was sure he would wipe his sweaty hands on his pants, plaster a smile on his face, and do it.

Rutherford sent two of the armed men up the underside of the ship, over the keel, and into the bowels of the wreck. We lost sight of them, but we listened to the wood creaking under their weight as they progressed through the ship. We heard a board snap, and there was silence. Rutherford looked at his watch. I looked at my watch, too, but I'd scratched the crystal on the slide down and it was difficult to read. After a couple beats we heard faint scuffing sounds. The men were back at work.

"What does your Magic 8 Ball say now?" I asked Glo.

" 'Tinkle tinkle little star I wonder where the bathrooms are,' " Glo said.

One of the men on the ship popped into sight.

"We found the treasure," he called down to us. "It's scattered around the captain's quarters."

"Up and over," Rutherford cheerfully said to me.

I stared at the keel looming above my head.

"Not gonna happen," I said. "There has to be another way to get on."

"Yes, yes, of course. We can find another way," Rutherford said. "I would have difficulty with that route as well."

We walked around the ship to where a gunwale was resting on the mix of sand and stone. A lot of this part of the ship was rotted, but I managed to climb around the rot on the slanted deck. I dropped through the hatch and into the salon, with the help of the man who was already in place. Everyone else followed. The interior was all sideways and cattywampus. The stairs were on the wall and the hallway led downward to an intricately engraved door. I made my way to the door and stepped into the captain's cabin. The ornate furnishings were tumbled over, but the elegant carving and gold inlays were intact. Light filtered into the room from the large bay window that filled the stern wall. We all looked up at the name carved above the window. GANJI-I-SAWA.

"This is the *Gunsway*," Rutherford said. "At one time there must have been a way to sail into here. We've circled the island several times in the past and never found an entrance."

"In the movies they blow up the entrance after they sail in so no one can find it," Glo said.

Rutherford looked like he wanted to hit her on the head with his flashlight. "That must be it," he said.

I crossed the tilted room to a huge overturned table and peered over the edge. The area behind the table was littered with gold and silver coins, jewelry, raw jewels, miniature icons, elaborate little bottles with stoppers, and carved gold platters. They had obviously spilled out of a heavy oak chest that had been smashed open. A skeleton was sprawled next to the chest. Bits of cloth clung to the yellowed bones, a filthy white wig lay next to the skull, and the man's boots were still attached to his feet.

"Most likely this is Palgrave Bellows," Rutherford said. "Those boots would have been very fancy back in the day."

My attention wasn't on his boots. My attention was drawn to the egg-sized rock in the man's hand.

"Pry the stone out of his fingers," Rutherford said to me. "Tell me if this is the holy stone of Mammon."

I attempted to take the stone away from the corpse, and accidentally snapped off two of his fingers. I gagged and broke out in a sweat.

"Oh my," Rutherford said, squeezing out a nugget of nervous laughter. "Ha-ha! That was something. They snapped right away. Ha-ha!" He shifted foot to foot. "Well, go ahead and pick it up. We have a schedule to keep. Let's see if this is the right stone."

I could feel the sweat trickle down my breastbone. The finger bones were still curled around the stone.

"Let's see," Rutherford said. "How can I make this easier for you? Oh, I know, we could distract you by shooting your friend. Nothing fatal, of course. Ha-ha."

"Don't worry, Lizzy," Glo said. "Broom would never allow it."

Broom was still stuck in Glo's tote bag. I wasn't sure I could count on Broom to save the day, so I sucked in some air and picked the stone up. It glowed green and hummed in my hand.

"I can tell from the expression on your face that this is the holy stone," Rutherford said. "This is the stone that will awaken Mammon!"

"And that would be Martin Ammon, right?" I asked. "Why isn't he with you?"

"Mr. Ammon is a busy, very, very important man. He can't be everywhere at once."

"I bet he's in a kennel," Glo said. "I swear it was an honest mistake. The page just sort of turned itself."

"A kennel?" Rutherford clasped his hands together. "Ha-ha, ha-ha! That's a good one."

"So he doesn't still think he's a dog?" Glo asked.

"A dog? Goodness, no. No, no. He's just fine. An occasional lapse, perhaps, but nothing serious. Nothing to worry about."

Rutherford took the stone from me and put it in a thick

leather pouch he'd obviously brought for the occasion. He attached the pouch to his wrist and tested it to make sure it was secure.

"We need to pack as much of the treasure as we can carry out of here," Rutherford said to his crew. "We can come back some other time for whatever is left behind. Right now I need to rush this stone to Mr. Ammon. I'm going to take the first helicopter out. By the time it returns I trust you'll have staged the most important items at the rim. Mr. Carter will be in charge of securing the ladies."

CHAPTER EIGHTEEN

Mr. Carter was balanced on the slanted floor of the ship, standing just in front of a trapdoor. He reached down and flipped the door open, and a dank odor of wood rot and seawater filled the room.

"How convenient," Carter said, shining his flashlight into the dark hold. "Chains for two." He looked over at me. "Ladies first."

"I don't think so," I said. "I'll pass."

"I haven't got time to play," Carter said, motioning to the two remaining men with his gun. "Take them down and chain them."

"I'm not really into the whole chained thing," Glo said. "I'd actually rather be a hostage."

"I was told to secure you, and that's what I'm going to do."

"He might not have meant that literally," I said to Carter. "He might have meant you should keep us safe."

"That's exactly what I'm going to do," he said. "I'm going to keep you safely secured so we can do our job."

One of the men dropped into the hold and another shoved Glo forward toward the trapdoor. Glo whacked the man with Broom. The man grabbed Broom away from Glo, and threw Glo and Broom into the hold. The second man followed Glo through the trapdoor. I heard splashing and shrieking and then a horrible quiet. After a couple beats the second man climbed out of the hold. He was soaking wet.

"You're next," Carter said to me. "You can voluntarily join your friend, or you can do it the hard way."

I lowered myself through the trapdoor and dropped into waist-high water. The second man splashed in after me. In the dim light I saw Glo chained by her wrists to the rough plank wall. There were several more sets of wrist chains. One of the sets of chains had a partial skeleton attached. The water in the hold was black, and the footing was treacherous. A man had me by my arm, guiding me to a set of chains, keeping me upright. The cuffs were snapped around my wrists and a second man tugged on the chains to make sure they were strong. The men sloshed away without a word, hoisted themselves out of the water, and disappeared through the trapdoor. The door slammed shut, and Glo and I were alone in the hold. It took a moment for my eyes to adjust to the dark. A small amount of light filtered through cracks in the captain's quarters' floorboards, and further down, in the bowels of the ship, I could see a gash in the side of the boat. Water and light flowed through the gash.

"I really hate this," Glo said. "The water is ruining my vintage skirt. It's not like these skirts grow on trees. And I don't know what happened to Broom. He's probably terrified. They just threw him down here."

As if on cue, Broom floated past us, without so much as a backward glance, and disappeared through the hole in the hold.

"He's probably going for help," Glo said.

"No doubt. I'm sure we'll be rescued any minute now."

A rat swam by, climbed onto a timber about three feet from me, and scurried away. I heard myself whimper, and I pulled against my chains.

"I'm starting to feel a little hysterical," Glo said. "I think I peed myself when the rat swam by."

"That could be good," I said. "It could drive him away. Can you wiggle your chains?"

"No. Can you?"

"No."

I looked down at the water. It was rising. It was now at chest level. The tide was coming in. The underground lake was a tidal pool, and somewhere on the island it became part of the sea.

"Either I'm getting shorter or the water is getting taller," Glo said. "It's almost up to my chin. And I'm c-c-cold."

"Maybe we should sing a song to keep our spirits up," I said.

"Row, row, row your boat . . ." Glo sang out.

I couldn't see my watch, but it seemed to me we sang "Row, Row, Row Your Boat" for about ten minutes. My teeth were chattering and my nose was running from fear and cold. My hands were numb in the rusted iron cuffs. I knew eventually Diesel and Wulf would find us, but I worried they wouldn't get to us in time.

"I'm getting tired," Glo said. "I'm standing on my tiptoes, and the water is almost up to my mouth. I don't want to die. I have stuff to do. I need to get my nails done. I need to punch Josh in the face. I haven't tried all the Ben and Jerry's ice cream flavors yet."

I had a lot of unfinished business, too, but I didn't want to think about it. It was too sad, too terrible, to go through the list.

"They're coming to get me," Glo said. "I'm done for. I hear the angels. They're walking around on the deck."

"I don't think you can hear angels walking," I said. "They have wings. They flutter."

"Well, I hear something up there."

We went still and listened.

Creak. Crrrrack.

Diesel fell through the rotted deck, splashed into the water, and resurfaced in front of me.

"C-c-crap on a cracker!" Glo said.

Diesel grabbed the iron bands on my wrists and the cuffs unlocked. He did the same for Glo. I swam to the trapdoor. Diesel shoved it open and boosted Glo through. A beat later I was on the dry slanted floor of the captain's quarters, and Diesel was next to me. I had a disorienting feeling that I was still chained, that the rusted cuffs were still in place. I looked down and saw that it was Diesel's hand I felt firmly wrapped around my wrist.

"I don't scare easily," Diesel said, "but these last couple hours were a ten when we couldn't find you."

I blinked away tears and took a deep breath. It was all okay. Glo hadn't drowned. The rats hadn't gotten to us. Diesel had been worried about me. And now I was safe beside him.

"I knew you would find me," I said.

"Honey, it wasn't easy. We had to swim to shore, towing Hatchet because he can't swim. Then we had to steal a boat so we could locate Devereaux's boat. Fortunately Josh found us just as we were shoving off, and he took us to the cove where Devereaux's boat was beached. After that it was the blind leading the blind since none of us was born with the tracking gene. We saw the helicopter land, and started to climb toward the helicopter, but it took off before we reached it. I stepped out onto a rock ledge, looked down at the water, and saw something floating. My first fear was that it was a body, but it turned out to be Broom."

"I told you he went for help!" Glo said.

"Long story short, since we weren't having any luck bushwhacking on the island, we decided to go with the hunch that there was a cave with water access, and that the cave was the logical place to hide treasure. We took the boat to the area where Broom was floating, saw that there was a strong current under a rock overhang, and here I am."

"The diamond led us to a tunnel that started at a high part of the island," I said to Diesel. "Rutherford spotted us from the air and followed us in. Devereaux fell to his death attempting to shoot Rutherford, and then Rutherford and his gang forced me to take them to the treasure. They got the SALIGIA Stone and left us to die."

"Was Martin Ammon with them?"

"No. Rutherford said he was too busy to be part of this treasure hunt, but I think he's still having an occasional lapse into Bow Wow Land."

"How'd Glo get here?"

"Rutherford brought her. He thought she'd be useful casting spells and whatever."

"How'd that work out?"

"There was a r-r-rat in the water," Glo said.

Diesel stood and pulled me to my feet. We got Glo standing up, and Diesel spotted the skeleton.

"Best guess is it's Palgrave Bellows," I said. "I had to pry the SALIGIA Stone out of his hand."

Diesel hooked his finger into the empty eye socket and lifted the skull off the floor. "We'll take this with us, so Nergal can talk to it."

Glo found her tote bag and hung it on her shoulder, and Diesel put the skull in it.

"Is Broom okay?" Glo asked. "Were you able to rescue him?"

"He's in the boat with Wulf and Josh."

We clambered down from the ship and stood on the rocks. The sand was covered by the high tide.

"The fastest way out is by water," Diesel said. "I'm going to tow you out one at a time. There's about a two-foot clearance between the water and the ledge, so watch your head."

He took Glo out first and returned for me. I closed my eyes when we passed under the ledge and opened them when a wave crashed over us. Ordinarily I'm a strong swimmer, but I was cold and exhausted, and happy to have Diesel ferry me to the boat that was bobbing beyond the surf.

They'd stolen a center console similar to the boat Devereaux had used. Josh was hunched on a bench seat, dabbing at a bloody nose. Glo was glaring at him from mid-ship. No explanation needed. That one was easy to figure out. No sign of Hatchet.

Diesel hauled himself out of the water. Wulf powered up the boat and steered around the island to the beach party.

"I thought we'd be heading for home," I said to Diesel.

"We have a helicopter picking us up. Apparently there's a flat patch of land that can be used as a helipad, and it's not far from the beach party. This isn't the off-the-charts island we expected."

Wulf anchored in shallow water, and we all slogged ashore. Hatchet was waiting at the water's edge, and he was naked, with the exception of his sword, which was in its scabbard and hung around his waist. He looked like a blob of marshmallow with stick legs and droopy doodles.

Wulf had his usual poker face, Diesel burst out laughing, and I thought I was going to have to pour bleach in my eyes to erase the sight.

"Welcome, sire," Hatchet said to Wulf. "The bird has not yet arrived."

"At least he has his sword sheathed," Glo said.

"I thought it best not to call attention to myself by being clothed," Hatchet said to Wulf. "If you are displeased you can whip me. I'll make a switch from a tree branch. I live to serve you."

"Lucky you," Diesel said to Wulf.

"This is my cross to bear," Wulf said.

"Sadly my garb hath disappeared," Hatchet said. "These wrinkled old folk have a mischievous side."

A helicopter buzzed the beach and disappeared behind a rock-strewn hill topped with a clump of trees. The beach party looked like it was winding down. The band was packing up, and the tiki hut was no longer serving drinks. Some of the partiers were sprawled on the beach, soaking up the last of the sun, and the rest were standing in small groups talking. They were still naked, and none of them were getting any younger. I saw a lot of gray hair, no hair, and skin cancer. The ravages of gravity on the human body over the years was sobering.

Several people waved to Hatchet when we crossed the beach to get to the helipad.

"Hey, Hatchet," one of the men yelled. "How's it hanging?"

"Yoo-hoo, Hatchet honey," a little white-haired lady called out. "Come over here and show us your sword."

"They be a wild and rowdy crowd," Hatchet said.

We reached the helicopter, and Hatchet got in first, giving us a view of the Grand Canyon when he bent over to take a seat.

"I'm not sitting next to him," I said to Diesel.

"Me, either," Glo said.

"Me, either," Josh said.

Wulf reached in and yanked Hatchet out of the helicopter.

The pilot wiped the seat down with hand sanitizer and sprayed the cabin with air freshener.

When we lifted off, Hatchet was on the ground, waving to us and shouting farewell.

"Will he be okay?" I asked Wulf. "He has no clothes and no money."

"He's quite resourceful," Wulf said. "He'll be fine."

It was dark when Diesel and I got home. We let ourselves in and went to the kitchen. Cat was on the counter, gnawing on a chicken potpie. Carl was eating peanut butter out of the jar with his finger. Cabinet doors were open and cereal boxes were on the floor.

"Looks like Carl made dinner," I said.

Carl looked over and smiled.

Diesel put the skull in the microwave for safekeeping. "First thing tomorrow we'll visit Nergal."

"I'm not sure we'll learn anything of value," I said. "This guy's been dead for hundreds of years, and the real task we have now is finding Martin Ammon and relieving him of the stone."

"You never know," Diesel said. "It could be interesting. You said you had to pry the stone out of his hand."

A chill ran down my spine at the memory. "It was creepy. I broke off two of his fingers!"

My clothes were still damp and caked with sea salt. My shoes squished when I walked. And I was starving. I made a cheese sandwich, told Diesel he was on his own, and took my sandwich upstairs with me. I locked myself in my bathroom and peeled my clothes off while I ate the sandwich. I stepped under a scalding hot shower, closed my eyes, and thought I was in heaven. I opened my eyes when Diesel stepped into the shower with me.

"Hey!" I said. "This is *my* shower."

"Not anymore," Diesel said. "Now it's *our* shower."

Diesel poured some of my shower gel into his hands and worked up a lather.

"This smells nice," Diesel said.

"It used to smell like lemon, but now it smells like cookies baking. How do you do that?"

"I don't do it. It just happens."

He ran his soapy hands over my shoulders and down my arms.

"Stop that," I said. "No fooling around!"

"I'm not fooling," Diesel said. "I'm deadly serious."

CHAPTER NINETEEN

I dragged myself out of bed at five A.M. My day had barely started and already I was late. I dressed in the dark so I wouldn't wake Diesel. Cat followed me down the stairs to the kitchen. I gave him fresh water and filled his bowl with kitty crunchies. I grabbed an apple and headed out. The street was quiet, but lights were blinking on in some of the houses. A car pulled into the parking lot for the shipyard at the bottom of my hill.

Clara was already at work when I got to the bakery. The big dough mixer was humming, and flour hung in the air like fairy dust.

"How'd it go yesterday?" Clara asked.

"First off, Josh and Devereaux broke into my house

and stole the map and the coin," I said. "We all raced to Penobscot Bay to see who could get there first and get the finder, which turned out to be the cursed Blue Diamond of Babur. We got the diamond but Devereaux blew our boat up with a rocket. Then Devereaux kidnapped me, and we went looking for the treasure. In the meantime, Rutherford kidnapped Glo, tracked us down, and followed us into the cave. Devereaux fell to his death, we found the treasure, which included the SALIGIA Stone, and Rutherford left Glo and me to die in the brig of a pirate ship. Diesel rescued us and here I am."

"So same old, same old," Clara said.

I buttoned myself into my white chef coat. "Pretty much."

"It's disappointing that Josh was working with Devereaux to steal the treasure," Clara said. "I guess you never know about people."

"It turned out that Devereaux was a really bad guy in disguise. Or maybe he changed when he took possession of the coin. At any rate, he was definitely insane at the time of death. I think Josh was just stupid. In the end Josh tried to help rescue Glo and me."

"Was Glo impressed with that?"

"She punched him in the nose the first chance she got. When we dropped them off here last night she still wasn't talking to him."

"Good for her," Clara said.

Glo arrived a little before nine. She parked Broom in a kitchen corner and set her Magic 8 Ball and tote bag on a workbench.

"I've been asking the Magic 8 Ball questions all morning," Glo said, "but it always has the same message. I think it might be waterlogged."

"What's the message?" Clara asked.

" 'Outlook not so good,' " Glo said.

Lucky thing I don't believe in the Magic 8 Ball or I might be depressed.

"Are you still seeing Josh?" Clara asked Glo.

Glo shook the 8 Ball and the message floated to the surface. "Outlook not so good."

Diesel sauntered in at eleven o'clock. He helped himself to a blueberry muffin and perched on a stool by my workstation.

"What's new?" Diesel asked.

"I need to finish glazing these cinnamon rolls, and then I'm done for the day."

Diesel grinned. "Do you want me to help?"

"No!"

"You'll never guess what I found this morning," Diesel said. "You left your wet clothes on the floor in the bathroom, and when I kicked them aside the Blue Diamond fell out of your jeans pocket."

"Omigosh. I stuffed it into my pocket and forgot about it."

"I'm sure Rutherford had a dark moment when he realized he'd left it behind. It's invaluable."

"I don't think Rutherford knew about the diamond," I said.

"Can you glaze those things faster? We have a lot of ground to cover today," Diesel said.

"Do you have a game plan?"

"I want to talk to Nergal. I have the skull with me."

"And after that?"

"No plan."

"So that doesn't seem to be a lot of ground."

"I'm working on it."

I finished my tray, cleaned my area, and asked Clara if she had anything else for me to do.

"Nope," she said. "It's a slow Monday. You might as well take off."

We stepped out of the bakery, and I looked around. "Where's your car?" I asked Diesel.

"It's the little black one," he said.

"That's a Porsche 911 Turbo. What happened to the last car?"

"It got swapped out. I parked it in front of your house last night, and this morning it was gone, and the Porsche was parked there."

"How do you know it's yours?"

"My cars always have similar license plates. 'DD0000.' Or some variation."

We drove the short distance to the hospital and found Nergal in his office.

"We brought you something," Diesel told him.

"I hope it's cupcakes."

"Sorry, no cupcakes," I said.

"It's something dead, isn't it?" Nergal said. "What is it with you people? You're like the death squad."

This from the man who decided to be a coroner.

Diesel pulled the skull out of his battered brown leather backpack and put it on Nergal's desk.

"I didn't have room to bring the rest of him home with me," Diesel said, "but this is probably all you need. We think he's Palgrave Bellows."

Nergal leaned forward and took a closer look at the skull. "The real Palgrave Bellows? That's pretty cool."

I nodded in agreement. "We found him in a cave."

Nergal put his hand on the skull, and his eyes got wide. "Whoa! This guy is nutty."

"What's he saying to you?"

"He's saying that it all makes sense. That it's all fallen into place. That he knew the power was within him. That he was destined to become the demon Mammon. And now he's going to eliminate all disbelievers and rule the world. That he's sure the crushing pain in his chest is Mammon being reborn in his body." Nergal removed his hand from the skull. "Personally, my money's on massive heart attack over the Mammon reborn theory."

"You get anything else from him?" Diesel asked.

"Nope. That's it. Can I keep the skull?"

"Sure," Diesel said. "Maybe someday I'll bring you the rest of him."

Neither of us said anything until we were out of the building and back in the Porsche.

"Bellows was holding the stone when he died," I said to Diesel. "It sounds to me like the stone makes you go nutty with the whole greed and Mammon thing. Devereaux had a similar reaction when he got the entire coin in his pocket."

"Where's the coin now?" Diesel asked me.

"So far as I know it's still with Devereaux. He had the coin on him when he fell. I suppose Rutherford or one of his men could have picked it up on their way out of the cave, but no one mentioned it when they were gathering up the treasure pieces, and I have a feeling it was forgotten."

"And the diary?"

"Ammon has the diary locked away somewhere. Probably in Marblehead."

"I see a road trip in my future."

"We're going back to the island?"

"Me. Not you. I can do this faster on my own. I want to get there before Ammon or Rutherford or whoever is running the show decides to send his minions back for the rest of the treasure."

"I don't think Rutherford runs anything. I think he's in damage-control mode, hanging on by his fingernails. I can tell you how to get to the tunnel. It might be easier than using the water entrance. Devereaux and I crept down a dangerous staircase carved out of the rock face. Rutherford and his men rappelled down. It was quicker and safer. Devereaux is at the bottom of the staircase. Another narrow tunnel connects the staircase to the cave and underground lake."

An hour later, Cat, Carl, and I watched Diesel drive off.

"Just the three of us today," I said to Cat and Carl. "What should we do? Clean the house?"

Cat pretended not to hear, and Carl climbed onto the couch and turned the television on.

I was halfway through vacuuming the living room rug when there was a lot of commotion on my front stoop and someone kicked my door down. It wasn't difficult to do, because the door was showing a couple hundred years of dry rot, and the lock was equally ancient.

Rutherford crept in around the mangled door. "Hello," he called. "Anybody home?"

"Yes, I'm home! What the heck do you think you're doing breaking my door down? That's a historic door. You'll be in big trouble with the Historical Commission."

"I knocked but no one answered."

"I was vacuuming. I didn't hear you."

"Yes, yes, I can see that. I'll have Mr. Ammon square

it with the historical commission. Mr. Ammon is a big contributor."

"I guess that would be okay," I said, inching my way toward the kitchen, where I had a big carving knife.

"I must say I'm relieved to see you somehow escaped from the cave. That was a mistake on my part. I should have been more clear with my directions to Mr. Carter. I meant for him to safely see you to the top of the canyon. When we realized the error we returned, but you were already gone. Very clever of you to take matters into your own hands. As you know, Mr. Ammon has plans for you. He just loves your cupcakes. And you'll play a very large role in our future."

"So you came to apologize?"

"Yes, yes, of course. But there is one other issue. It's the coin. We don't seem to have the coin."

"Devereaux had the coin."

"Mr. Carter assures me that the coin wasn't on Devereaux. Of course, Mr. Carter is no longer with us. He's been . . . um, reassigned. But we feel confident that the coin was removed."

"Not by me," I said. "I don't have the coin."

"I totally believe you. Totally. But I'm sure you realize how important this coin is to our lord Mammon. We must have all essential elements to complete the awakening ceremony. And the coin seems to be one of those elements."

"You realize this is all nuts, right?"

"Ha-ha, nuts. No, no, I assure you it's not nuts. Mr. Ammon has fully researched this. He's had a vision."

"And you believe Mr. Ammon?"

"Of course. Totally."

"And you believe in Mammon?"

"Ah, Mammon. Yes, he is . . . the prince."

"Well, I'm sorry but the prince is going to have to wake up without the coin because I don't have it."

Rutherford was smiling and sweating. "That would be lovely. We would all like for that to happen, but it might not be possible. So you are going to have to bring the coin to us. You're the only one who can recognize it. Mr. Ammon is very set on this. I know this is going to sound extreme, but you must keep in mind the importance of the ceremony. I'm afraid we will be forced to wreck havoc if you don't bring us the coin. I admit that *havoc* is a very strong word, but Mr. Ammon has been quite specific about this."

"Can you explain *havoc*?"

"My understanding is that it would involve torture and death. Possibly mutilation." Rutherford took a photo out of his suit jacket and handed it to me. "As you can see, this is a picture of the elderly gentleman related to your boss. I believe he's her grandfather."

It was a picture of Gramps waving at the camera. Two armed men in suits were standing behind him. Their faces had been blotted out.

"He's a character," Rutherford said. "You never know

what he'll say. Very entertaining. I would feel terrible if we had to cut his ear off."

"That's disgusting."

"It is. I absolutely agree. But we must do what we must do. Responsibility is a heavy burden." He clapped his hands together. "I guess that about sums it up. I should be leaving so you can get on with it."

"How do I reach you?"

"I've sent contact information to your cellphone."

I watched him leave and saw that there were several men in suits standing at attention by an SUV. Rutherford got in. His thugs followed.

I had a range of emotions wash over me. They were jumbled and hard to identify individually, but anger was clearly at the top of the list. I was angry that Rutherford would kidnap Gramps, and I was angry that I was involved. Diesel was wrong. I didn't like the adventure. I liked dull and boring. I wanted my life to be *pleasant*. I wanted Gramps's life to be *pleasant*. Hell, I wanted the *world* to be *pleasant*.

Sitting side by side with the anger was ice cold heart-grabbing fear, because I knew Rutherford and Ammon were dangerous and capable of just about anything. And I suspected that the stone was slowly turning them from merely dangerous into crazy psychopaths.

I took a look at my door and blew out a sigh. The jamb was splintered and there was a long crack running from the doorknob almost to the bottom of the door. I managed to get the door to stay closed, but I couldn't lock it. As if it mattered. One good kick and the door was toast.

"We need a plan," I said to Carl and Cat. "Hopefully Diesel will be back with the coin before they hurt Gramps. In the meantime I need to keep everyone else safe."

I called Clara, gave her the short version of what was happening, and asked her to check on Gramps just to make sure he'd truly been snatched. Glo had already left the bakery, so I tried her cellphone. No answer. I called Diesel. No answer there, either. I was tempted to get in touch with Wulf, but I had no idea where to begin. I didn't know his phone number or where he lived. And you know it was a scary day in hell when I was thinking about asking Wulf for help.

I finished vacuuming and was contemplating laundry when Glo called.

"The Pirate Museum is on fire," Glo said. "I'm half a block away. I can't get any closer. I hope Josh is okay. I'm still mad at him, but I hope he's out of the building. I tried his phone and he isn't answering."

"Rutherford and Ammon are on a rampage, and you could be in danger," I told Glo. "Go back to the bakery and stay with Clara until I get there."

I poured out a big bowl of kitty crunchies and set an extra water bowl on the floor for Cat.

"I'm going to leave the kitchen window open," I told

him. "Do *not* guard the house. If someone breaks in I want you to jump out the window and hide. I probably won't be back tonight. I'm going to stay with Clara and Glo."

I threw extra undies, my sweatshirt, and my toothbrush into my tote bag along with all the usual junk I always carry. I hung the bag on my shoulder, grabbed Carl, and went out the back door. I drove to the bakery and saw the black smoke from the Pirate Museum when I rolled into Salem. In my gut I knew Rutherford had started the fire, either to smoke Josh out or to send me another scary message. Most likely it was both of those things.

Lights were on in the bakery when I parked in the lot. Clara opened the door for Carl and me, and closed and locked it after we were safely inside. She had an assault rifle hanging from her shoulder and a semiautomatic handgun shoved into her jeans waistband.

"I didn't know you were a gun person," I said to Clara.

"The Dazzles have been locked and loaded since before the Revolution."

"Did you check on Gramps?"

"Yes. He's not at home, and he's not with his caregiver."

Glo was perched on a stool. "These people are sick," she said. "Gramps is such a sweetie. I hate to think he was kidnapped. Did you tell the police?"

Clara and I exchanged glances.

"Not yet," I said. "I was hoping Diesel would return with the coin, and we could make a trade. I'd rather not explain this whole bizarre mess to the police. I doubt they would even believe me. Martin Ammon has money and power, and I just have cupcakes."

"Yes, but they aren't ordinary cupcakes," Glo said. "Your cupcakes are *extraordinary.*"

"Yeah, I don't want to have to explain that to the police, either," I said.

Baking exceptional cupcakes, it turns out, is my other ability that is slightly beyond normal. So I wasn't kidding when I told Ammon that the ingredient I'd left out of the cupcakes recipe was magic.

There was a lot of loud banging on the front door to the bakery, and Glo went to investigate.

"It's Josh," she said, unlocking the door and letting him in.

Josh was soot smudged and sweaty. His puffy pirate shirt was untucked and streaked with black grime, his striped pants had a hole in the knee, and his hair was an unruly mess.

"They're freaking crazy!" Josh said. "They set a match to the Pirate Museum. I barely got out alive. Had to crawl out the basement window."

Broom smacked Josh in the head.

"Ow!" Josh said. "That hurt."

"It was Broom," Glo said.

"It was *you*," Josh said. "You're holding Broom."

"Were you the only one in the museum?" I asked him.

"Yes. The museum manager got a call to pick up a package, so I shut the doors for a spell. Too difficult to run the show alone. It's a slow time for us anyway. People are thinking about dinner and not pirates. It picks up again when the ghost tour starts."

"How did the fire start?"

Josh got whacked with the broom again.

"Okay, I get it," Josh said to Glo. "You're mad at me. I'm sorry. I was a jerk. I don't know what the heck I was thinking."

"About the fire," I said.

"We were all locked up, but someone was knocking and knocking and knocking, and, like an idiot, I went to the door. It was three guys in suits. They pushed me back into the museum, and one of them hit me on the head with his gun. When I came around there was fire everywhere. Lucky I was near the trapdoor that goes to the basement. It's just a crawl space down there with the rats and the spiders, but I got to the small half window that's on the back alley side and managed to squeeze out. The police were out front and the fire trucks were pulling up, but all I could think of was putting distance between me and the men in suits. I figured they were lurking somewhere close, waiting until someone discovered my charred remains."

"They kidnapped Clara's grandfather," Glo said.

"That's horrible," Josh said. "Is he okay?"

"We don't know," I said.

Rutherford called on my cellphone. "Good evening," he said. "Mr. Ammon would like to speak to you."

There were some scuffling sounds and Ammon came on the phone. "I trust you've heard the news by now that there was a fire at the Pirate Museum. I thought the symbolism was appropriate since we seem to have a theme of fire and brimstone. *Rrrruff, ruff.* Excuse me. Remnants of my concussion. I trust you're working hard to find the coin for me. We'll have a wonderful future together once you've found the coin. *Aaarooo.*"

More scuffling, and Rutherford took over. "Mr. Ammon has gone to get a cough drop," Rutherford said, "but it sounds like the conversation went well. I have to say I saw some of the fire at the museum, and it was spectacular. Did you get to see any of it?"

"No."

"Well, there will be other opportunities. Mr. Ammon has a list of activities prepared to demonstrate his commitment to completing Mammon's holy ceremony."

"More fires and kidnappings?"

"Very definitely. Mr. Ammon is still a bit under the weather from time to time, but he's a master at planning a campaign such as this. He would have made a wonderful general. A regular Napoleon."

There was some offstage growling and a muffled conversation.

"One last thing," Rutherford said, returning to the

phone. "Mr. Ammon would like to order a dozen cupcakes. Six chocolate and six red velvet with cream cheese icing. I'll send someone over to pick them up."

I disconnected, grabbed a cupcake container, and filled it with the dozen cupcakes. I wrote "Martin Ammon" on the container, and set it out front next to the door.

"Gather up some food and kill the lights," I said to Clara, Josh, and Glo. "We're going underground until Diesel returns."

Five minutes later we locked the bakery, took the stairs to the storeroom, and moved into the tunnel. I pulled the shelves back in place, so the tunnel entrance wasn't visible. Clara led the way with the big spotlight. Glo and I had smaller flashlights tucked into our tote bags. Carl skipped alongside me. Josh carried two large freezer bags filled with meat pies and muffins. We would be able to get water at the speakeasy.

"These tunnels go for miles and miles under Salem," Clara said. "The speakeasy is the most elaborate of the hidey-holes, but there are storerooms and bunk rooms all over the place. Houses and office buildings have changed hands and been renovated, and the current owners probably have no idea they're living over tunnel entrances."

We reached the speakeasy and settled in, allowing ourselves light from just one lightbulb in case Rutherford returned to Gramps's house.

"We'll know if someone is in the house," Clara said. "You can hear people walking overhead on the creaky floorboards. And if you climb the stairs and stand in front of the door, you might be able to get cell service."

We ate meat pies and played checkers. I tried to reach Diesel a couple times but had no success. At nine o'clock Clara wanted to check on the bakery, so we left Josh and Glo and Carl at the speakeasy, and Clara led me through the tunnels to a trapdoor. We unlatched the door and popped up in a dark, musty shed that was housing a lawnmower.

"This shed belongs to Myra Belkar," Clara said. "It's a total wreck, and Myra would love to demolish it and put up a garage. Unfortunately for Myra, the shed is deemed historic, so she can't change it, and she can't tear it down."

We crept out of the unlocked shed and looked around. There were no streetlights on the narrow street. The small houses crammed into small pieces of land were in dark shadow. Lights were on in the houses. None had shades drawn. We could see Myra in her kitchen, at the sink. The bakery was a block away. We walked to the corner and looked down the street. We didn't see any fire-blackened buildings. No fire trucks. No yellow crime scene tape. No lunatic Ammon employees hanging out. It all felt benign. I supposed Martin Ammon was happy with the cupcakes.

"At least they didn't attack the bakery," Clara said. "It

would be painful to see it destroyed. My first instinct is to stand my ground and protect it, but I know that's not smart. It's just a building after all. It can be rebuilt."

My phone chirped with a text message from Diesel. It was just one word . . . *success*. He had the coin. I messaged back that there were problems, and we'd gone underground. *Look before you shoot* was his answer. I assumed that meant he'd try to find us.

Clara and I retraced our steps and returned to the speakeasy. Josh and Carl were playing checkers in the dim light.

"Who's winning?" I asked.

"Carl is winning," Glo said. "If we don't let him win he pitches a tantrum and throws the checkers all around the room."

CHAPTER TWENTY

When you're underground, the only way to know if it's day or night is to check your watch. And I imagine if you were underground long enough even your watch wouldn't keep you from being disoriented. It was close to midnight when I fell asleep. I was on the floor, using my tote bag as a pillow. I awoke at five, drifted back into a restless sleep, and woke up again at seven.

Glo was up and pacing, Josh was playing solitaire, and Carl was sprawled on top of a poker table sound asleep.

"Where's Clara?" I asked Glo.

"In the tunnels. She said she needed exercise. Personally I think it's a creepy place to go for a walk."

"Not for Clara. She played in these tunnels when she

was a kid. And she's probably freaked out that the bakery is closed. The bakery is *never* closed."

Clara returned at seven-thirty, and moments later we heard someone walking overhead. We snapped the light off and froze. No one spoke. I looked at my cellphone. No bars. If it was Diesel upstairs, looking for the entrance to the speakeasy, he couldn't reach me. I tiptoed to the stairs and crept up to the door. A text message flashed on from Diesel. *Can't find entrance.*

I texted back *broom closet.* A moment later I heard the broom closet door open and mops and a bucket getting kicked around. I opened the secret door at the back of the closet, and Diesel handed me a cardboard box with four coffees from Starbucks.

"Morning," Diesel said. "You look like you got run over by a truck."

"I slept on the floor last night."

"There are these things in the house called beds," Diesel said.

"We were afraid Rutherford and his men would return. They kidnapped Gramps, tried to kill Josh, and burned down the Pirate Museum."

"I go away for a couple hours and the world falls apart," Diesel said.

Carl woke up at Diesel's voice. He stretched, scratched his ass, and ambled off to the rest room. Everyone else took a coffee.

"Did you have trouble finding the coin?" I asked Diesel.

"No. It was in Devereaux's pocket. I helicoptered to the island, but the pilot decided it was too dangerous to land at the top of the bowl, so he set me down by the tiki hut. I hiked to the bowl, found the tunnel entrance, and rappelled down the shaft. The ropes were still there from Rutherford's excursion. I found the coin and heard a chopper in the distance. Obviously its pilot had more guts than mine because it landed on the rim and dropped a bunch of Ammon's zombies into the bowl. I didn't feel like taking on the zombie army, so I hid in an alcove and waited for them to leave."

"They went back for the coin," I said.

"The coin and the rest of the treasure," Diesel said. "They packed it all out. Took them hours. They were like worker ants. They even took Devereaux. Maybe they thought he hid the coin on him . . . or in him. They took their ropes, too, so I had to use the stairs. They weren't bad going up, but I'm glad I didn't have to use them going down."

"We need to get Gramps," Clara said. "He needs his blood pressure medicine."

"Do you have any idea where they're holding him?" Diesel asked.

"No," I said. "They sent me a photo but there's nothing recognizable in it."

I showed Diesel the photo of Gramps waving. There were no background objects. Just a white wall and two faceless thugs.

"I have a list of all properties owned by Ammon Enterprises," Diesel said. "There are four in Salem, seven in Boston, one in southern New Hampshire, and Ammon's personal house in Marblehead. I got the list because I thought Ammon would be at least temporarily storing the treasure in one of his buildings, and the stone might be with it."

Clara put a bag of muffins on the bar, and we all took one.

"The best candidate for treasure storage is Ammon's property on Green Street," Diesel said. "He owns a four-story office building that used to be a bank, complete with a vault. The building is currently empty, slated for renovation."

"I know where that is," Clara said. "One of the tunnels runs under it, and then the tunnel continues on to the harbor. It meets up with another tunnel that goes to the lighthouse."

"How long would it take us to get from here to the bank building using the tunnel system?" Diesel asked Clara.

"Maybe forty-five minutes. The tunnels don't go in a straight line."

Diesel pulled a map of Salem out of his backpack. "I've marked Ammon's properties in orange," he said to Clara. "Are any of these other addresses accessible by tunnel?"

Clara looked at the map. "I'm not familiar with the whole tunnel system. I only know the area around the bakery, the waterfront, and the area around Gramps's house. A tunnel would run under the house on Marjorie Street, and the warehouse on First Avenue definitely has access."

Diesel took the Blue Diamond out of his pack and handed it to me. "It found the stone on the island. Maybe it can find the stone in Salem. And if we're lucky, Gramps will be with the stone."

We all left the speakeasy and followed Clara through the tunnels.

"We're like the seven dwarfs going off to work in the mine," Glo said. "Except there are only six of us."

I didn't feel up to dwarf level. The dwarfs knew where they were going every day. I was blindly walking behind Diesel. If I were a dwarf my name would be Clueless.

I checked the diamond from time to time, but nothing was registering. No blue glow. Not even a flicker. We walked for over a half hour, and Clara finally stopped and looked around. We were at yet another fork in the tunnel system.

"The left fork goes to the Wessel House," Clara said. "The house has been in the Wessel family for generations. Jerome Wessel was a ship's captain when the house was built. Bitsy Wessel ran a boardinghouse there during Prohibition and never lacked for boarders since there was a steady flow of rum punch coming out of the root cellar in the backyard. I dated Kenny Wessel when I was in high school, and we used to make out in the tunnel. The Wessel House is a block from Ammon's bank building. I'm pretty sure the tunnel runs under the bank building, but I don't think there's access. The men who built the tunnels didn't care about robbing a bank. That part of the tunnel dead-ends two blocks beyond the bank at the corner of Marjorie and Clinton. The right fork goes to the warehouse on First. The rumrunners brought their small boats into the shallow water or to the lighthouse. From those two points the hooch was transferred to the warehouse and beyond."

We went left, walking under the Wessel House and under the bank building. We continued on to the end of the tunnel. We didn't see any access points beyond the Wessel House, and the diamond never glowed or flickered or felt warm. We retraced our steps and took the right fork. We walked past the warehouse entrance and went all the way to the lighthouse. Again, no sign from the diamond.

"Okay, we go to plan B," Diesel said. "We're not picking up any vibes in the tunnels, so Lizzy and I will go aboveground. Everyone else will go back to the speakeasy."

"Check for text messages once in a while," I said to Clara. "I'll keep you in the loop."

Diesel and I exited through the root cellar in the Wessels' backyard. It was locked from the outside, but that wasn't a problem for Diesel. No one was out and about when we emerged. We walked toward the bank building and watched it from half a block away. It looked abandoned. Windows and doors were boarded over. No one stood guard at the door. We continued on to the warehouse on First. It had no doubt been impressive when it was built. Today it looked quaintly historic. A single loading dock in the back. Two stories. Lettering on the door said AMMON ENTERPRISES. No guys standing guard. No tingles. No glow from the rock.

"I don't think he's here," I said. "I don't think anyone is here."

"Ammon has a house in southern New Hampshire that's a fortress. It's a huge stone monstrosity set in the middle of a hundred acres. I have someone checking it out. In the meantime, I think we should negotiate for Gramps."

"Are you willing to give them the coin for Gramps?"

"Yeah. They have the stone. I don't see where the coin is going to make a difference. The stone, the coin, and all the tea in China isn't going to awaken Mammon. Rutherford, Ammon, and their followers are already delusional and greedy. A couple more degrees of greed won't make a big difference. Ultimately I need to get the stone and the coin back anyway."

"I have Rutherford's number programmed into my phone."

"Make a deal."

I called Rutherford and told him I had the coin.

"I want to swap the coin for Gramps," I said.

"I knew we could count on you. Mr. Ammon will be pleased. He'll insist that we prove the authenticity of the coin, of course."

"The coin is divided into eight pieces, and it has the chop

marks needed to read the map. Beyond that, I don't know how to prove its authenticity to you, since I'm the only one able to sense the power of the stone."

"As luck would have it we picked up a gentleman named Hatchet. He's a little odd, but we've been assured he's your equal. We found him wandering around naked on Brimstone Island, and he's now in service to Mammon."

"I think he's already in service to someone else."

"Finders keepers," Rutherford said. Very jovial.

Good luck with that one, I thought. I wouldn't want to tangle with Wulf.

"Where do you want to make the swap?" I asked Rutherford.

"We would like the transaction to take place at Mr. Ammon's country residence in southern New Hampshire. You can come at your convenience. And you must come alone."

"Okeydokey," I said. "See you soon."

I disconnected and looked over at Diesel. "He's in the New Hampshire house. They want me to come alone. And they have Hatchet."

Diesel's face creased into a wide grin. "They have Hatchet?"

"Rutherford said they picked him up naked on Brimstone and you know . . . 'finders keepers.'"

"It'll be more like 'finders weepers' when Wulf shows up. He's not good at sharing."

I texted Clara that we had a lead on Gramps, but that they should still stay underground until we returned.

"We need to use your car," Diesel said to me. "We can't fit Gramps in the Porsche."

"I'm supposed to go alone."

"I'll wait by the car. I'm not sending you off completely alone."

That sounded like an okay plan. I didn't want to go alone. And I wasn't sure my junker car could make it to New Hampshire and back. At least I'd have Diesel to push me to a service station or zap up a new car.

It wasn't a far walk to the bakery. Diesel let us in, and we packed a lunch for us and a bag of food for Clara, Glo, Josh, and Carl. I texted Clara that food was waiting for her in the tunnel. We locked up behind ourselves and chugged off in my car. We made a fast stop at my house, so I could take a shower and change my clothes. Men can be heroic when they're wrinkled and smell bad. Women work better with a little lip gloss and clean hair. I gave Cat fresh water and a new bowl of food. I grabbed my tote bag, and Diesel and I took off for New Hampshire.

The driveway wasn't well marked from the road. There was a rusted mailbox with the house number on it, and a single-lane gravel road leading into the woods. We followed the road for a half mile as it gradually wound its way uphill.

When we broke out of the woods into rolling pastureland we could see the house looming in front of us. It looked like a downscale, builder-grade version of an old Scottish castle with dark, water-stained stone walls and minimal landscaping. Halfway to the House of Doom there was a guardhouse, complete with a man wearing black fatigues and carrying an assault rifle.

"Lizzy Tucker to see Martin Ammon," I said to the guard.

The guard looked in at Diesel and then at me. "You were supposed to come alone."

"I'm almost alone," I said. "He's going to wait in the car."

The guard made a phone call and waved us through.

A second guy with an assault rifle met us when we approached the house. He directed us to a parking place and silently watched while I left the car and Diesel settled in to wait for my return.

The interior of the house was even gloomier than the outside. It was all gray stone, heavy columns, dark red over-stuffed furniture, and dark wood trims. The front door opened into a massive foyer with an ornate staircase. I had the diamond in a leather pouch in my sweatshirt pocket. I put my hand to it and felt it hum. The stone was here some-where.

Rutherford came to greet me. "Again, so sorry about that misunderstanding in the cave," he said. "We certainly didn't want to leave Mr. Ammon's favorite cupcake baker behind." Large smile.

I looked around the room. "Where is Mr. Ammon?"

"He's out and about somewhere on the grounds. This is the time of day when he likes to get a little exercise. It's important to Mr. Ammon that he stay fit."

"I bet Mammon likes that, too."

"Ha, yes. We all want a fit Mammon. Speaking of which, did you bring the coin?"

"Yes. Do you have Gramps?"

He nodded. "Yes. And he's been a delight."

"I'd like to see him."

"Of course."

There were several men in suits standing at parade rest around the room. Rutherford motioned to one of them, and a moment later Gramps was led in.

"This hotel is a disgrace," Gramps said to Rutherford. "I don't have a bathtub in my room and my eggs were cold this morning."

"Oh dear," Rutherford said. "Apologies. I'll speak to the household staff about it." He turned back to me. "Do you have the coin?"

I handed the coin over, and Hatchet stepped out of the shadows. He was wearing khakis, a white dress shirt, and a red tie with the Ammon logo.

I gave him a little wave. "Heard from Wulf lately?"

"Not lately," Hatchet said. "My new lord doth forbid other contact. I now live to serve Mammon."

Hatchet made a whirly sign alongside his head to

indicate *crazy*. I smiled and Hatchet nervously shifted from foot to foot. We both knew there would be hell to pay when Wulf found him. And we both knew Rutherford was no match for Wulf.

Hatchet came forward and touched the coin. "It doth vibrate," Hatchet said. "It is truly enchanted."

Rutherford told his man to release Gramps into my custody, and Hatchet stepped back into the shadows.

"So glad you were successful in finding the coin," Rutherford said to me. "Of course we'll be seeing you again, very soon I expect. Mr. Ammon has mentioned that he would like to invite you to participate in the final ceremony. It will be quite the occasion. Very festive."

Lucky me. I led Gramps out of the house to my car, where Diesel was waiting behind the wheel. I buckled Gramps into the backseat and jumped in beside Diesel, and he took off.

"That didn't take long," Diesel said.

"Rutherford got what he wanted. I got what I wanted. End of story."

"Not exactly," Diesel said. "I don't have what I want."

"The stone."

"Yes. We're going to hand Gramps over to Clara, and then we're going back for the stone."

"The diamond was humming, so I'm pretty sure the stone is there, but that place is a fortress guarded by a bunch of armed men in suits. It's not going to be easy to get in and get the stone out. Plus, I'm guessing the stone is with Ammon. I didn't see him, but Rutherford said he was on the grounds."

"Maybe he's walking the dog," Gramps said. "What kind of hotel lets a dog howl all night long? I couldn't get a wink of sleep."

I looked over at Diesel and caught him smiling. "It's not funny," I said. "The poor man still thinks he's a dog!"

"It could be worse," Diesel said. "He could think he's Mammon."

I texted Clara that we had Gramps. I told her we were going to bring him back to his house, but we wanted everyone to remain underground for a while longer.

CHAPTER TWENTY-ONE

"Look at this," Gramps said. "Everyone's here in my rumpus room. Is it my birthday?"

"I don't know how much longer I can stay down here," Glo said. "Broom is getting twitchy."

"Where's my cake?" Gramps asked. "And the ice cream? I want vanilla."

Josh gave him a muffin and sang "Happy Birthday" to him.

"That's lame," Gramps said, "but I appreciate the effort."

"We need to go back to get the stone," I said. "Hopefully this will all be over soon."

"Rumpus room living is getting old," Clara said. "And I don't see Gramps sleeping on the floor tonight."

"If we don't resolve this by the end of the day, we'll find a better place to stash you," Diesel said.

Minutes later we were in Diesel's Porsche, on our way back to New Hampshire.

"Exactly how are you going to pull this off?" I asked Diesel.

"No clue."

I was thinking I should have taken some of Gramps's medicine. My blood pressure was probably in the red zone. I know Diesel's a big, strong sort of smart guy with special abilities, but I didn't know what abilities we were going to need. For instance, I know it would be hard to kill Diesel but not impossible. I know he can open locks and give me an orgasm. I know with some assistance he can pop in and out of places like Captain Kirk on *Star Trek*. Beyond that, it's uncharted territory.

"I can't help but notice we're all alone without military assistance," I said to Diesel. "The men in suits had assault rifles."

"Yeah, but I have my charming personality."

Oh boy.

The sun was low in the sky when we got to Ammon's driveway. Diesel drove out of the dark woods and into the sunlit field and stopped. The guardhouse was empty, and in the distance, where the monstrous mansion once stood, was a huge pile of smoking rubble.

"Looks like Wulf's been here," Diesel said.

231

"Seriously?"

"Once when he was a kid he got so mad he self-combusted, and we had to throw water on him."

We moved closer and approached a small group of dazed women and men in gray and white uniforms.

"What happened?" Diesel asked.

"It exploded," one of the men said. "This vampire-looking guy showed up and asked for Hatchet. We said he wasn't here, that he helicoptered out with Rutherford and Ammon. I guess that was the wrong answer because the vampire guy got real still, and I swear there was some smoke curling out of his head, and the whole house started to shake. And he told us we had three minutes to get everyone out of the house."

"Did he have fangs?" I asked.

"No," the guy said. "But he was real white, and had long black hair, and he was dressed all in black."

"Did everyone get out of the house in time?" Diesel asked.

"Yes. I think so. The security people left when Rutherford and Ammon left. What you see here is the household staff, but I guess we're all out of a job since there's no house."

"Do you know where Ammon is now?"

"No. They just took off. They didn't say."

We made a U-turn and Diesel sped down the driveway. We were on paved road when the first of the police cars and fire trucks passed us, heading for Ammon's property.

"Wulf isn't making my job any easier," Diesel said. "It's bad enough *we're* underground. . . . I don't want to drive Ammon underground."

"Maybe it wasn't Wulf. I mean, it's hard to believe he could pitch a fit and blow up a house. I'm going with gas leak. I thought I smelled gas when I was in the house."

"Were you standing by Hatchet?"

There was mutiny in the rumpus room when we returned, so we sent everyone home. It seemed like Rutherford and Ammon had what they wanted anyway, and the danger level was insignificant. Broom whacked Josh one last time, but it was halfhearted, and Glo thought Broom might not be all that mad anymore. If it was me, I wouldn't be so forgiving. But then Glo dated guys with snakes tattooed on their foreheads, and I wouldn't do that, either.

Cat was waiting at the door when Diesel and I stepped into the house. I picked him up and held him close, and carried him into the kitchen.

"I'm glad you weren't in any danger," I said. "I was worried about you."

Cat probably thought this was stupid. He was self-sufficient. It was unclear how many lives he'd already had, but clearly this wasn't his first. Still, I wanted him to know I cared. Cat and I had become family.

"Eeep," Carl said.

I looked down at him. "Yep," I said. "You, too."

"How about me?" Diesel asked.

"What about you?"

"Am I included in this happy family?"

"Sure. What the heck."

He grabbed me and kissed me. "What's for dinner?"

"Something from the freezer."

"Is there dessert?"

"I can arrange it."

My phone rang, and I saw that it was Glo.

"Help," she said. "Oh crap. Low battery."

And the phone went dead.

"Glo's in trouble," I said to Diesel.

"Where is she?"

"Don't know."

"This doesn't look good for the dessert, does it?" Diesel said.

"We should go over to her apartment and see if she's okay."

Diesel took a box of cereal out of the cupboard and handed it to Carl.

"Knock yourself out," Diesel said. "Bananas Foster when we get back."

Carl grabbed the box and gave Diesel the finger.

I snagged a sweatshirt out of the coat closet and hung my tote bag on my shoulder. It had started to rain and the temperature was dropping.

"Search and rescue of senior citizens isn't in my job description," Diesel said.

"You only do what's in your job description?"

He opened the door to the Porsche for me. "Apparently not."

Diesel drove through Marblehead and crossed into Salem. He was a block from Glo's apartment when she darted into the road in front of the car. Diesel hit the brakes, and I was thrown against my shoulder harness.

"You gotta love the ceramic brakes," Diesel said. "I have a distant relative in New Jersey who drives a black Porsche Turbo, and I'm beginning to see why. I'm liking this car."

Glo yanked my door open. "Let me in. They're after me!"

I jumped out, and Glo climbed into the miniseat in the back, taking Broom and her bag with her. I got back in, and Diesel cruised down the block, past Glo's apartment. She lives in a large house that had been built for a single family in the '50s and converted into four apartments in the '70s. There was some paint peeling off the window frames, and the yard was minimally maintained, but it was in a relatively safe part of town, and it was in Glo's budget.

A black Cadillac Escalade was parked in front of the house. Headlights were on and windshield wipers were working. Windows were tinted. No way to know who was inside. Diesel made a U-turn and pulled to the curb a block away, so we could watch the Escalade.

"It was Rutherford," Glo said. "I saw him through my peephole, and I wouldn't let him in, so he broke down my door. Honestly, that is so rude."

"What did he want?" I asked.

"He said he feared somehow Mr. Ammon had been put under an evil spell, and he wanted me to lift it. I tried to explain that it wasn't so simple, but he wasn't listening. He kept saying how Mammon was angry. And time was short. That Mammon had awakened but wasn't able to achieve his full potential in his present form."

"His present form being that he thinks he's a poodle?" Diesel asked.

"More like a rabid honey badger," Glo said. "Rutherford had a big bite mark on his hand. When he saw me looking at the bite mark he said that Mammon had a hunger that needed feeding. And then he mumbled something about human sacrifice."

"Human sacrifice isn't good," I said. "That never ends well."

"How did you get away?" Diesel asked.

"Rutherford was explaining his predicament to me, and all of a sudden Martin Ammon burst into my apartment. He was totally nutso. Wild eyed and drooly. His shirt was all wrinkled and not tucked in and full of food stains, and his hair was a mess. There were two security men who came in with him, but they looked like they were afraid to get too close. Ammon was making growly sounds, and between the growly sounds he was saying 'Mammon wants. Mammon wants.' It was really creepy."

"And then what happened?"

"I'd just made myself a ham and cheese sandwich. It was sitting on my kitchen counter, and Ammon ate it. He sniffed the air, spied the sandwich, and dove for it. In two seconds there was nothing left of the sandwich. No crumbs. Nothing. He looked over at Rutherford and growled and snapped at him. And then he turned and ran out of my apartment."

"And?"

"Everyone ran after him. I could hear them trying to catch him in the hall, and I didn't waste any time getting out. I grabbed Broom and my tote bag and went out the window. I called Lizzy, but my phone went dead."

The front door to Glo's apartment building crashed open and Ammon ran out, chased by three men in suits. Rutherford ran behind them, doing his best to keep up. They ran down the street, cut into a yard, and disappeared in the misting rain.

"I've seen some weird stuff since I've had this job," Diesel said, "but this is right up there at the top of the list."

"On the bright side, we know Ammon is in Salem," I said. "And I think we can be pretty sure he has the stone on him."

Diesel pulled into traffic and headed for Marblehead. "It's even better. We have something Rutherford desperately wants. We have Glo."

CHAPTER TWENTY-TWO

By the time we got home the wind and rain had picked up and streetlights were on. Everyone huddled in my kitchen while I made grilled cheese sandwiches and opened a bottle of wine.

"This would be fun if only I wasn't terrified that I was going to be attacked by a grinning lunatic and a deranged dog," Glo said.

I gave Carl the first sandwich. He smiled a hideous monkey smile at me, took his food into the living room, and turned the television on.

"We need a plan," I said, buttering the frying pan and sliding another sandwich into it.

Diesel sipped his wine. "I *have* a plan."

I looked over at him.

"We have Glo, and Rutherford needs her to remove the spell," Diesel said. "So we lure him out with Glo."

"And what do we do when they come after Glo?" I asked. "Do we drop a big net over them and wrestle the stone away from Ammon?"

"The net could be a problem," Diesel said. "I don't know where to get a big net. I was thinking Taser."

"I've seen videos of people getting tased," I said. "It's awful."

"I like it," Glo said, taking the second grilled cheese. "I wouldn't mind seeing Rutherford tased, but I think you should use a tranquilizer dart on Ammon. We don't want animal rights people coming after us."

"I need to create a situation where the stone capture is controlled," Diesel said. "I don't want Ammon's henchmen in the mix. And I need to make sure that Rutherford and Ammon are neutralized."

"And you have a plan for all this?" I asked him.

"I want to have the spell undone at the lighthouse. The condition will be that only Glo, Lizzy, Rutherford, and Ammon will be present. Rutherford can watch the lighthouse beforehand and have his men stand down at a distance. I can access the lighthouse through the tunnel system, and I'll take Rutherford and Ammon down while they're distracted by Glo performing her spell removal."

I gave Diesel his sandwich. "That's a pretty good plan. Tell me about the neutralizing."

"That hasn't totally come together for me yet."

"It doesn't involve death, does it?"

"Not by my hand."

Carl came into the kitchen, handed me his empty plate, and looked up at me.

"He was promised bananas Foster," Diesel said.

I looked over at my fruit bowl. "Your monkey ate all my bananas."

"You ate all the bananas," Diesel said to Carl.

Carl gave him the finger.

"Someone needs to go to the store," I said to Diesel.

He glanced at the window. "It's raining."

"How bad do you want bananas Foster?"

"Can you make cookies?"

"Not unless you go to the store. I'm out of everything. I'll give you a list."

"I'd go," Glo said, "but I'm afraid I'll get snatched."

"Yeah, and I'd go, but I'm not motivated," I said.

Diesel drained his wine glass. "I'm motivated. Give me the list."

Ten minutes later we watched him jog to the sexy black car and disappear inside.

"Freaking awesome," Glo said.

"The car?"

"That, too."

We returned to the kitchen, I topped off Glo's wine, and washed the frying pan. I gave the pan to Glo to dry, and the back door crashed open and two men in suits rushed in. Glo and I jumped and yelped. Carl hid in a corner and put his hands over his eyes. Cat sat hunched and slitty-eyed, his tail twitching.

"What the heck?" I said. "Are you kidding me?"

One of the men looked over at Glo. "Excuse me, ma'am. Are you Glo?"

Glo nodded. "Uh-huh."

"We'd like you to come with us."

"I don't think so," Glo said.

He lunged at her, and Glo smacked him in the face with the frying pan. Blood spurted out of his nose, and he crumpled to the floor. I snatched the big butcher knife out of the rack and moved beside Glo. Cat rose to a crouch.

The remaining man went rigid.

"Jeez," he said. "Look what you did to Steve. He could be dead."

Glo toed the guy on the floor. "I don't think he's dead. I just flattened his nose a little."

Rutherford appeared in the doorway. "Knock, knock."

"She killed Steve," the man said to Rutherford.

"I did *not* kill Steve," Glo said. "I'm almost sure of it."

Rutherford looked down at Steve. "Steve's a great kidder.

I'm sure he's fine. We'll just trundle him out of here, so he's not underfoot." He turned to the man who was still standing just in front of the door. "Perhaps you could help Steve to the car."

"He's bleeding," the man said.

"Thank you. That's a good observation. You might want to put him in the trunk, so we don't ruin Mr. Ammon's upholstery."

Rutherford stepped aside, and Steve got dragged out of the house.

"Where's Martin Ammon?" I asked.

"He's sleeping," Rutherford said. "He's had an exhausting day."

"He ate my sandwich," Glo said. "And you ruined my door. You owe me a new door."

"Absolutely, we'll get you a new door. My apologies. It's just that the men get carried away, and before you know it . . . no door. Ha-ha."

"It turns out it's not that easy to undo a spell," Glo said to Rutherford. "Especially when you don't know all the details of the original. Not that I'm sure he has a spell cast on him. I'm just saying."

"I'm sure you can figure it out," Rutherford said.

"I'll help her," I said to Rutherford. "I know something about these things, but we'll need a little time to do some research and shopping. Most spells require specialty aids, like hummingbird wings and troll snot."

"Yes, and not just any old troll snot, either," Glo said. "Romanian troll snot is best. I tried to use French troll snot once and it didn't work at all."

"Understood," Rutherford said. "We wouldn't want to use inferior troll snot. Mr. Ammon always insists on the best."

"Four o'clock tomorrow at the lighthouse," I said.

"Ah-hah, the lighthouse. I was hoping for a more private location. Perhaps at Mr. Ammon's house in Marblehead."

"Nope," Glo said. "It has to be the lighthouse."

Rutherford looked like he was making a maximum effort to keep it together. "Right, the lighthouse. Perfect."

He gingerly stepped around the broken door and moments later I heard his car drive away.

"Great," I said, "now I have *two* broken doors."

Rain was blowing in, so I propped a kitchen stool against the door to hold it closed. Carl left his corner, scuttled across the room, and hopped up onto the stool. Glo mopped the blood off the floor.

"Maybe you should thumb through *Ripple's* and see if you can find a general all-purpose undoing spell," I said to Glo. "Just in case things don't go as planned, it might be good if we could get the dog thing out of Martin Ammon's head."

Glo took the Magic 8 Ball and *Ripple's Book of Spells* out of her tote bag and placed them on the counter. She had the 8 Ball in a plastic baggie because it was oozing liquid. "Outlook not so good" floated to the surface.

"The 8 Ball's seen better days," I said.

Glo bit into her lower lip. "It's so sad. I tried sealing it with nail polish, but it's still leaking."

Diesel rapped on the back door, and I moved Carl and the stool to let him in.

"What happened here?" he asked, setting the grocery bags on the counter.

"Rutherford happened," I told him. "He came with two of his men. They were after Glo, but one of the men walked into a frying pan Glo happened to be holding."

"Nice," Diesel said. "And they went away?"

"Temporarily. We set up a meeting at the lighthouse for tomorrow at four o'clock. In the meantime I thought it would be good for Glo to find a way to get rid of the dog spell. Just in case."

"Can't hurt," Diesel said.

I put the groceries away and started the bananas Foster.

"Here's one," Glo said, reading from *Ripple's*. "'Good to reverse all spells unless those spells are deemed irreversible.'"

"How do you know if a spell is irreversible?"

"I think they're the ones with a skull and crossbones next to them," Glo said. "I try to avoid them."

I splashed some rum into the saucepan with the bananas and lit it all on fire. Cat arched his back and hissed, and Carl clapped his hands.

"I don't have all the ingredients for this spell," Glo said. "I need spider legs and dried primate gonad."

We all glanced over at Carl.

"What size gonad are we looking for?" Diesel asked. "Gorilla gonad or monkey gonad?"

"It's nonspecific. It just calls for a teaspoon of powdered primate gonad."

"Eeep!" Carl said.

"I imagine it takes days to dry out a gonad," Glo said.

"Yeah, and I don't think you'd get a teaspoon out of what Carl's showing us," Diesel said.

Carl gave him the finger and mooned him. Easy to do since Carl didn't wear pants.

I portioned out the bananas Foster, and Glo scooped vanilla ice cream.

Diesel and Carl took Glo home, and Cat and I cleaned the kitchen. Glo had mopped up the blood, but I went over the floor again with disinfectant. This was more for my own mental health than for cleanliness.

"This was fun," I said to Cat. "Not necessarily the part about smashing Steve's nose, but the rest of it. I like cooking for my friends. It's especially fun when it's last-minute like this."

We moved to the living room, and I was surfing for a

television show when Diesel and Carl walked in and shook the rain off.

"I thought you were going home," I said to Diesel.

He sat next to me and slouched back. "You thought wrong. I took Glo home and did a temporary fix on her door. I don't think she's in danger until four o'clock tomorrow."

"Me, either."

"Honey, you're holding your back door closed with a barstool. Any knuckle dragger can walk in."

Carl cut his eyes to Diesel and gave him the finger.

"Nothing personal," Diesel said. "It's an expression."

"Can you fix my door?"

"I can fix it tomorrow. Tonight I'm going to keep you safe by staying close."

"Oh boy."

"It's going to be way better than *oh boy*."

"Wowee kazowee?"

"Yeah, more like wowee kazowee."

Carl took the television remote from me and changed the channel to National Geographic.

"What will we do if Ammon doesn't have the stone on him?" I asked Diesel.

"We'll go to plan B."

"Would you like to share plan B with me?"

"No."

"There isn't a plan B, is there?"

"Not at the moment."

"Have you talked to Wulf lately?"

"No."

"Do you know where he lives?"

"No."

"Do you know how to get in touch with him?"

"You ask a lot of questions."

"The answers aren't reassuring."

"You need to lower your expectations."

CHAPTER TWENTY-THREE

The bakery was back in business Wednesday morning. Clara and I had been working since five, Glo and Broom were behind the counter at nine, and customers came and went in a steady trickle, as usual. On the outside it all looked normal. On the inside we were struggling to stay calm.

"I spent the night combing through *Ripple's*," Glo said. "I was hoping to find an undoing spell that was less complicated. I don't know if I'm going to be able to get all the ingredients for the spell I have. What if I can't change Ammon back?"

"Rutherford will get Martin the best kennel money can buy," I said.

"It's two o'clock," Clara said to Glo. "I'll take over the counter. You and Lizzy should go to the Exotica Shoppe to get your ingredients, and then you can go directly to the lighthouse. I'm closing the bakery at three o'clock so I can lead Diesel through the tunnels."

I drove the short distance to Ye Olde Exotica Shoppe and parked on the street. Nina Wortley is the store's owner-manager. She's in her early sixties, has long frizzed snow-white hair, and her face looks like it's been dusted with cake flour. Today Nina was wearing Birkenstock clogs and a yellow Belle gown from her Disney collection.

Every nook and cranny of Exotica was crammed with the strange and wonderful. Wolfsbane, bats' wings, gummy bears, snail entrails, warthog hoof, powdered bridge troll penis, Snickers bars, Pringles, vulture claw, pickled brown cow tongue, rotted beetle brain, kosher salt. There was a special section for vegan witches who needed tofu substitutes for animal parts. And there was also a rack with Harry Potter wizard wands for the tourists.

"I have a list," Glo told Nina.

"You must be working on a special spell if you have a list," Nina said.

Glo gave her the list. "It's an undoing spell."

"Undoing spells are tricky. Let's see what you need." Nina snagged a basket and began to fill it. "Gonads, lizard beak, dingleberries." She moved to a different part of the shop and searched a cluttered shelf. "Extract of dragon tail, my last bottle. I must remember to reorder." She unscrewed the lid on a big jar filled with eyeballs. "One blue eyeball."

"Where do the blue eyeballs come from?" I asked Nina.

"China, of course. They do all the eyeball manufacturing."

"Do they clone them?" I asked.

Nina put the eyeball in a plastic baggie and dropped it into the basket. "Heavens no. Eyeballs are just for effect. They're plastic."

"It's for my goldfish," Glo said. "They float."

Nina carried the basket to the register. "I had everything but the toad tongue. I substituted chopped newt. It should work just fine."

"I just have to put all this together now," Glo said.

"I can do that for you," Nina said. "I can mix it together in the back room."

"That would be great," Glo said, handing Nina *Ripple's Book of Spells.* "I'm not good at the mixing part."

Nina returned in five minutes and handed Glo a screw-cap jar. "The recipient only needs to drink about a teaspoon of this. The rest should be poured in a circle around him. When he steps out of the circle the spell should be complete."

Glo settled her account, and we left the store.

"It's hard to believe some of these things are real," I said. "Where does she get extract of dragon tail?"

"I asked her that one time and she said Slovakia."

It had stopped raining but the sky was overcast and the

air was unseasonably cool. I was wearing a sweatshirt over my jeans and T-shirt. Glo was wearing a bright pink fluffy rabbit fur jacket, her usual motorcycle boots, black tights, and a short black tunic. We jumped in my car, buckled ourselves in, and headed for the lighthouse.

"You're driving super slow," Glo said. "The car behind us isn't happy."

"How do you know he's not happy?"

"He's honking his horn."

I blew out a sigh. "I didn't notice. I'm distracted. I don't want to get to the lighthouse. I'd like to get onto the highway and not stop until I reach California."

"I'm game for California. I'm not crazy about this gig, either. What if my undo spell doesn't work and Martin Ammon tears me to shreds?"

"That would be a bummer."

"No kidding."

I'd been driving at a snail's pace, but I still managed to reach Derby Street.

"I suppose I should park," I said.

"Yeah," Glo said, gathering her things together. "Showtime."

We left the car and walked the length of the pier to the lighthouse. Two men in suits stood midway. I nodded to them, and they nodded back.

"Freaking creepy," Glo said.

Hardly anyone ever visited the lighthouse. It didn't

look historic or interesting, and there were no signs to indicate that it was open to the public, so the public never showed up.

I pushed the door open and flipped the light on. Nobody home. We were ten minutes early. A text message from Diesel came in on my phone. *Conduct the ceremony on the second floor by the beacon. I'm in place.*

The lighthouse floor was cement, as were the walls. Hidden behind the spiral staircase was a door. I opened the door and saw circuit breakers and electrical feeds crammed into a small closet. The floor was wood planking. Trapdoor, I thought.

We climbed the spiral stairs. Glo set Broom aside by the door leading to the balcony and then got busy setting up her workstation. She turned *Ripple's* to the appropriate page and placed the jar next to the book of spells.

"It seems bare," Glo said. "I should have brought a candle or some flowers."

"It's fine," I said. "It's not like it's a dinner party."

I left Glo in the beacon room, and I went downstairs to wait for Rutherford and Ammon. They arrived precisely on time, both dressed in black with red ties. I supposed this was the standard Mammon wardrobe. Ammon's eyes were glazed, and he looked totally tranquilized.

"Is he okay?" I asked Rutherford. "He's a little zoned out."

"Mr. Ammon? Zoned out? No, no, he's just relaxing," Rutherford said.

"Glo needs to do this upstairs where there's less interference from the earthly stuff that, um, interferes."

Rutherford looked at the spiral staircase, gauging if he could get Ammon to climb it.

"It would be more convenient to perform the ceremony down here," Rutherford said.

"Glo can't guarantee it will work if Mr. Ammon's feet are on terra firma."

We led Ammon to the staircase and eased him up step-by-step. I had no clue what Rutherford had given Ammon, but I was thinking I wouldn't mind having some. My palms were sweating, and my heart was skipping beats. I was terrified that Ammon would wake up and go into mad-dog mode or worse. What if he actually became Mammon? Crap on a cracker!

I positioned Rutherford and Ammon in front of the table with their backs to the beacon and the stairs.

"Okay," I said to Glo. "Do your thing."

"Undo, undo what's been done," Glo read from the book. "All spells be cast aside, all demons be banished . . ."

"Oh, um, excuse me," Rutherford said. "That won't work. We don't want *all* demons banished. Ha-ha. No, no. This man holds the sleeping Prince of Avarice. The sacred demon Mammon is poised to emerge and assume his kingdom."

"Silly me," Glo said. "What was I thinking? Let me start over. Undo, undo what's been done. All spells be cast aside, all demons with the exception of the Prince of Avarice our good friend Mammon be banished." Glo looked at Rutherford and he nodded his approval. "Lickety lickety down it goes, round and round, step aside, spell be gone."

Ammon was panting and drooling.

"Now what?" Rutherford said. "Is that it?"

"We have to get him to drink a teaspoon of the potion. And then we have to pour it in a circle around him. And then when he steps out of the circle the spell should be broken."

"Should be?" Rutherford said.

"Hey," Glo said. "This isn't a cake recipe. This is hocus-pocus."

I thought I heard the trapdoor open and close downstairs. No one else seemed to notice.

Glo poured out a teaspoon and offered it to Ammon. He sniffed it and growled.

"Maybe he needs just a tad more tranq," Glo said to Rutherford.

"I left the dart gun in the car," Rutherford said. "Just get on with it."

"Have you got any rawhide treats with you? Any bacon bits?"

"Is it essential that he drink it?" Rutherford asked.

"Yes! This isn't cough syrup I've got here. This is spider

legs and monkey gonads. It's not like you can get this at Rite Aid. It's a critical part of the ceremony."

"Try again."

Glo held the spoon out to Ammon, and Ammon knocked it out of her hand. He sniffed at her jacket and growled.

"Bad dog," Glo said to Ammon. "Sit!"

Ammon lunged at Glo and sunk his teeth into the hem of her jacket. Glo grabbed *Ripple's* and smacked Ammon on the top of his head with the book. Ammon growled and tugged at the jacket.

"It's rabbit," I said to Glo. "Take it off and give it to him before he mauls you."

Glo shrugged out of the jacket, and Ammon ran to the other side of the room with it. Diesel appeared in the middle of the confusion and grabbed Ammon by the scruff of his neck. Ammon yelped and dropped the jacket.

"Search him," Diesel said to me.

Two red spots appeared on Rutherford's cheeks. "Foul! Foul! This wasn't allowed. This is terrible. I can't allow this. Oh my goodness."

I ran my hands over Ammon. "The stone isn't on him," I said.

"We feared the stone would interfere with today's treatment, so we stored it someplace safe," Rutherford said.

"So then you don't mind if we search you, too?" Diesel said.

"This is outrageous. I'm appalled. Truly appalled. You people have no honor. We had an agreement."

"Actually we had no agreement," I said, running my hands over Rutherford. "We never discussed this."

"It was understood."

"He's clean," I said.

"You will never get the stone," Rutherford said. "Never. Mammon is guarding the stone."

"I thought Mammon was trapped inside Martin Ammon," I said.

"Yes, technically I suppose that's true," Rutherford said. "Still, you won't be able to steal it away from him. We've taken precautions."

Glo had another spoonful of potion ready for Ammon. "Nice doggy," she said.

Ammon wriggled away from Diesel and for a moment looked like he was going to lick the spoon, but he leaned forward and licked Glo instead. He *woofed*, grabbed the jacket off the floor, and bolted for the balcony that surrounded the beacon room. He tripped over Broom when he went through the door, stumbled, and flipped over the wrought iron railing.

Everyone gasped and froze for a beat before rushing out and looking down at Ammon. He was laying spread eagle on his back.

"Holy bejeezus," Glo said. "Do you think he's okay?"

Ammon's eyes fluttered open. *"Aaarooo,"* he said.

The two men that had been standing guard halfway down the jetty were running toward Ammon.

"Bacon," Ammon said. "What? Who?"

Rutherford rushed into the beacon room, snatched the jar of potion off the table, hurtled down the stairs, and ran out of the building. We looked over the railing and saw Rutherford pouring the contents of the jar into Ammon's mouth.

"Whoa," Glo said. "That's a lot of gonad he's giving him. He's going to get diarrhea."

People were gawking from the restaurant at the water's edge and from the ship museum. An EMT truck pulled onto the wharf with lights flashing. A cop hustled down the wharf toward Ammon.

"Time to go," Diesel said.

We ran down the stairs, crammed ourselves into the electrical closet, and squeezed through the trapdoor.

Clara was waiting for us in the tunnel. "How'd it go?" she asked.

"It was mixed," I said. "Ammon did a flip off the lighthouse balcony."

"Is he okay?"

"Okay is relative," I said. "He's not dead. And it looked like he might be coming out of the dog thing."

"I saw him move his foot," Glo said. "And he sort of had

a spasm when Rutherford was pouring the potion into him."

I wasn't sure how I felt about all this. Ammon wasn't a good person, but I didn't wish him dead or paralyzed or thinking he was a dog for the rest of his life. I mostly just wished he would go back to being a self-absorbed billionaire and leave me alone.

"Even if Ammon is perfectly okay, this is going to occupy everyone's attention for a couple hours," Diesel said. "We should use the opportunity to look for the stone. They have it someplace safe. The first safe place that comes to mind is Ammon's bank vault."

"I'll take you to the Wessel House exit," Clara said. "Then I'm going back to the bakery."

"I'll go to the bakery, too," Glo said. "My bike is there, and Broom could use a cupcake."

CHAPTER TWENTY-FOUR

We left the tunnel system at the Wessel House and walked to the bank building. Two men in suits were lounging at the building's front door. No assault rifles in sight. They didn't look especially worried about an attack. In fact, they didn't look worried about anything . . . maybe because they were both sucking in weed. I guess Mammon took a lenient view on recreational drug use. We were standing downwind, and I was getting a contact high.

Diesel took the Blue Diamond out of its pouch and dropped it into my hand. "Anything?"

"No."

"Won't hurt to check anyway," Diesel said.

We moved to the side of the building where a paved driveway led to a rear metal fire door.

"Can you open it?" I asked Diesel.

"Yeah, and I'm guessing they're not bothering to set the alarm. The building isn't in use, and there's a construction dumpster here. The guys out front are just window dressing. If Ammon is using the safe he probably feels it's secure enough."

He slid his hand over the door, and I heard the lock click. He pushed the door open, and I held my breath and waited. All was silent. No alarm. I stepped in and looked at the control panel beside the door. No blinking lights. The alarm had been deactivated.

The back door opened into an empty storage room. No windows. Dark interior. Another door stood open at the far end, and there was some dim light beyond it. We crossed the room and looked out into what used to be the bank lobby. Light was coming from a skylight and from two small windows in the front of the building. The lobby had been gutted. The floor tiles were chipped and covered with dust. There was an elaborately scrolled wrought iron gate on the back wall. We went to the gate and looked inside at a small foyer leading to a massive vault door with a lock that looked like it was straight off a movie lot.

"Well?" I said to Diesel.

Diesel opened the gate and walked up to the vault. He

put his hand on the lock, fingers first, then the flat of his hand.

"I'm guessing this is the original lock installed when the building was completed," Diesel said. "That's good because I can't do a lot with a computer chip beyond scramble it."

He moved his hand a little and listened. He did this three times, spun the dial, and the door creaked open.

Diesel grinned. "Am I good, or what?"

It was a large walk-in vault. Plastic tubs with snap-on lids were stacked against the wall. The tubs were clear and I could see that they were filled with gold and silver coins. Some tubs were bigger than others, and the big ones looked like they held an assortment of jewels, hammered gold goblets, and fancy perfume and spice bottles. The treasure from the *Gunsway*. Very impressive, but not what caught my attention. Hatchet had my attention. He was sitting on a folding chair in the middle of the room. He was dressed up like an insurance salesman in a cheap suit, and he was holding a samurai-type sword. He had a mask attached to an oxygen tank on the floor beside him.

"Hey," Diesel said.

Hatchet gave a curt nod.

"So this is a new look for you," I said.

"I feel the fool," Hatchet said. "'Tis a sorry day when I must wear such cloth as this. Hatchet is of another age, and this is foreign garb for Hatchet."

"Are you supposed to be guarding the treasure?" I asked him.

He slumped in his seat. "I will guard *nothing* without tights and tunic." He blew out a sigh. "Truth is, I have not been asked to guard the treasure. I am locked away here as *part* of the treasure."

"You have a sword."

"I found it in a bin."

"We need the stone," I said to Hatchet.

"It is not here. I would have captured it for my true liege lord if given the chance."

"Do you know where it is?"

"Nay, I do not. It was on Ammon for a while, but the dog part of him grew too vicious under the stone's influence. Rutherford sometimes transports it in a thick leather pouch. I believe it is currently locked away in a safe, but I don't know where."

I looked at the plastic bins stacked against the wall. "So this is what one hundred and ninety million dollars' worth of treasure looks like."

"Actually it is a lot less," Hatchet said. "As in many tales of adventure, the facts have changed with the telling. When evaluated and tallied it was determined this amounted to a mere twenty-five million."

"Hardly worth worrying about," Diesel said. "No wonder Ammon left it unguarded in this vault."

"It's not unguarded," Hatchet said. "The silly security men come to check on it from time to time."

"How long have you been locked in here?" I asked him.

"Since midafternoon. 'Tis getting tiresome." He looked over at the vault door, which was slightly ajar. "Am I to stay?" Hatchet asked.

"Your choice," Diesel said.

Hatchet jumped off the chair and rushed to the door. For a moment I was afraid he would lock us inside, but he scurried away.

"Sometimes he really creeps me out," Diesel said. "He's like a big, pudgy rodent."

"This stone search is dragging," I said. "I vote we let Rutherford and Ammon have it. Not to mention, we don't even get to keep it. You gave it away to Wulf. So let *him* get the stupid stone from Rutherford and Ammon if he wants it so bad."

"I like your thinking, and I'd like nothing better than to get zapped off to an island and a palm tree."

"But?"

"But it's not gonna happen. The stone is dangerous in the wrong hands. And it's my job to put it out of circulation."

"Are you telling me you have a work ethic?"

"No. I'm telling you my boss is almost as crazy as Rutherford, and I wouldn't want to piss him off."

"What would happen?"

"I'd have to fly commercial, for starters."

"Gee, that's awful."

"You want to try it with a monkey?" Diesel was back on his heels, staring at the treasure bins. "We should take this."

"The treasure?"

"Yeah. All twenty-five million of it."

"That would be stealing," I said.

"This stuff has been stolen so many times over the centuries I don't think it matters anymore."

"What would we do with it?"

"I guess we could eventually donate it to a museum, but in the short term it might turn out to be useful. We might be able to bargain with it. Or maybe we just use it to make the bad guys mad. Throw them off their game while we search for the stone."

I didn't want to steal the treasure. I wanted to get out of the vault. I wanted to go home or back to the bakery. I wanted to be someplace that felt safe and happy.

"Just thinking about stealing the treasure makes me nauseous," I said.

"You're probably just hungry. I'll buy you an ice cream cone when we're done."

I glanced at my watch. If we were going to do this we needed to get it done quickly.

"The bins look heavy," I said. "How are we going to get them out of here?"

"The same way they got them in here. Hand truck. There's one in the corner. It's still got three bins stacked up on it."

"Then what? We can't truck them all the way to the Wessel House."

"Call Clara and tell her to bring the van."

Twenty minutes later we had all the bins, plus the hand truck, loaded into the van. Diesel locked the vault and the back door to the bank, and we took off.

"Where am I going?" Clara asked.

"We need to stash this somewhere," Diesel said.

Clara stopped at an intersection. "We could put it in the speakeasy. There's a second entrance in Gramps's garage. No one would see us unloading."

Diesel shoved the last bin into place against the bar. "It should be okay to leave these here short-term. I have other, more pressing problems."

"Such as?" I asked him.

"Food. I'm starving. I need a burger. One of those fancy little meat pies isn't going to do it."

"I'll drive you back to the bakery and you can get your car," Clara said.

We filed out of the speakeasy into the short sloping tunnel that led to the one-car garage. Clara was parked behind the Rascal scooter.

"How does Gramps get his Rascal to the aquarium?" I asked Clara.

"Benita has a van with a hydraulic lift. And I hate to say this, but sometimes Gramps sets off on his own."

"It doesn't look like he's home. There aren't any lights on, and I didn't hear anyone walking overhead."

"He has a heavy social calendar," Clara said. "He's probably at the senior center cheating at cards."

Ten minutes later Diesel parked his Porsche in a lot off Lafayette Street, and we walked the short distance to a pub.

"They better have ice cream here," I said. "You promised me ice cream."

"They have ice cream everywhere."

We slid into a corner booth and ordered burgers, fries, onion rings, and beer.

Diesel waited for the waitress to leave before looking over at me. "Call Nergal and see what the deal is with Ammon. I'm sure he's tapped in to hospital gossip."

"Why can't you make the call?"

"Nergal thinks you're cute," Diesel said. "He's more likely to do something unpleasant for you."

This was obnoxious but probably true.

"Hey," I said when Nergal picked up.

"Let me guess," Nergal said. "You want to know about Martin Ammon."

"Yes! How did you know that?"

"*Everyone* wants to know. My *mother* called me."

"Is he dead?"

"No. He's in a private room with some idiot in a suit standing guard at his door."

"Does he think he's a dog?"

"A what?"

"Dog. Like, is he barking or anything?"

"I haven't heard anything about barking. The information I got is that they're keeping him here overnight for observation. He has a concussion."

"Nothing unusual?"

"There's a rumor going around that he was covered in pink rabbit fur when he was brought in, but that's about it."

I thanked Nergal and relayed the information to Diesel.

"So the stone isn't on Ammon, and it's not with Rutherford, and it's not in the vault," Diesel said. "My second-best guess would be the Marblehead house."

"I see where this is going, and I'm not searching the Marblehead house until I've had my ice cream."

"You can take your time with the ice cream," Diesel said. "I think it will be just about impossible to search the Marblehead house without the distraction of a party and a fire. We're going to have to find a way to make the stone come to us."

"That shouldn't be difficult. Ammon will get out of the

hospital and retrieve the stone. All we have to do is snatch Ammon and rip the stone out of his demon hands."

"Yeah. Why didn't I think of that?"

"Or we could snatch Rutherford," I said. "He probably helped hide the stone."

"Even better."

The waitress brought our food, and we stopped talking and concentrated on eating.

"Anything else?" she asked when we were done.

"Ice cream," I said.

"We have vanilla, chocolate, strawberry, coffee, tutti-frutti, butter pecan, and chocolate chip."

"Yes," I said. "That's what I want."

"Which one?"

"All of them."

Twenty minutes later Diesel was slouched in the booth, smiling at me. "You ate all that ice cream," he said. "Impressive."

"Yeah, but I'm feeling sick."

"My original plan was to have you lure Rutherford away from the hospital tonight, so you could sweet-talk the information out of him. I'm thinking that just went out the window."

Upchucking tutti-frutti seemed like an okay trade-off to sweet-talking Rutherford. He wasn't as evil as Ammon, but he creeped me out. All that smiling and good cheer and the *ha-ha* laughing made me want to kick him in the knee. Not to mention, I was pretty sure I lacked the sweet-talking gene.

"I need to go home and lie down or throw up or something," I said.

CHAPTER TWENTY-FIVE

I t was five in the morning, I was at the bakery, and so far my day was looking good. I had woken up to a house that felt relatively normal. Just Cat and me in the velvety darkness. Diesel had patched my doors the night before, so they would at least stay closed. He promised to get me new ones today. My kitchen felt welcoming when I switched the light on. No sign of Mammon. No Rutherford. No Wulf.

Clara bustled in and went to her workbench. "Four dozen cupcakes for Mr. Dooley today," she said.

"Four dozen cupcakes coming up."

She looked over at me. "Have you heard any more about Ammon?"

"So far as I know he's in the hospital with a concussion."

"You seem very chipper today."

"I know. I woke up feeling terrific, and everything has been perfect this morning. Perfect coffee. Perfect toasted bagel. Every light was green on the way to work." I gave up a huge sigh of contentment. "It's going to be a good day."

Glo showed up a couple hours later. She was all in black, including lipstick and nail polish.

"You look like goth girl," I said to her.

"I'm in mourning. The 8 Ball died."

"Gee, that's awful," I said. "Sorry."

"Yeah, condolences," Clara said.

"I sort of expected it," Glo said. "He'd been leaking for a while. And to tell you the truth, I'm not so sure he was magical. Still, it's sad. I paid two bucks for that 8 Ball. You'd think for that kind of money he would have lasted longer."

Glo took a tray of almond croissants out to the shop and unlocked the front door. Jennie Bell came in for a blueberry muffin, and Mrs. Kuzak bought a loaf of rye. I moved on to cookie dough, and I heard Nergal's voice at the counter.

"Hey," Glo yelled back to me. "Guess who's here?"

Nergal smiled and gave me a finger wave when I came to the counter.

"I felt like a cupcake this morning," he said.

"Red velvet?" I asked him.

"Yes. I'll take two. And a lemon chiffon."

"Wow, you must be having a good day."

"A suicide, an accidental overdose, a gang-related

shooting, and Quentin Devereaux was found on the side of a road. And it's only nine in the morning."

I gave Nergal his three cupcakes in a little box and pulled him aside. "Tell me about Devereaux."

"He was gutted, but all of his organs had been shoved back in. And that wasn't the way he died. It happened some time after death."

"His last thoughts?"

"'Be sure to drink your Ovaltine.'" Nergal gave me his credit card. "Sometimes last thoughts don't make a lot of sense."

I gave the card back to him. "No charge for the cupcakes," I said. "I owed them to you."

"Thanks. It was nice seeing you again. Let me know if you ever want to see an autopsy or go out to dinner or something."

I returned to my cookie making and was about to slide the first tray into the oven when Rutherford knocked politely on the side door, and let himself in.

"It's gone," he said. "Poof! Gone!"

He was pacing back and forth, wringing his hands. Everything was perfectly ironed and in place. His hair was slicked down. His pants had a razor-sharp crease. His tie was expertly tied. His expression was sheer panic.

"I went to check on our guest, Mr. Hatchet, last night. I had to make sure he had enough oxygen, and he wasn't there. *Nothing* was there! The door was locked. The vault was locked, but nothing was there. How could that happen? I went back this morning to see if anything had changed, but it hasn't. It's all gone."

"And?" I asked.

Rutherford stopped pacing. "It had to be magic. There's no other explanation. Mr. Ammon and I were the only ones who knew the combination. Mr. Ammon is in the hospital. He's hooked up to tubes and things. He never left. And I'm pretty sure it wasn't me who opened the vault. I guess I could have had a moment, but I don't think that's it."

"You think it's magic?"

"Yes. So of course I thought of you and your friend. She could have put a spell on the vault."

"Did the vault growl at you?"

"No."

"Then it wasn't Glo."

"I see your point," Rutherford said. "Then it must have been Mr. Hatchet. He clearly has a strong magical component." More pacing. "This is very bad. Mr. Ammon is in the hospital. The Prince of Avarice is waiting at the threshold. And I've failed them. This happened on my watch. They're going to be very disappointed in me."

Glo had come into the kitchen. "What happens when they're disappointed?" she asked.

"I don't know," Rutherford said. "I've never disappointed them at this level. This is big. I think something catastrophic might happen. Biblical even."

"Wow," Glo said. "Biblical is huge!"

Rutherford nodded. "I would prefer to avoid it."

"I can ask Hatchet," I said. "I might be able to talk him into making a deal."

Rutherford looked like he might explode with happiness. "Really? What kind of deal?" He leaned forward and whispered at me. "I would be willing to do anything. *Anything.*"

"That covers a lot of ground," Clara said.

"Would you have something to trade for the treasure?" I asked Rutherford.

"I have a car. It's a Ford. Very reliable."

"Hatchet might not care about a car. Hatchet lives to serve his master, Wulf. He would want something that would make Wulf happy. It would have to be something unique. Something Wulf might desire."

"Gosh, I don't know," Rutherford said. "I've never had the pleasure of meeting Wulf."

"What about the stone?" I said to Rutherford. "It's not nearly as valuable as the treasure, but Wulf might like it."

"The Avaritia Stone? The Stone of Avarice? The stone that will set Mammon free?"

"You don't really believe all that, do you?" I asked him.

"I don't know. Mr. Ammon believes it."

"Yes, but so far it hasn't done squat for him. I mean, let's face it, it's just a stone."

"Maybe."

"Do you know where the stone is hidden?"

"Not exactly. We put it in a safe place, but it isn't there anymore. I think Mr. Ammon re-hid it."

"Do you know where he re-hid it?"

"I have my suspicions."

"Which are?"

Rutherford smiled his big, wide Rutherford smile. "Lately, since Mr. Ammon is . . . sometimes doglike, he likes to dig in the flower beds at Cupiditas."

My first reaction was to burst out laughing, but I checked it and simply nodded at Rutherford. "If you could find the stone I think I might be able to get the treasure back into the vault before Ammon realizes it was stolen."

"Oh wow," Rutherford said. "That would be amazing. That would make Mr. Ammon very happy."

"And the Prince of Avarice," Glo said. "He'd be happy, too."

"Yes, yes," Rutherford said. "It would be excellent. The Prince of Avarice is very big on treasure."

I gave Rutherford a chocolate cupcake and ushered him out the door. "Let me know when you find the stone, and I'll get in touch with Hatchet."

"Thank you so much," Rutherford said. "Thank you. Thank you."

"Pretty slick," Clara said when I closed the door on Rutherford.

"It's not a given that he can find the stone," I said.

Clara went back to bagging the fresh bread. "He'll have every member of Ammon's household staff out there digging up the garden."

Diesel strolled in at noon.

"I got word on Ammon," he said. "He's still in the hospital. They were going to release him, but they found him drinking out of the toilet bowl and decided the concussion was more serious than they'd originally thought. So he's there for another day."

I told him about Rutherford, and Diesel grinned.

"Good work," Diesel said.

"We'll see," I told him. "There's no guarantee that Ammon buried the stone."

"True, but it'll give Rutherford something to do." Diesel helped himself to a cookie. "I have a small job to do for the Exalted One, but I'll be back for dinner."

"Who's the Exalted One?"

"My boss."

"Does he have a name?"

"Sidney."

"Last name?"

"I don't know his last name."

He gave me a kiss on the top of my head and walked out of the shop.

"I see what you mean about this being a good day," Clara said when Diesel left. "If he kissed me I'd think it was a good day, too."

I finished up a batch of cookies, cleaned my workstation, and headed for home. I stopped at the store and got steak and baking potatoes for dinner. I rolled into my house a little after three.

Rutherford knocked on my back door ten minutes later. "So sorry to bother you," he said. "I thought you would want to know that we're planning to bring Mr. Ammon home late tomorrow morning. He seems much improved."

"Not drinking out of the toilet bowl anymore?"

"Ha-ha. No, no. None of that, I'm happy to report." He looked over my shoulder at the food on the counter. "Steak and baked potatoes. Excellent choice for a meal. I see you're expecting a guest."

"Diesel."

"Of course. I imagine he more or less lives here."

"More or less."

Rutherford clasped his hands together and went serious. "About the treasure. Have you located it? Is a trade actually possible?"

"Yes and yes."

He looked around. "I don't suppose you have it here?"

"No. I'm just a go-between."

"Of course again."

"Have you found the stone?" I asked him.

"Ah, that's the thing. It seems that without your special ability, all stones look alike. We have, in fact, found many stones that are the appropriate size. Unfortunately, I don't know if any of them are the stone. I was wondering if you would come out to the car to examine the rock collection."

"You brought them with you?"

"It seemed like the least I could do since you're helping me get the treasure back. I wouldn't want to inconvenience you any more than is necessary."

A black Cadillac Escalade was parked at the curb. The back gate was open and two suited henchmen stood on either side of the SUV. I peeked inside at three boxes of rocks.

"That's a lot of rocks," I said to Rutherford.

"There are a lot of flower beds."

I put my hand to the rocks one by one. None of them were empowered.

"Sorry," I said.

"I don't suppose you would want to give me the treasure anyway?" Rutherford said.

"I don't have it. Someone else has it."

"Someone who wants a stone."

"Yes."

"Couldn't you give them one of these?"

"I don't think that would work out."

Rutherford packed up and left, and I returned to my house, where Cat was waiting.

"No luck," I said to Cat. "They were all just plain old rocks."

Cat looked at me with his one eye, thought about it for a beat, and gave his foot a lick.

"Well, I had to look," I said to Cat. "You never know. The stone could have been there."

Cat looked like he didn't think so.

I stashed the food in the fridge, and Nergal called on my cellphone.

"I have something to show you," he said. "I went to the bakery, but you'd already left."

"What is it?"

"You have to see it in person. I'd bring it over to you, but I don't know where you live."

I gave him my address, and twenty minutes later he was at my door.

"Are you done with work for the day?" I asked him.

"I'm on call. My job is like that. Anyway, I went to that specialty grocery store that just opened on Fifth Street. They have an amazing deli. The egg salad has lots of mayo, and the tuna salad is full of celery."

"I know the store you're talking about. They make their own terrine out of olives and baloney. It's awesome."

"Yeah, so I'm in there, and I'm walking around and what do I see? Lizzy's Cookies! I'm sure you know all about this, but I was excited. These are my favorite cookies. Mint chocolate chip." He handed me a bag. "And now I can buy them at the grocery store!"

I pulled a packet of cookies out of the bag. They had the

Ammon Enterprises logo on them. In small black letters under the large black and gold logo it said LIZZY'S COOKIES. I opened the packet and tried one.

"This is great," I said. "These are my cookies all right."

Except I didn't feel great. I felt deflated. Like someone had let all the air out of my balloon. I'd given away my cookie recipe to a man who was trying to turn into a demon. I read the ingredients label. Red dye number seventeen and something I couldn't pronounce. If I stabbed myself in the eye with the butcher knife it would be less painful.

"There were a bunch of other Lizzy's Cookies there, too, but I only bought these," Nergal said. "They were pricey, and coroners don't make all that much money."

I led him into the kitchen, cracked open a bottle of red wine, and poured out two glasses. I heard the front door open and close, Carl raced in, and Diesel followed.

"Theodore brought me cookies," I told Diesel.

"They're Lizzy's Cookies," Nergal said. "I found them in the grocery store."

Diesel took a cookie from the bag and ate it. "Yep, they're Lizzy's Cookies all right." He looked over at me. "No wonder you're drinking."

"We're celebrating," I said.

Diesel grinned. "I bet."

Nergal's phone buzzed with a text message.

"Jeez," he said. "They're dropping like flies today. I have to go."

I added a couple of my chocolate peanut butter chip cookies to his bag and handed it back to him. "Thanks for stopping by to show this to me," I said. "We'll have to get together sometime when you're not on call."

"Yeah, that would be great," Nergal said. "I bet you have all sorts of fun stories about your adventures to save the world and everything."

I closed the door after him and drained my wine glass. "He's going to get another text tonight," I said to Diesel, "because I'm going to kill Ammon."

"Ammon didn't waste any time getting these cookies into production."

"They have artificial ingredients! He added coloring and preservatives."

"No one will notice. The writing on the bag was very small. It's the American way."

"It's *not* the American way. The American way is to have quality and purity."

Diesel refilled my wine glass. "I like your thinking," he said. "What's for dinner?"

"Steak and potatoes."

"I *really* like your thinking."

I went to the kitchen, turned the oven on, and put the potatoes in.

"Would you still like me if I couldn't cook?"

"Yeah, you're cute. Cooking is the icing on the cupcake."

"Okay, suppose I wasn't cute. Suppose I was fat and ugly. Would you like me then?"

"Let me get this straight. You can't cook and you're fat and ugly?"

"Yeah."

"Are you mean?"

"No. I'm nice."

I put an onion on the chopping block and started to slice it.

"What about special talents?" he asked. "Are you good in bed? Can you give a deep-tissue massage?"

"Good grief."

"I'm just trying to get a grip on this," Diesel said. "Suppose the situation was reversed, and I was fat and ugly. Would you still like me?"

"Half the time I don't even like you *now*."

"I get that, but what about the other half?"

"I don't know. What are *your* skills? Can you give a deep-tissue massage?"

"Honey, I'm going so deep on you tonight I might not be able to find my way out."

I almost sliced my finger off.

"Looks like you nicked yourself," Diesel said. "Want me to kiss it and make it better?"

"No! I want you to go into the living room and watch television with Carl. I'll call you when dinner is ready."

CHAPTER TWENTY-SIX

The dinner dishes were in the dishwasher, the kitchen was clean, and we were watching a ball game drag on between the Red Sox and the Mets. Diesel stood and stretched. When he stretched he raised his arms and his T-shirt rode up giving me a glimpse of tanned, perfectly defined abs. I'd seen them before, plus a lot more, but it didn't matter . . . it was always good.

"Do you need anything from the kitchen?" he asked.

"Nope, I'm okay," I said.

Diesel ambled off and Rutherford called me.

"I found it! I found the stone. I know it's the stone because it's in the leather pouch. It was buried under an azalea bush. How soon can we get the treasure moved back to the vault?"

"I'll need at least a couple hours to gather it together. I'll call you when we can arrange the transfer."

"Remember, we need to do this before Mr. Ammon is released from the hospital."

"No problem. I'll get back to you later tonight."

Diesel returned to the living room with a couple cookies. "What's up?"

"Rutherford found the stone. He wants to make the trade tonight so everything is in place when Ammon leaves the hospital tomorrow morning."

"Call Clara and ask her to bring the van to Gramps's garage."

Clara was waiting for us when we pulled up to the garage. The van was parked inside.

"We have a problem," Clara said. "Follow me."

We entered the tunnel through the garage and walked the short distance to the speakeasy. The door was open and Gramps was inside, sitting in one of the comfy club chairs.

"Howdy," Gramps said. "Welcome to my rumpus room."

We looked around and immediately saw the problem. The treasure was gone. Only one plastic bin was left.

"What happened to all the bins?" I asked.

"Got rid of them," Gramps said. "They were taking up

too much space. Kept the one that had the pretty green jar in it."

"Where'd the bins go?" I asked him.

"I gave them to the Pirate Museum. They had a fire and lost a lot of stuff. Terrible. The pirate ship burned up and everything. The junk in the bins looked like pirate loot, so I handed it over. Pirates are my second favorite thing. When I gave all that junk over to the museum people they said they were going to name a room after me. Can you imagine that? I'm going to be famous."

Diesel was back on his heels, smiling. "Easy come, easy go," he said.

"What are we going to do about Rutherford?" I asked him.

"We'll give Gramps the pretty green jar and give the rest of the bin to Rutherford," Diesel said. "If he doesn't want to hand over the stone we'll jump him and take it."

"Suppose he has a bunch of armed men with him?"

"We'll wait until he's alone, and then we'll jump him."

"Okay," I said. "I like it."

I called Rutherford and told him to meet us at the front entrance to the bank building Ammon owned.

"Excellent," Rutherford said. "This is a wonderful plan. A lifesaver. Ha-ha. Literally. Ha-ha."

I disconnected and turned to Diesel. "He's losing it. He did two of those awful *ha-ha* laughs. Two. There was definitely hysteria involved."

"With good reason."

We loaded the single bin into Clara's van and drove to the bank building.

"Keep the motor running, and if I give you the sign you take off," Diesel said to Clara. "Lizzy has to verify that we've actually got the Avaritia Stone before we hand over what's left of the treasure."

We sat there at idle for ten minutes before a black Escalade drove up, and Rutherford got out followed by two men in suits. The street was dark, lit by pools of light from streetlights. Rutherford stood at the building's front door, and the two men stayed by the car. Diesel and I got out of the van and crossed the street.

Rutherford took in a huge, deep breath and exhaled. "Well, this is such a relief. Oh my goodness, you can't imagine what this means to me. This is large. Massive!" He leaned forward and lowered his voice. "This will be our little secret. No need to let the men know the full extent of the transaction."

"Understood," I said. "Do you have it?"

He turned his back on the men and carefully extracted the leather pouch from his suit jacket.

"We need to be discreet about this," he said, handing the pouch over to me.

I opened the pouch and looked inside. It was hard to tell on the dark street, but the stone was the right size and I could see some silver glinting off it. I touched it with my fingertip and felt nothing.

"Uh-oh," I said.

I dropped the stone out of the pouch, into my hand. Nothing.

"It's not the stone," I said.

Rutherford looked stricken. "What do you mean? Of course it's the stone. I found it in the garden. It was in the leather pouch."

"Sorry," I said. "It's a dud."

"Ha-ha, you're pranking me, right? You're kidding. That's marvelous. I love it."

"No, I'm really sorry. This isn't the stone."

I put the stone back into the pouch and handed it over to Rutherford.

"Oh dear," he said. "Oh dear. Oh dear."

He stumbled back and sat down hard on the cement step leading to the bank's front door.

I looked down at him. "Are you okay?"

"I'm a dead man," he said. "I lost the treasure. I lost the weird little guy with the red hair, and I can't find the stone. I'm done. Dead. Maybe worse than dead."

"You have a couple hours," I said. "You could keep digging."

"We've dug up everything. There's nothing left to dig. The yard looks like it's been bombed." He looked up at me.

"You have to give me the treasure. Please. Please, please with sugar on it."

"The truth is, there's not much left," I said. "We could only recover one bin."

"Truly?"

"Yes."

"Ha-ha, ha-ha, ha. Only one bin. Ha-ha, ha. You mean it's all gone?"

I nodded.

"Gone! Where did it go? Wait, I don't care. Doesn't matter, does it? It's gone."

"Okay, you should calm yourself," I said. "It's not that bad. Things happen."

"No, no. You don't understand. This is Mammon we're talking about. The God of Greed. He doesn't like when he loses treasure."

"It's not Mammon," I said. "It's Martin Ammon. What's the worst that can happen?"

"I don't know. Ha-ha. Anal probes? Ha-ha."

"Maybe he still has the tranq gun in the car," Diesel said. "We could plant one on him."

"We're going to leave now," I said to Rutherford. "If you find the stone you can call anytime."

"Yes, yes. I'll do that. Of course. Yes, yes."

Diesel and I walked calmly across the road, got into the van, and told Clara what happened.

"Drive off as if everything is perfectly normal," I said to

Clara. "We don't want to alarm the men with the guns. And we especially don't want the crazy man who's pacing back and forth in front of the building to go completely gonzo."

"Too late," Diesel said. "That ship has sailed."

"Now what?" Clara asked, winding her way around Salem.

"I guess we take the treasure back to Gramps," Diesel said. "He's the expert at treasure redistribution."

It was hard to drag myself out of bed in the morning. It had been a late night. Diesel was warm next to me. Cat was curled at the foot of the bed. Carl was in the laundry basket. I oozed out from under the quilt, trying not to disturb anyone, and shuffled into the bathroom. I stood in the shower until the room was steamy and I was pretty much awake. When I finally tiptoed out of the bathroom Carl and Diesel were still asleep. Cat was at the door, waiting for me.

Cat and I went downstairs and I fixed Cat's breakfast. "My life is a big mess," I said to Cat. "I set drapes on fire and lose treasures and hook up with the wrong men. And I'm not just talking about romantic hookups. I'm talking about cookbook hookups, too."

Cat didn't seem especially concerned. Cat was happy to have his half can of cat food.

I was a half hour late getting to the bakery, and Clara had already started the yeast dough.

"I'm not up to saving the world after eight o'clock at night," Clara said. "Just take the keys next time you need the van."

"I'm hoping there won't be a next time. It seems to me we're at a dead end with the Avaritia Stone."

"Ammon must know where it is."

"I'm not sure what Ammon knows. I'm told dogs don't have good short-term memory."

At eleven o'clock I was finishing the frosting on a batch of cupcakes, and Glo stuck her head in the kitchen.

"He's here!" Glo said.

"Who?"

"Martin Ammon! He wants to see you."

I made my way to the counter and tried my best to smile. "Hey," I said. "How's it going?"

"I had a concussion. Nothing serious, but they wanted me to stay in the hospital for observation. I'm sure you heard."

I nodded. "Yup."

"I'm on my way home, but I wanted to stop by and personally invite you to the house to discuss the cookbook. We've gotten behind schedule."

"You still want to publish my cookbook?"

"Of course. It's a large part of the campaign. We have decisions to make. We need cover art and an author photo. I was thinking three o'clock. Does that work for you?"

More head nodding. "Three is good."

We all watched him leave. He walked out on two legs and climbed into the backseat of a black Mercedes sedan. He didn't bark or lift his leg on the tire. It looked like Rutherford was at the wheel.

"You aren't going to his house, are you?" Clara asked. "It could be a trap."

"Yeah," Glo said. "Mammon could be waiting for you."

"He didn't look like Mammon," I said.

"He didn't look like a dog, either," Glo said. "But I wouldn't wear a rabbit jacket around him."

"He caught me off guard," I said. "I'll send him a text and tell him something came up."

CHAPTER TWENTY-SEVEN

At one o'clock I tossed my chef coat in the laundry bin, hung my tote bag on my shoulder, and waved good-bye to Clara.

"See you tomorrow," I said.

"Hope so," Clara said.

I walked to my car and realized Rutherford was hovering a short distance away.

"A moment?" he said.

"Sure. I guess Ammon understood about the missing treasure."

"Oh, of course, well, actually he doesn't know. Just not enough hours in the day to get to everything. Lots of time to tell him about the treasure. Lots of time. The more pressing issue is to schedule a meeting between the two of you. Mr. Ammon received your text and was very disappointed. Perhaps you would be able to attend a meeting later today. Four o'clock or five o'clock, perhaps?"

"No."

"Ha-ha. No? Ha-ha. That's a good one. Just *no.*" He smoothed out his tie. "The thing is, Mr. Ammon has tasked me with ensuring your presence at Cupiditas sometime today."

"It's not going to happen."

Rutherford pressed his lips together. He removed his pocket handkerchief and waved it, and four men in suits appeared out of nowhere. One of them tagged me with a stun gun, there was a loud buzzing in my head, and my legs collapsed. I was scooped up and tossed into the back of an Escalade.

By the time my nerve endings stopped tingling and my muscles started working again, I was at Martin Ammon's doorstep.

"Oh my, that was something, wasn't it?" Rutherford said, smiling wide, like this had been the fun experience of a lifetime. "I've never seen that before. Very impressive display of weaponry."

"You're an idiot."

"Yes, yes. Ha-ha. I've heard that before." He motioned to the men. "Help Miss Tucker into Mr. Ammon's office. He would like to have a moment with her before the ceremony."

"Ceremony?"

Rutherford pressed his hands together. Hard to tell what it signified since he was always grinning. Glee? Terror? Nervous excitement?

"Yes!" he said. "Finally. This is the day we've all been waiting for. This is to be the rebirth of Mammon. Very exciting. Very wonderful. Yes, indeed. Big day. Big, big."

"You've found the Avaritia Stone."

"Mr. Ammon knew exactly where he'd left it. It was in his sock drawer! *Imagine!* It just brings a smile to my face."

I went slack-jawed. Didn't he know his face was in a perpetual grin? The man looked like the Joker. He had to have cheek muscles that could crack a walnut.

I was marched into Ammon's office and placed in front of his desk like a seven-year-old standing in front of the principal. The security force and Rutherford retreated to the far wall and stood at parade rest.

"Miss Tucker," Ammon said. "I'm glad you could find time for this meeting. It's really very important to me. I like to keep everything neat and tidy. Now that I'm recovered from my concussion, I thought we should have this meeting prior to the ceremony. I want your mind to be at ease. As you know, I have your signed contract, which gives me total control over everything you've ever owned or created. In fact, I've already begun to produce products under your brand. So you can rest easy when you're gone that your legacy will live on."

"You put coloring and preservatives into my cookies!"

"It makes the product much more cost-effective. When I put your picture on the label with all your wholesome blondness the consumer will never think to check the label. It's genius, isn't it?"

"It's awful!"

"Now that you understand all this, we can move on to the real reason you're here. The holy ceremony to release our lord Mammon requires that all elements be in place at the time of the ceremony. We need the human who carries Mammon and will assume his very soul. That would be me. We need the Avaritia Stone. I have it here on my desk. And as you can see, I also have the coin and the Blue Diamond. At the last moment we realized we'd completely forgotten about the diamond. Fortunately we were able to locate it in your kitchen."

"We didn't want to disturb you while you were at work," Rutherford said. "I was sure you wouldn't mind if we looked around your house. We were very careful not to disturb anything. Although I'm afraid we did slightly destroy your door, but we'll reimburse you for the repairs. And goodness, your cat is quite ferocious. Ha-ha. He's quite the attack cat."

"You better not have hurt him," I said.

"Oh no. No, no. Goodness, he's a delightful creature. I gave him a bite of muffin before we left. I hope that was all right."

"And last but not least," Ammon said, "we need to sacrifice a high priestess with special abilities. That will be you."

Oh boy.

"I'm not a high priestess," I said. "I'm a baker."

"You're too modest. Your abilities are apparent."

"You won't get away with this. You'll be arrested and sent to jail."

"I'll be Mammon. I'll own the world. I'll be untouchable."

"Yeah, but what if you don't turn into Mammon? You'll just be some nutcase who killed someone." I looked over at Rutherford. "You, too."

Rutherford wiped his hands on his slacks. "Ha-ha! Good one. Very funny. That's why we're so fond of you."

"Take her away and prepare her," Ammon said.

Prepare me? What did that mean?

I had a man on either side of me, plus Rutherford.

"We have a lovely chapel in the basement," Rutherford said, guiding me out of Ammon's office. "We'll hold the ceremony there. It's nice and quiet. Very private."

"So no one will hear me screaming?"

"Oh goodness, you won't be screaming. It's a very moving ceremony. You'll be honored. You're a lucky young woman. Very lucky."

"I'm surprised you're still here," I said to Rutherford. "It will be even worse for you if he actually turns into Mammon. Imagine how angry he'll be to learn he's lost that treasure."

"Oh no, no. I'm sure he'll understand. And I've taken measures to get the treasure back. It's only a matter of time."

We went down a flight of stairs to a short hallway that led to a small vestibule. The floor was marble. There were candles lit in wall niches. Double doors led into a medium-sized room with stained-glass windows. There was an altar and several rows of pews. To one side of the double doors was another single door. Rutherford opened it to a large powder room. A white gown had been draped over an elaborate gilt chair.

"We're ready to begin," Rutherford said. "This lovely white gown has been prepared for you."

"You're kidding."

"No, no. We're quite serious. Mr. Ammon has spared no expense to make this ceremony perfect. And once you're sacrificed to Mammon you'll be a queen in his kingdom. It will be fabulous. Just fabulous."

"I'm not putting the dress on."

"Oh dear, Mr. Ammon will be disappointed. And there's no telling what Mammon might think. Honestly, I don't think you want to make Mammon angry. He is, after all, one of the seven princes of hell."

So here's the honest-to-gosh truth. I'm terrified, and all I can think to do is stall. Time is my friend, right? If I'm down here in this loony bin long enough, surely Diesel will find me.

"Okay, I'll put the dress on, but I need privacy."

"Of course," Rutherford said. "Come out when you're ready."

After five minutes Rutherford knocked on the door. "How's it going?"

"I'm almost ready."

Five minutes more and there was another knock on the door. "Do you need help?"

"No!"

"Everyone is in place."

"Mammon's waited this long. He can wait a little longer."

"Ha-ha, that's why we love you. Wonderful sense of humor. Seriously, I'm going to have to send some men in to get you."

I blew out a sigh and dropped the white gown over my head. It looked like a choir robe with a plunging neckline. I stepped out of the powder room and stood in front of Rutherford.

"You have your clothes on under the gown," he said. "You were supposed to take your clothes off."

"I don't want to take my clothes off."

"Of course. I understand completely. Maybe no one will notice."

We walked into the chapel and I noticed Hatchet was there. He was naked, hanging upside down from a hook in the ceiling.

"Greetings, wench," Hatchet said. "I fear you doth have thrown me under the bus."

"Sorry," I said. "I wasn't thinking. It was one of those spur-of-the-moment things."

"You can take your place of honor, here by the altar," Rutherford said to me.

I was trying to stay calm. I needed to be vigilant. If an opportunity arose for escape I had to be ready.

"How is this going to happen?" I asked Rutherford.

"I believe Mr. Ammon has settled on strangulation. It's much less messy than a bullet or a knife. This is our first human sacrifice, so we're learning as we go."

"How long are you going to have Hatchet hanging there?"

"Until he tells us where he hid the treasure."

"He didn't hide the treasure. I lied to you. Diesel and I took the bins out of the vault and gave the treasure away."

"Very admirable. Noble, even, that you should want to help Mr. Hatchet. I would expect no less from you. A charming gesture."

"Thou be a pig's behind," Hatchet said to Rutherford.

"Ha-ha. Yes, yes. Good one," Rutherford said.

Martin Ammon entered and pretended not to notice Hatchet. "Her hands aren't tied," Ammon said to Rutherford. "Honestly, what have you been doing all this time? Mammon is impatient."

"Well, ah, ha-ha, I was never instructed to tie her hands," Rutherford said.

"Standard protocol is to tie the victim's hands," Ammon said.

"My mistake," Rutherford said. "I'll have them tied immediately." He looked over at the four men standing guard at the door. "Charles, would you be so kind as to secure Miss Tucker for us."

Charles stepped forward, took a flexible plastic handcuff from his back pocket, and tied my hands behind my back. Rutherford smiled and looked expectantly at Ammon.

"Much better," Ammon said, "but she should be kneeling."

Rutherford rushed to my side and helped me kneel.

"We can now begin," Ammon said, very solemnly. "Rutherford, clear the room."

Rutherford nodded to the four men standing to one side, and they silently left the room and closed the door.

"Do you have the Book of Mammon?" Ammon asked Rutherford.

"Indeed," Rutherford said, all smiles. "Yes, yes. It's right here on the altar, turned to the appropriate page."

"And the Avaritia Stone?"

"Also on the altar in its special container."

Ammon stepped forward and removed the stone from an engraved silver container, and I could see it was glowing a brilliant green.

"Ahhhh," Ammon said. "I feel the power. Who am I, Rutherford?"

Rutherford clasped his hands together. "You're a fallen angel. Yes, yes. You're the Lord God of Pandemonium. One of the seven princes of hell."

"Suddenly it all makes sense," Ammon said. "I always knew, of course. I always knew that I mattered more than others. That what I wanted was more important. That my desires were to be honored above those of others. That I was on a higher plane. I never said it aloud before this, because, well, you know, I might have come off as a sociopath. I would have been misunderstood. But now I understand. I've always felt more important than others because I *am* more important. I am *Mammon*!"

"Well, ah, technically, we haven't performed the ceremony yet," Rutherford said.

"Get on with it, then," Ammon said. "Perform the Ceremony of the Opening of the Gates."

Rutherford took the Book of Mammon off the altar and began reading. " 'Oh, Mammon, I call upon you to welcome this sacrifice and take your place upon this earth.' " He leaned forward, toward Ammon. "This is where you kill her, sir."

"Very well," Ammon said. "Where's the garrote?"

"I thought you were bringing the garrote," Rutherford said.

Ammon rolled his eyes. "Idiot! I'm the demon god.

I can't be expected to bring my own garrote. Do we have a length of rope?"

Ammon and Rutherford scanned the room. No rope.

"Perhaps we could use my tie or my belt," Rutherford said.

Ammon shook his head. "That would be inappropriate."

"Of course," Rutherford said. "What was I thinking?"

"We'll have to shoot her," Ammon said. "Give me your gun."

"Um, I don't carry a gun," Rutherford said.

"Well, *get* one! Do I have to always think of everything?"

Rutherford blinked and gasped, ran to the door, and wrenched it open. "I need someone's gun!" he said to the men waiting in the vestibule. "I need it now!"

He returned with a gun and offered it to Ammon.

"I think you should do this," Ammon said. "I have to be ready for Mammon to emerge."

"Um, excuse me? What?"

"Shoot her."

"Yes, yes. Ha-ha. You want *me* to shoot her. Ahhh, well, this will be a new experience." A trickle of sweat ran down the side of his face. "I don't . . . that is, ha-ha." He aimed the gun at me. "Uh, where would you like me to place the bullet?"

"Oh for Pete's sake! In the head. No, wait. In the heart."

"The heart. Are you sure? It's um, behind a breast. And, uh, let's see how we work this gun. I've never actually shot a gun before."

"It's easy," Ammon said. "You pull the trigger."

Rutherford's hand was shaking and sweat was dripping into his eyes. "Yes, yes, of course, but, ha-ha, am I holding this correctly?" He turned to Ammon. "Do I, ah, have the proper grip? I really think it would be best if you did this, sir. I don't feel entirely, ha-ha, competent here."

Ammon's face went scarlet. His fists were clenched and his face was contorted with anger. *"Just freaking pull the trigger and shoot her!"*

Ammon grabbed at the gun, there was a small awkward wrestling match, and *BANG!*

Ammon's face went blank and a red stain began to spread across his chest.

"Oops," Rutherford said.

Ammon crashed to the floor, and Rutherford bent over him.

"Mr. Mammon?" Rutherford asked. "Hello?"

No one answered. Rutherford carefully placed the gun on the floor. He stood and smoothed his tie.

"Ha-ha," Rutherford said, backing up, moving toward the door. "My bad. Ha-ha. Well, I'm just going to leave now. I, uh, I actually have a job offer in . . . Tasmania. And, um, I might consider it. So it's been lovely. And you have a fabulous day. The weather should be outstanding today. Outstanding."

Rutherford slipped out of the room and carefully closed the door behind him. Words were said in the vestibule, but

I couldn't make them out. There was the sound of footsteps and then it was quiet.

I looked over at Hatchet. "Okay, then," I said. "That went well."

"I think I hath pooped myself," Hatchet said.

CHAPTER TWENTY-EIGHT

The door opened and Diesel walked in. "Are you okay?" he asked.

I nodded. I'd been running on bravado up to this point, but it was fast disappearing, getting replaced with a wash of relief that had me close to tears.

"Who shot Ammon?"

"Rutherford," I said. "Not entirely intentional."

"He was running out of the house when I arrived. *Everyone* was running out of the house. I grabbed him, and he said you were in the basement chapel and you were lovely in your white gown and waiting for me."

"The waiting part is true. Not sure about the gown," I said.

Josh and Glo and Clara rushed in.

"Whoops," Clara said, spotting Ammon. "Looks like we're late for the party."

Diesel got Hatchet off the hook and dumped him onto the floor.

"A thousand thanks, sire," Hatchet said. "I fear I have no blood in the lower half of my body."

Josh was bent over Ammon. "Whoa, he's holding a rock. I bet it's the Stone of Avarice." Josh took the stone away from Ammon. "You know, I always felt I was on a higher plane than everyone else," Josh said, holding the stone. "And now I know why. It's because I really am superior. I was meant to own this stone. I was meant to own *everything*, to rule the world."

"Good grief," I said. "Someone take the stone away from him and put it in the silver box on the altar."

Diesel removed the stone and dropped it into the box. He took a pocketknife out of his jeans, lifted me to my feet, and cut my cuffs away. A tear leaked out of my eye, and he wiped it away with his thumb.

"Sorry I didn't get here sooner," he said, wrapping an arm around me, holding me close to him.

"How did you know I was kidnapped?"

"Josh was standing in front of the bakery, letting some tourists take pictures of him, and he saw Rutherford and his men drive off with you. He ran inside and told Glo, and Glo called me. I was on my way back from Boston when I got the call."

"We were worried Diesel was too far away, so we jumped in Clara's van, and took off to save you!" Glo said.

"Boy, have I got good friends, or what?" I said.

Diesel looked over at Ammon. "Nergal's going to love talking to this one."

I spent the night next to Diesel. The danger was over but the fear stayed with me, and I didn't want to be alone. I didn't set the alarm, but in the morning I woke up on time anyway. The room was dark. Cat was at the foot of the bed. Diesel was still asleep. I crept out from beneath the covers, took a shower, and dressed in my usual uniform of jeans and a T-shirt. I went downstairs and made coffee. My kitchen was cheerful and my world felt good again. Everything would be fine until another stone found its way to Salem. I fed Cat, and when I turned around I was face to face with Wulf.

"Good morning, Lizzy," Wulf said.

He was very close to me, and his personal space hummed with energy.

"You missed the finale," I said.

His eyes were dark and intense but his mouth curved into the hint of a smile. "We haven't seen the finale yet," he said. "Hatchet filled me in on yesterday's ceremony. An inevitable outcome. Ammon was never meant to have the stone."

When Diesel and I went to bed we'd hidden the silver box that contained the stone, the coin, and the Blue Diamond in the microwave. Wulf went to the microwave and took the silver box. He looked inside, seemed satisfied with what he saw, and snapped the lid closed.

"Thank you for retrieving this for me," he said.

"Diesel won't be happy to hear you broke in and took the stone."

"My cousin understands that a deal was made. And I'm sure he knows I'm here."

"The stone and the Blue Diamond are said to be cursed."

"Then they're in the right hands." Wulf smiled again. "I have a way with cursed things."

He stepped in and drew me close against him. His lips brushed mine, the kiss became more intimate, and I felt fire curl through me.

"We have a mission to find the lost stones," Wulf said. "There are four left. When the last stone is found it will be *our* time. And I'll come to finish what I've started here."

He stepped back and *poof* he was gone. I turned and saw Diesel lounging against a doorjamb, arms crossed over his chest, hair still mussed from sleep.

"I don't think so," Diesel said.

ABOUT THE AUTHORS

JANET EVANOVICH is the #1 *New York Times* bestselling author of the Stephanie Plum series, the Lizzy and Diesel series, twelve romance novels, the Alexandra Barnaby novels and Troublemaker graphic novel, and *How I Write: Secrets of a Bestselling Author,* as well as the Fox and O'Hare series with co-author Lee Goldberg.

www.evanovich.com

Facebook.com/JanetEvanovich

@JanetEvanovich

PHOEF SUTTON is a writer, producer, and novelist who's written for shows such as *Cheers, NewsRadio,* and *Boston Legal.* Sutton is the winner of two Emmy Awards, a Golden Globe, and a Peabody Award.

www.phoefsutton.com

Facebook.com/PhoefSuttonWriter

@PhoefSutton

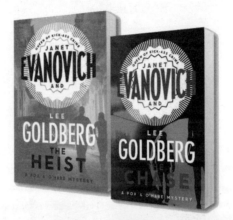
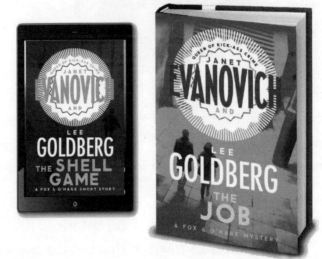

Have you read the new Stephanie Plum adventure from Janet Evanovich?

THE DEAD ENDS ARE TURNING INTO DEAD BODIES IN . . .

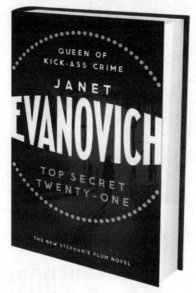

Stephanie Plum is getting desperate. She's running out of leads in her search for a dangerous wheeler dealer and even Joe Morelli, the city's hottest cop, can't help.

And Ranger, Stephanie's No. 1 temptation, needs her help. There's a killer in town with a personal vendetta against him. If he wants to survive, he'll finally need to reveal a piece of his mysterious past . . .

Order it now at
www.headline.co.uk

And don't miss . . .

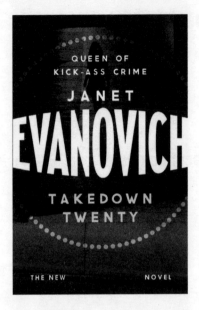

QUEEN OF
KICK-ASS CRIME

JANET
EVANOVICH

TAKEDOWN
TWENTY

THE NEW   NOVEL

KEEPING IT IN THE FAMILY CAN BE MURDER . . .

Stephanie is angry. Someone is killing old women and leaving them in dumpsters, and she's risking the wrath of the local police by investigating behind their backs. And to top that, her latest bounty is the town's much-beloved vicious mobster, 'Uncle Sunny' Sunucchi.

Stephanie doesn't mind (that much) that the local Godfather is her boyfriend Morelli's actual godfather – but since they are almost her in-laws, she could do with the Family not trying to kill her for a while . . .

Order it now at
www.headline.co.uk

headline
review

Join **JANET EVANOVICH**
on social media!

Facebook.com/JanetEvanovich

@janetevanovich

Pinterest.com/JanetEvanovich

Google+JanetEvanovichOfficial

instagram.com/janetevanovich

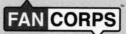

janetevanovich.fancorps.com

Visit **Evanovich.com**
and sign up for Janet's eNewsletter.